Great story! Readers will enjoy the rocky and surprising journey behind the façade of normalcy in a family plagued with tensions and distrust. Waiting is the turmoil that can stifle souls when we live lives of contradictions and hypocrisy. This is a real human story of a woman struggling to protect her inner core from the ravages of secrecy and emotional abuse, and emerging with renewed zest for life. Loved it!

—Dunbar Campbell, Author
The Bianca C Still Burns: A Grenada Novel
Blood of Belvedere: A Grenada Novel

Sylvia Dickey Smith's stated mission is to "write strong women," and this book measures up to that yardstick, and to many others. Beginning with the clever title and lovely cover art, the reader is immersed in the inner workings of the church in which the main character finds herself an emotional prisoner. But it's worse than she thinks.

These fully drawn characters had me believing they were real, partly because they reminded me of real people I have known in similar situations, and entirely because of the skill with which they were portrayed. The setting in the Deep South only adds to the tension and ultimate resolution of the highly charged crisis the reader is drawn into. Based in current societal issues, this story will have you eagerly turning pages to find out what happens next.

—Mike Gadell

Author of *Navy Blues* This is a very thought-provoking novel. It is a story of forgiveness, redemption, tolerance, and I could go on and on. The author is an accomplished writer. I have read several of her other novels and recommend them all, but this is the best yet. I would encourage those who might shy away from writing that takes on religion to stick with this one. Your views may be tested. Very tastefully done!

—Larry Watts, Author

Original Cyn is clearly a book that needed to be written. Around the world today there seems to be so much intolerance and exclusiveness, I have found myself wondering, "Is there anywhere a voice of inclusiveness, openness, and respect for another's journey?" Well, in Sylvia Dickey Smith, I have found such a voice. Finally. In this outstanding and thought-provoking book, we are invited to join Cyn on her amazing journey of the sacred and of self-discovery, where there are surprises at every turn. Our lives often have twists and unexpected turns as well, and Cyn keeps us with her through all of hers. This is a book for anyone who has ever been on their own spiritual journey, a journey where there are more questions than answers. My hope is that every reader will find themselves on their own journey, and explore the wonder of embracing another's journey, especially when it is different than one's own. Therein lies the power of Original Cyn. I am a much broader and open human being as a result of reading this book. I can think of no greater end than that.

—Rev. James T. Hogg,

When I first started reading Original Cyn, I expected a typical story targeting 'women of a certain age.' After all, Cyn was at that stage in life when her son was leaving home. Her husband neglected her and obsessed over obeying the rules and living up to what his church expected of their pastor. Neglected and frustrated, Cyn deserved a romantic interlude, and the opportunity is hinted at. It wasn't long before I realized this book was much deeper than that. I was hooked. The author took on a difficult subject and handled it with sensitivity and insight. Her characters survive the unthinkable, and grow. This timely story will open minds and hearts and keep you hooked right to the end."

—Holly Sullivan McClure
Ordained Celtic Christian Minister,
Literary Agent & Published Author

When the preacher is in his pulpit and his dutiful wife sits in the front row performing as his support and helpmate, their lives seem perfect and full. When the sermon is over, Cyn Carter's life is far from full and she doesn't know why. Why does she feel that over the years her life was sucked dry and she became an empty shell? The answer comes suddenly in an avalanche of revelations, which turn her life not only upside down but inside out. She finds herself flooded in a tsunami of truths about love, sex, marriage, hypocrisy and narrow-minded intolerance and is forced into a challenging journey of examination and discovery

Sylvia Dickey Smith is uniquely qualified to write a story as powerful and revealing as this one. Like Cyn, she was a pastor's wife for a number of years. At the same time, while raising four children and still serving as the pastor's wife and missionary, she earned a BA in Sociology and a Masters in Educational Psychology. This led her to a new career in private practice as a licensed professional counselor and marriage and family therapist.

Her next career goal was to become a writer. In the process of writing a successful and highly praised series of novels and becoming a state and national award winning novelist, she found her niche in creating strong female characters forced to face overwhelming adversity.

In ORIGINAL CYN, she has combined her psychological education and experience as a professional counselor with her writing skill and crafted a compelling story that will keep any reader turning pages.

This book is highly recommended for both men and women.

—Earl Staggs, Author
Derrigner Award-winner

Original Cyn

Sylvia Dickey Smith

White Bird Publications
P.O. Box 90145
Austin, Texas 78709
http://www.whitebirdpublications.com

ISBN: 978-1-63363-149-6
LCCN: 2015960750

PRINTED IN THE UNITED STATES OF AMERICA

Dedication:

Marty Cormier and Barry Wright,
without you, this story might never
have been written.

Acknowledgements

"No man is an island," nor is a book. A multitude of people and life situations make up any work of art, including this book. Author, Cindy Phillips suggested the book title. Critique partners—Randy, Earl, Joan, Joy and D.C. kept me on track. Christina Wiggins, a beta reader, gave invaluable feedback. Rev. Jim Hogg contributed invaluable input and monitored the storyline for authenticity.

My Bill—I can never say enough about this man and the positive effects his unconditional love has made on my life.

Visit Sylvia
At

http://www.sylviadickeysmith.com

https://www.facebook.com/sylvia.d.smith.142

https://www.facebook.com/SylviaDickeySmithAuthor/?fref=ts

https://goo.gl/nB7Snc

https://twitter.com/SmithSyl

http://www.amazon.com/Sylvia-Dickey-Smith/e/B002ZE9Q8Q/ref=sr_ntt_srch_lnk_1?qid=1451057775&sr=8-1

Original Cyn

White Bird
Publications

The essential questions have no answers
You are my question and I am yours
And then there is dialogue
The moment we have answers
There is no dialogue
Questions unite people
Answers divide them
So why have answers
When we can live without them

~Elie Wiesel

CHAPTER ONE

When the sun came up that morning, Cyn Carter did what every other burned-out unambiguous preacher's wife did. She crawled out of bed, threw on yesterday's jeans and tee shirt, and did a quick finger-comb as Wilburn strolled out of the bathroom. "If you don't mind Cynthia," he said, "can you get a move on? I have an appointment at eight o'clock, and you haven't even gone downstairs yet, much less started my breakfast." Sarcasm dripped from his words.

Big fat hairy deal. Cyn hustled down the hall toward the stairs. Same story, same attitude, every single solitary day.

Out of habit, she paused just inside the door to her son's bedroom. His recent departure to college left the house feeling so empty, so quiet.

"I said get a move on, Cynthia," Wilburn barked as he came up behind her, then stopped to check his reflection in the full-length mirror. After a quick adjustment to his tie, he spun on his heels and walked on, an overdose of aftershave trailing behind him.

Cyn took a long deep breath, as if his departure returned oxygen to the room.

He waited for her at the bottom of the stairs worry lines creasing his forehead. Cyn followed him into the kitchen where he went straight to the coffee pot, prepared and set the night before. He often teased that he expected the coffee ready when he got up every morning, much like the cruse of oil in the Bible. As the story went, the cruse remained full of oil, regardless of how much the poor widow used, implying, of course, that God kept the righteous woman supplied with oil. Guess that made a statement about Cyn's righteousness, or the lack thereof, for she supplied their coffee.

"I see you're still moping around like you lost your best friend." He spooned a heaping teaspoon of sugar into his coffee and stirred, stirred—and stirred.

It made her want to grab the spoon out of his hand and shove it up his butt.

"I wish you'd get over this notion of having nothing more to live for since Justice left for college." He tapped the spoon against the rim of the cup and tossed it on the granite counter top.

"Don't be stupid." Her sharp words startled her. She wasn't accustomed to talking back.

"Then stop acting like he died. I get depressed just looking at you."

"You make it sound like I can simply wish away whatever bothers me," she said through clenched teeth. "That bugs the heck out of me."

"You watch that pronoun curse word, young lady." Finger-quotes bracketed his words.

"It's not a pronoun." She did her own bracketing.

"Maybe not, but you use it in place of a curse word, so it counts as the same thing." He tapped his forehead as he spoke as if any idiot should know that. "I never said you could wish anything away, but you sure can do something about it."

He took a few sips of coffee then ambled to the breakfast table, newspaper in hand. "What I said was to get out and go do something—get it off your mind. Mrs. Turner and a couple of other ladies fold the bulletins on Thursdays. Why don't you come help them? At least it'll get you out of the house."

"No thanks." She bit her tongue before it released the dictum that a snowball had a greater chance in hell. Mama's words bounced around in her head. *You can think it, Cynthia Ann, but that doesn't mean you have to say it.*

She'd cooked Wilburn's breakfast so many times she could do it blindfolded, and might as well today, for all the interest and energy she had in doing so. True to form, however, the smell of frying bacon soon filled the house, half-cooked, the way he liked it. After plating the bacon, she basted the eggs, whites firm, and yolks soft.

All while Wilburn read the newspaper and slurped coffee.

As she moved the eggs from the skillet to Wilburn's plate, being careful not to break the yolks, her mind drifted to the night before. In their twenty-plus years, she'd never known him to take much notice of his dreams, but he'd awakened at straight up 3:00 o'clock in a cold sweat brought on, he'd said, by the image of her vaporizing like an early-morning fog exposed to bright sunlight.

"It's only a dream," she'd said, trying to comfort him. She stopped short of admitting how close his dream touched reality, that as of late she felt herself fading into someone else. No, more like exploding into it.

When she put his food in front of him, he folded the paper and laid it beside his plate, eyes still glued on the article he'd been reading. Approaching his mid-forties, Wilburn looked every bit as handsome as he did the day she first laid eyes on him talking to a group of girls at her hometown church. His trim frame and impeccable taste in clothing still made him stand out, regardless of the crowd. The sprinkling of gray at the temples didn't hurt either. Women, young and old, worshipped him and envied her.

They needn't have bothered. Although she worshipped him herself before they married, afterward, she'd sworn someone kidnapped him and replaced him with a stranger. Like once he caught her, the romance ended and doing God's work began. Over the years, he kept her at an emotional arm's length. Except for the God-talk, she had no idea what went on inside the man's head.

But she knew what went on inside hers. The day stretched painfully in her thoughts—clean the kitchen, make the bed, wash the clothes, and have Wilburn's lunch on the table at straight up noon. She poked her eggs with a fork and bit into a slice of toast.

"Cynthia." His voice was strident.

"What?" She glanced up to see him glaring at her.

"Shame on you. You know we never eat without first saying grace."

Good lord, she'd broken the cardinal rule of the parsonage, a rule, without a doubt, written on tablets of stone hidden somewhere in the house.

Tempted to say "Grace," and get on with eating, Cyn thought better of it. Instead, when he bowed his head and closed his eyes, she kept hers up and open, fork in midair. The memory of Justice doing the same thing years ago, and the shame heaped upon him by his father, still rattled her heartstrings.

However, what bothered her the most was Wilburn's so-called prayers always—always—targeted more than one agenda item, each intended not for God, but for Wilburn's audience and more often than not, her.

After the blessing, Wilburn glanced her way then back at his food. "You haven't said anything about my sermon yesterday." He reached for the blackberry jam and spooned a mound onto his toast. "Didn't you like it?"

The *exact* same question, word for word, he'd asked her over breakfast every blessed Monday for the last twenty years. This time, she said nothing. Just kept eating, but not tasting.

An uncomfortable silence filled the room.

Wilburn broke it. "It's evident you're still thinking of no one but yourself." He shoveled in another mouthful of eggs. "You've acted like this ever since Justice left for college."

Their son Justice, a young teen when they first moved to Mobile and into the century-old parsonage, soon started calling his dad's church the "Do Right Be Good Church," but never in front of his father.

"I miss Justice, yes, but the boy leaving for college has nothing to do with what I'm going through." She tried to explain the unexplainable. "It's not the empty nest that bothers me. It's me. I'm empty."

"You're just depressed. Probably time for your period or something." He shrugged. "Anyway, if you want something to do, as I said, every Thursday, several women get together and have fun folding the bulletins. If you want to—"

"I don't want to fold your damn bulletins." She spat the words through clenched teeth.

Wilburn stood and slung his napkin onto the table. "Watch your language, young lady." He stormed out of the kitchen, slinging words over his shoulder as he tromped down the hall. "I'll be home for lunch, Cynthia. See that it's ready on time. Think you can at least do that much?"

The front door slammed behind him, leaving a tension she could pierce with one of Justice's epées. Did other dutiful preachers' wives ever daydream about murder?

Over the years, Cyn had learned not to push. After growing up with an abusive father, Wilburn shied away from physical violence, but he learned the more manipulative ways of his mother. Add to that, he suffered the aggravation of an older brother who acted like Mr. Perfect in front of their parents, and tormented Wilburn without mercy behind their backs.

To say Wilburn never crossed the line wasn't totally accurate. On occasion, he resorted to his father's ways of dealing with frustration. He never hit her or Justice, but a couple of times he came mighty close when she questioned one of his religious beliefs, and he couldn't convince her to see it his way.

Addicts filled their cravings with something. His father used alcohol. At times, Cyn wondered if Wilburn's extreme religiosity was a type of addiction. The thought of that bothered her as much as his lack of intimacy. The distance between them wasn't new, but it hadn't improved over the years either. In fact, it seemed to have grown worse.

She'd vowed to be the submissive wife, to honor and obey him at every turn, and Lord knew she'd done that— for decades. So why hadn't it worked? Why, instead, did she feel like some soul-sucking monster slipped in and gobbled her up from the inside out?

Cyn shoved the chilling questions aside, shifted her brain into zombie-mode, and loaded the dishwasher, wiped the table, made the bed, and started a load of laundry, her 14,200,656[th] load—but who's counting?

After the laundry, she ran the vacuum, boiled a couple of eggs for the tuna salad she'd make later for their lunch, and then headed outside with a mug of hot coffee. Strolling through her flower garden, the one place where she found peace, she cupped a late-blooming gardenia in her palm and inhaled, letting the fragrance soothe her soul.

She wished Wilburn understood her feelings. Wished he wanted to understand them. Perhaps if he did, he might not resent her reluctance to go to church every time someone unlocked the frigging doors. Instead, he nagged about the responsibility she'd accepted when she married a preacher. "He forgets he wasn't a pastor when we married," she muttered, "and he certainly didn't consult me before enrolling in seminary."

She felt trapped, like she lived inside the world

rather than outside where the air smelled fresh, where possibilities came true, or had the chance of doing so. She longed to breathe, to flap her wings like the baby bird after it outgrows its shell and pecks its way out.

Lost in rumination, she hadn't heard the back gate open and close until a familiar voice called out, "So that's why you didn't answer the doorbell. I hoped I'd catch you out here."

"Dee?" Cyn dumped her coffee into the thirsty soil and hurried to meet her younger sister. "Sweetheart, I thought you were headed to Europe or something."

"Operative word, headed, until they diverted my flight to Mobile. Mechanical problems they claimed. Canceled the whole trip until tomorrow. I stood in line at the ticket counter for over half an hour trying to make a connecting flight before my boss texted and said, 'Hold off, complications of some kind.' So, anyway, I took a taxi and here I am."

They embraced for the longest, each bubbling with the joy shared by sisters, who couldn't be more different, yet never got enough of each other.

As a baby learning to talk, Dee struggled to pronounce her older sister's name, but could only manage the first syllable, Cyn. The nickname stuck, much to Cynthia's delight and their mother's horror. From then on, everyone except Cynthia's mother called her Cyn. That is until she married Wilburn.

He swore no one would ever call his wife Cyn again. A person might be born in sin, but that didn't mean he'd let someone call his wife that ugly word.

However, with Dee, Wilburn met his match. She simply ignored his order, acted like she hadn't heard him.

The girl knew no fear. All her life, she slashed through any obstacles in her way as if they existed to encourage her, to prod her into action. Perhaps the red hair and freckles had something to do with it. She spent her childhood fighting and scratching through taunts in elementary school until the bullies ran. Unlike Cyn, she did not tolerate bad behavior or fools.

Arm in arm, Cyn and Dee strolled into the house while Dee chattered about her adventures as a foreign correspondent. "You should see my new cameraman." She flicked her fingers, laughing. "Hot, hot, hot."

Cyn smiled, wondering what it might feel like for a man to turn her on again, or to be more accurate, for her to turn on a man.

"Now, tell me about my favorite nephew. How's Justice? He's in college now, right? What a neat kid— takes after his mom, that's for sure." Dee gave Cyn's waist a gentle squeeze.

"I'm afraid he takes more after his Aunt Dee." Cyn laughed. "A thought goes in his head and comes out his mouth. Got himself in trouble a few times because of it too."

Dee raised her eyebrows in question.

"I remember one night at a church picnic when a bossy deacon ordered Justice to go gather wood for the bonfire." Cyn smiled at the memory. "Justice felt demeaned by the way the guy spoke to him and countered with, 'You want firewood, go get it yourself.'"

Dee doubled over with laughter. "He didn't? Really? Good Lord, I'll bet Wilburn had a coronary."

"Wilburn wanted to beat the kid black and blue, but thank goodness he didn't. Ate a big piece of humility pie with the deacon, though, that's for sure. And Justice received a heated lecture from his dad on the topic of courtesy." Cyn smiled, remembering how embarrassed she and Wilburn were over their son's behavior. Later that same night, Justice had asked Cyn why he should treat someone he did not respect with that same courtesy and respect his dad yelled about. Put Cyn back on her heels for a few seconds, but when she felt the answer in her heart, she knew it to be true. "Justice, you treat all people with courtesy and respect, not because of who they are, but because of who you are, a person who treats others with—"

"Respect and dignity," he said, finishing her sentence. "Okay. I see what you mean, Mom. Thanks." He'd given her a big hug and went on his way.

She never needed to talk to him about courtesy again.

Cyn and Dee spent the day catching up on the goings-on of family and friends. That, plus Dee's latest love interest, which changed as frequently as the weather.

Wilburn always asked why Dee didn't pick one man and settle down. What did she want to do, hump every man in the country? Cyn hated it when he started in on Dee.

The two sisters dropped any further mention of Wilburn until he called after lunch to cancel lunch. "And don't bother about dinner either," he added. "I've got a building committee meeting this evening and will likely go straight from it to the deacon's meeting."

"And you're just now telling me? I already prepared—"

"The building committee, Cynthia," he said as if his

precious committee took precedence over everything else, especially her. For months, the committee had been working on an expansion project and planned to present their proposal to the deacons for approval later that evening. Last minute rehearsal, she guessed, but she figured he knew about the meeting before now.

She slammed the phone down and threw the spatula across the room. Before it landed, however, she realized with him not home for dinner she and Dee could breathe easier, longer.

Dee shrugged. "Well, at least you've already got tomorrow night's dinner done." She stood at the sink cleaning up after Cyn's prep for a canceled dinner. "I swear, girl, I don't know what you ever saw in the man. He's good-looking, if you like that type, but he's a turd, big sister. I know it. You know it."

"He's not that bad." Cyn laughed, but her words felt like fish bones in her throat.

Dee glanced over her shoulder. "If he isn't, why didn't you tell him his call came too late. Look at this mess, all for a man who surely knew of a committee meeting before now. Good Lord, if I didn't know better, I'd think we still lived in the twentieth century."

Relieved when Dee's ringing cell phone and her subsequent exit of the room ended the conversation, Cyn moved to the sink full of dirty dishes, took one look, and shuddered. Bits of greasy food floated to the top. Not-so-greasy bits swam around the bottom, waiting.

She shuddered at the thought of putting her hands in that mess under the pretext of cleaning the dishes. It stood to reason, use dirty water, get dirty dishes. Oh, they might look clean, but without a doubt, they contained more germs than before they took the plunge.

All her life, Dee argued dishwashing should be done one way, and one way only. Put in a stopper, fill the sink with hot, soapy water, and plunge every filthy dish into the depths and scrub. Voila, the dishes came out clean.

Not on Cyn's watch. She pulled the plug and loaded the dishes in the dishwasher.

A few minutes later Dee returned to the kitchen. "My boss called. Former boss, I guess I should say."

"He fired you?"

"Used the term cutbacks."

The two stood with their mouths open, staring at each other. Then, Dee cracked a smile. "Look on the bright side, you'll get to tell dipshit I'm here after all."

"Don't act ugly." Cyn turned her back to hide a grin.

"I'm just sayin'..."

"Well, I'm just saying let's take a glass of ice tea outside and sit on the front porch."

What she'd say to Wilburn about her sister visiting, she hadn't a clue. One thing she did know, she had to tell him before he walked in and saw Dee, or else he'd pout for a week.

Once outside, the sounds of a creaking swing and the rapid-moving wings of a hummingbird soothed the silence until Dee spoke up.

"You know what? I've heard Catholic nuns consider themselves married to Jesus, right? Thing is, you're not a nun. You're not even Catholic. But I get the idea you married Jesus all the same, or at least to a man who sees himself as second-in-command."

Weary of the topic, Cyn didn't respond. How could she, and stay loyal to her husband? Plus, she hated to admit her sister spoke the truth.

Cyn's silence, however, did not discourage Dee. "I guess when you go to church you still sit on the front pew like Wilburn tells you to, so you can catch his drippings from the pulpit. That's the silliest thing I ever heard." Dee laughed so hard she almost spilled her tea.

"He laughs when he says that, and you know it." Cyn sucked through her teeth.

He joked all right, but Cyn had come to realize that, once again, the joke fell on her. Most church members pooh-poohed the New Age phenomenon of channeling. Humph—nothing new to her. Wilburn channeled God every service and most times in between.

However, she certainly wasn't going to admit that to Dee. Instead, she changed the subject.

"There's a women's circle meeting at church tonight. I'm expected to attend. Hope you won't mind staying here alone. Wilburn is at a deacon's meeting, so I should get home before him. You won't have to face him by yourself."

"Why don't I go with you?"

"That'd be great, but are you sure you really want to?" Cyn shuddered to think what Dee might say or do at a group like that. Shock the conservative women right out of their pantyhose and padded bras.

"Better than sitting here by myself. Besides, I'll make sure those biddies don't take pot shots at my older sister."

"Careful on that older stuff."

It felt good to laugh. Cyn couldn't remember doing so since Justice left. His antics always gave her comic relief.

CHAPTER TWO

Cyn spotted Wilburn's car in the church parking lot as soon as she pulled in. She glanced at the clock on the dash. "I guess the building committee is meeting right now."

"Sounds like fun to me," Dee said. "I'd rather have a root canal."

"It may not be fun, but it's not the toughest part of his evening. After that meeting ends, he and the chairman present the building expansion proposal to the deacons."

"Uh-oh. Do I hear dread in that tone?"

Cyn didn't confirm or deny, nor did she elaborate on how high nerves ran when big money came up for discussion at deacon's meetings. Some deacons supported expansion, others didn't. For Dee's sake, Cyn hoped the proposal passed. Otherwise, when Wilburn came home...well, she hated to think of his mood.

Cyn led the way to the church parlor full of overstuffed chairs and an air-conditioner that chilled the room to a year-round temperature frigid enough to entertain fur coats and penguins.

President Hazel Harrison met them at the door, her hair plastered in its usual survive any hurricane style. Cyn cringed at the woman's swift head-to-toe sweep of Dee. Cyn preferred giving Hazel a wide berth, but that wasn't always possible since the pious woman served on the parsonage committee and acted like the century-old house belonged to her.

Obliged to introduce Dee, Cyn said, "Mrs. Harrison, I'd like you to meet my sister, Dee Rogers. She's visiting from out of town."

"So nice to meet you," Mrs. Harrison gushed. "There's coffee and cookies on the table. Make yourself at home. We'll start in a couple of minutes."

Eager for the excuse to move on, Cyn took Dee's elbow and steered her toward the refreshment table. "Oh, look, there's Ginger Goodman. I want you to meet her before the program begins."

"Who is she?"

"My best friend," Cyn whispered. "Her husband, Stephen, chairs the board of deacons. She's someone I can talk to and know it won't go anywhere."

"Oh, Sis, don't you know there isn't a soul in this building you can trust that much? Believe me. I know church gossip—especially among women."

"What makes you such an authority on gossiping church women?" Cyn asked, poking Dee in the ribs with her elbow.

Dee didn't answer. Just smiled.

"Regardless, I want you to meet Ginger. She's not like that."

"Yeah, right, she's—"

"Ladies?" Lorene Harvey called from the front of the room. "It's time for us to begin. Can we all take a seat?"

Lorene, a small, mild-mannered woman, and her husband, Bud, had one child, a son named Marcus. Over the last five years, Marcus spent more time hanging out at the parsonage with Justice than he did at home with his parents. Then, Justice and Sophie became an item, and the twosome became a threesome. You saw one; you saw the other two.

Marcus' dad, Bud, owned a construction business, and from what Justice said, ruled the home like he ran his business, with a firm, no-nonsense fist.

The chairs filled up quickly. By the time Dee and Cyn gulped down their punch, the only seats available were on the front row.

The room grew quiet until Lorene, Prayer Chairman of the group, began reading a list of names of foreign missionaries from their denomination who celebrated a birthday that day. Along with the names, she also recounted the countries where each served, and then asked the group to bow their heads while she led a prayer.

After the prayer, Hazel Harrison moved to the front and flashed a tight smile. "Everyone, if you haven't met our visitor, please meet Dee Rogers, the sister of our beloved pastor's wife, Cynthia." She gave a quick nod Cyn's way. "Welcome, Mrs. Rogers, and welcome to you, Mrs. Carter. We're glad you made it tonight." Hazel ducked her head and cut a quick glance at the vice president.

Cyn saw their eyes meet and hold for a millisecond. Long enough that Cyn got the message. Pastor's Wife always was and forever remained their favorite topic of conversation—and judgment. It didn't matter what she said or did, or how she dressed, someone criticized her. Much of Wilburn's success depended on her, but despite all her efforts over the years, it seemed she always failed him in one way or another.

Hands in prayer pose, Hazel flashed an aren't-we-holy-smile straight at Dee. "We want you to know how much we love your sister. We always love our pastors' wives—especially the last one. She never missed a single women's function in this church. Not only did she attend, she also took charge of most of the events. Course some people thought she did too much, but not me. I respected what that woman did. She organized food drives, set up the promotion and collection of our annual Easter and Christmas mission offerings. Why, we didn't have to lift a finger. All that, and kept the parsonage looking like a model home. I don't know how she did it."

Cyn squeezed Dee's hand. Dee squeezed back.

"Never missed a worship service," Hazel continued—just when Cyn thought Hazel had finished the praise list. "Why, at Christmas she sponsored an open house at the parsonage, cooked all the food herself. Wouldn't let any of us lift a finger."

Okay, Cyn wondered, how many fingers did the group not lift?

Dee must have read Cyn's thoughts, for before Cyn could stop her, Dee chimed in with "Wow that sounds like a lot of fingers missed a chance to participate."

If not for the plush carpet, a hairpin would have sounded like a cannon ball when it hit the floor.

Cyn glanced at Ginger, who made a slit her throat motion. Cyn didn't know whether to defend Dee or Hazel. Or run for the door.

One woman rushed to the bathroom. Another went to refill her coffee. Lots of throat clearing and butt squirming.

"I'm just sayin'..." Dee flashed a bright smile.

Hazel cleared her throat again. "Thank you for your comment, Mrs. Rogers." Ice crystals coated Hazel's words.

Cyn's toenails felt like they curled back in on themselves. She knew Dee's opinion of the title Mrs., but before she could elbow her sister to shut up, Dee opened her mouth again. By then, there wasn't anything Cyn could do but hang onto the bungee cord and wait for the rebound.

"Ms. Rogers, please. Even if I do marry, I'll never use Mrs. as a title. After all, Mister doesn't declare whether a man is married or not. Why should we have to? It's another example of sexism, that's for sure."

Hazel glanced from one woman to the next, but not Cyn. She looked right over her. Sputtering, stumbling over her words, Hazel declared, "No disrespect, Ms. Rogers, but, but..."

The vice president picked up the conversation from there. "What Hazel is trying to say is, we women of the church are proud to be married, and to let people know we feel that way. After all, God created woman as man's helpmeet, and marriage as the first institution. If Adam hadn't needed a wife, God might not even have created us."

Cyn prayed for the floor to open up. Even if the hole went all the way to hell, at that moment, she'd take her chances. She needn't have wasted the prayer, however. By the look on Dee's face, nothing short of a second coming would stop her sister from picking up that gauntlet.

Keep breathing, Cyn told herself. *Breathe.* She tried to pinch Dee into silence just as Dee shifted and crossed her legs, the flame-red miniskirt riding higher.

"Give me a break." Ridicule waltzed around the edges of Dee's words. "You ladies need to go back to school and study your biology. Every man born in this world started out in the womb as a female. Didn't you know that?"

"That's a lie," someone hissed.

Grumblings around the room told Cyn she had best get Dee out of there, and fast. "Ladies," she said, "excuse us, please." She clamped Dee's hand in hers and despite Dee's reluctance, yanked her out of the parlor, down the hall, and to the car while the hounds of hell nipped at their heels.

Cyn bustled Dee into the passenger seat and raced to get behind the wheel. The two sat in utter silence for a couple of seconds, but when Cyn pushed the auto-lock button, the sound of all four doors locking in unison set off a simultaneous explosion of gut-wrenching, hiccupping, nose-dripping laughter.

In the midst of the euphoria, however, Cyn knew she had yet to pay the devil. Regardless, she held her belly and choked out, "I can't...believe you...you really said that to those women. I'll...never live this down. Not to mention Wilburn. He's gonna be furious."

Each looked at the other for a second and then tumbled deeper into hysterics.

"But you know..." Cyn sniffed, wiped her nose on her sleeve. "...at the moment, I don't really care. I'm so sick of all those religious clichés of the righteous."

Dee sniffed, gripped Cyn's arm. "Or how...'bout...righteous...clichés of the...religious?"

"That, too." Cyn shook her head, trying to get the laughter under control. "Whatever, I'm sick of all the masks people wear and then act like they're so holy—like they have all the answers to every question ever asked."

"Wonder how many of those biddies wear a mask?" Dee settled into the occasional hiccup. "One, for sure, is your friend, Ginger. I'd watch her. Besides, she reeks of cologne. I like a little sweet-smelling stuff but, geesh—bathing in it?"

Cyn headed out of the parking lot, shooting a quick glance Dee's way. "Oh, I think you're wrong there. She's nicer to me than—"

"That's my point. What's in it for her?"

"Well...my friendship, I suppose."

"Get real, Cyn. You're a great person, but you forget these people make Wilburn their God...or at least God's representative. So what does that make you?"

"What do you mean?"

"Think about it, sweetheart. God—wife?" Dee held her palms up like balance scales. "That makes you the second most important person out of what, five-six hundred people? If Ginger is close to you, that raises her status. I figure the biggest majority of his female parishioners manipulate you like all get out because they have a crush on the preacher. They don't see his imperfections. To them, he's perfect. He always listens to what they say. He's handsome, helpful, friendly, loyal, courteous, kind. An omniscient boy scout, that's how they see him."

"Guess I never looked at it that way." Cyn took the freeway exit and turned left at the light.

"Remember, Cyn, when I was a little kid, how you stood up to all the neighborhood bullies?"

"I...guess I don't."

"Sure. Remember the time you called out that blond kid for teasing me about my red hair?"

Cyn chuckled. "Oh, yeah, I forgot about that."

"You dug into Mama's drawer, found her rouge, and took off outside. After you tracked down the kid, you straddled his back, dug your fingers into the bright red color, and coated his blond hair until it turned hot pink."

Cyn smiled. "I did, didn't I? We stood in their front yard and listened to him bawl after his mama yanked him inside by his ear and scrubbed his head with Dutch Cleanser."

"Nothing stopped you from standing up for yourself before Wilburn came along. Then, you even let him change your name."

"I stood up to him when Justice was born. Wanted to name him Jude. Biblical, he said. Told him Justice was too." Cyn smiled, remembering Wilburn's anger that she filled out the forms when he wasn't there. She never regretted doing it, for Justice certainly lived up to his name. The boy spoke for justice regardless of who a person was or wasn't. Got him in trouble a few times when he'd taken an unpopular stand, but she couldn't argue with his reasoning.

"Besides, Dee, what do you expect me to do? I can't make Wilburn call me Cyn."

"Sure you can, and you aren't that Hazel woman's doormat, either. You've walked on eggshells ever since I got here. Even when Wilburn's not in the room, you rush around trying to outguess what he expects from you."

"I don't need to guess." Cyn laughed at truth as she knew it. She turned on her street and slowed the car. "Anyway, you don't visit often enough to know what I do."

"And why do you think that is, my dear sweet sister?"

"Because Wilburn acts superior to you?"

"Got it—and superior to you, too. That, and I get tired hearing him quote scripture for every blessed thing. What's wrong with living like you believe the Bible, instead of talking to people like they're idiots? Like he's so much more holy than me or—"

"Okay, that's enough." Cyn breathed a heavy sigh. "We're home, and I don't want to talk about all this in front of him."

"God, no, let's not do that."

Cyn ignored the sarcasm in Dee's voice as she parked and turned off the ignition. Only then did she realize Wilburn's car wasn't in the driveway. She shuddered at the thought that by now someone had called him and reported his sister-in-law's behavior at the women's circle meeting. Regardless of what he said or did, Cyn wouldn't have missed the evening for anything in the world. She hadn't laughed like that in a long time. Come to think of it, not since Dee's last visit.

"Looks like we lucked out and beat Wilburn home," Dee said, opening the car door. "Maybe he's got a girlfriend."

Cyn swiped away the suggestion as ridiculous, even though she couldn't remember the last time he'd shown any amorous attention to her.

Once inside, Dee blamed exhaustion and excused herself to the guest room for the night. Cyn figured Dee's self-described fatigue might connect to not wanting to face Wilburn when he got home. Cyn didn't want to either.

Chilled from the night air and an evening spent in the freezer-for-a-parlor, Cyn longed to flop in bed. But she dared not sleep until Wilburn came home and had his say. Get it over with—or at least get it started. If he waited until morning, he'd stew all night and be even more upset.

After dressing for bed, she lit the gas logs and cuddled up with an afghan and a cup of cocoa while Dee's admonitions battled her own thoughts. Was Dee right? Had Cyn sold herself for a lump of security—like their mom?

Numbness wrapped her like a warm blanket as she lay staring into the flames until she saw herself walking around in a shroud-covered, lifeless body watching the world turn. No one saw her, for as she passed, both she and the shroud crumbled into a heap of ashes dusting the toes of strangers.

CHAPTER THREE

Awakened by the sound of banging cabinet doors coming from the kitchen, Cyn sat straight up surprised to see she'd spent the night on the sofa. Someone had turned off the gas logs, but no one had turned off the uneasiness in her gut.

Was that Wilburn? Or Dee?

Cyn put on her slippers and eased to the kitchen door.

Wilburn fiddled with the empty coffee maker.

She wanted to run. Instead, she straightened her shoulders and headed into perdition. "Good morning. Sorry about the coffee pot. I forgot to set it. Why didn't you wake me when you came in last night?"

Wilburn didn't turn around. Nor did he speak.

"Can I get you some breakfast?"

Silence.

"I know you're angry, but—"

"I'm not angry, Cynthia, I'm trying to figure out this stupid coffeepot."

"Here, let me." She took the bag of coffee out of his hands and soon had the pot gurgling.

"Why didn't you tell me Dee was here? That way I could warn folks about her big mouth." His words sounded tight, clipped. "Her inexcusable behavior last night couldn't have come at a worse time or made a bigger ass of herself."

"She didn't mean anything by it, Wilburn." Cyn collected mugs for the coffee and grabbed the sugar bowl. "You know her. She's impulsive. Mother always said she came out of the womb feet first and raring to go. Surely she didn't cause that much damage."

"Didn't cause too much damage?" he yelled. "You've got to be kidding. One of the most important deacon's meetings of my career and you think her behavior didn't screw it up?"

Cyn fiddled with a dishtowel.

"Her visit came on the worst day possible. She's rude, Cynthia. She was a guest in my church, in my home."

"Don't you mean our home?" Wasted words. Regardless of what she said, Wilburn would never understand how second-class she felt.

Wilburn sucked through his teeth. "You know what I mean. The parsonage, which the church owns, anyway."

Irritation coated his words. No, more than irritation, ridicule.

"I know what you mean," Cyn said, "and it has

nothing to do with the house being owned by the church. You never let me forget you are the king of the castle, and that this is your home—not mine. Between you and certain women at the church, there is always someone ready to make sure I don't forget."

"That's ridiculous. Anyway, when does she plan to leave?" Wilburn poured himself a cup of coffee and stepped to the kitchen table.

"I assume you are talking about my sister. She has a name, you know."

"Who else would I be talking about? Got any more surprise guests stashed somewhere in the house?"

Cyn sucked in a deep breath and released it, slow and easy. "I'm...not sure how long she'll be here. She lost her job yesterday." She cast a furtive glance Wilburn's way. He seemed not to connect with the news. Hadn't he heard her? Maybe he simply didn't care.

"These people pay my salary, Cynthia. If we don't keep them happy, I'm out of a job same as her."

So he had heard. He just didn't care, at least about Dee's circumstances.

"Even if she doesn't like what they say," he continued, "as a guest in our church she must not antagonize them. You know that. She should, too."

Cyn fiddled with the belt on her housecoat. "Are folks that mad?"

"You know how women are," he said, gesturing with his hand. "They get upset at another woman, and they go straight to their husbands and demand they do something. Last night, we'd no sooner adjourned the building committee than a bunch of women waylaid me in the hall. I finally escaped them, and then walked straight into a hostile deacon's meeting."

Wilburn sat at the table and buried his face in his hands. "I made my mind up to not mention this to you, but I think I better."

"What?"

"Things don't look so good for us right now," he said. "Seems some of the deacons are turning on me."

Cyn hadn't expected that. Truth be known, it didn't even make the list. "Turning on you? I...I don't understand."

"After getting chewed up and spit out by the women, I walked into that deacon's meeting and the minute I did, everyone in the room stopped talking."

"Hmmm. That's odd. What did you make of it?"

"That the meeting started without me, that's what." Wilburn sighed and fell back in his chair.

"You're imagining things. Your precious chairman wouldn't let them do that."

"Right. Well, seems like...Get this. Soon as I walk in, Stephen says to the group, 'Gentlemen, as I said a few minutes ago, whatever you have to say about Pastor, you should say to his face instead of behind his back.'"

"What? Wow, what was going on?" Cyn looked at Wilburn's hands propped on the table. His entwined fingers didn't move, but his thumbs twiddled to beat sixty.

"Seems several deacons bad-mouthed the building plan and me, before I joined the meeting."

"Who? I thought they supported it."

"Harris Harrison for one." Wilburn grabbed the newspaper and threw it to the floor. "The man shot daggers at Stephen. Then, Bud Harvey sat over there shaking his head like he couldn't believe Stephen told me, while others squirmed in their seats."

"No one said anything?"

"Not a one, but they wouldn't look at me either. After a couple of minutes, Randy, who chairs the building committee, cleared his throat, straightened that ugly bowtie he always wears, and said since no one had anything to say, we might as well consider the building committee's proposal." Wilburn looked Cyn in the eye. "And you know as well as I do, if we don't get that new building, and soon, attendance will continue to decline."

Cyn listened, knowing he did not want her opinion, especially if it differed from his.

"So, since no one still hadn't said anything, Randy made the motion that the deacons accept the recommendations. That's when Bud Harvey brought up how all these parents drop their kids off at church and then go shopping. Said the church was nothing more than glorified babysitters to a bunch of undisciplined kids."

"I'm sure you showed them the divide-and-multiply statistics."

"Yes, we showed them the diagrams. Explained how four years ago our attendance ranked the highest in its history. We had so many kids they were hanging from the ceiling. Went on to show how, from that point till now, our attendance declined."

"I guess that fed Bud's argument."

"Yep, Bud made his point, and that drove it home."

Wilburn paced the room. "Then Harris started raving about what his wife said. Seems Hazel likes her class and her teacher, and she's not moving to a different class regardless of how many we create," he said, mocking

Hazel.

"They went from that to attacking me because the offerings have been down. That really ticked me off, so I asked Harris what he planned to do to bring in more money."

Cyn chuckled. "You didn't?"

"Sure did."

"What did he say?"

"Just what I expected. He said, 'Seems to me, that's what we pay you to do. You're the preacher, and I can't remember the last time you preached a hot sermon on tithing. Anybody else remember?' Then he looked at the others as if for support. No one looked back, so he kept talking." Wilburn did a perfect Harris imitation. "'Besides, since our attendance is falling off, why go spend money on another building? We're not using all the space we have now.'"

Wilburn raised his palms to the ceiling. "Why, indeed."

He sat stunned, looking, as if in his mind's eye, he saw a bad situation dissolve to a worse case, end-of-the-world scenario. "Then, to make matters worse, Hazel Harrison barged into the deacon's meeting demanding that I 'never let that Dee woman darken the doors of the church again.'"

"She didn't?" Cyn suppressed a laugh. Now wasn't the time for that.

"Hazel even threatened if she saw Dee there again, she'd never put another penny in the offering plate. That closed down the whole meeting."

Cyn moved to the sink and made busy washing her coffee cup so Wilburn wouldn't see the grin on her face.

Not because she didn't feel sorry for him, but because the whole thing sounded like a carnival, especially combined with what she and Dee went through earlier that evening.

"As if that wasn't bad enough, all the work we did is now down the drain."

"That's too bad. I'm truly sorry." She turned back to Wilburn. "I know getting that plan approved stood to make a big difference, but I'm not sure we can blame all that on Dee."

"No, but it sure didn't help." Wilburn stared at his now-empty cup and let out a heavy, hopeless-sounding sigh. "That building program held the key to the future of the church. I guess I don't know what they want." He shoved his cup aside. "Oh, well, enough about that for now. Nothing more I can do, or if there is, I don't know what it is."

Wilburn never seemed to express his true feelings. Cyn wished he'd said, "They really pissed me off." But he didn't, and she knew they had. She also knew he hurt.

"Right now, I've got to get to the hospital before Mrs. Baker goes into surgery." He walked to the door and then turned back to Cyn. "Whatever you do, don't let Dee set foot inside the church again. If you have to, tie her up, leave her here by herself. Maybe she'll get the picture and leave."

His words were stern, uncompromising. This time, when he left the room, it felt like he took all the oxygen with him.

Dee brought the air back when she stepped into the kitchen a few minutes later. She looked Cyn in the eyes as if trying to read her mind in case the words didn't match.

"So does he want me to leave?"

"I'm thinking you might want to leave," Cyn said, unable to imagine her wanting to stay.

Dee shuffled to the coffee pot, filled two cups, and handed one to Cyn. "You want me, I'm here, except I have a flight out later this morning to clean out my office and deal with an apartment I can't afford now. Let me do that, and then touch base with you."

"Only problem with you leaving is I don't want the women to think they won." Cyn grinned.

Dee raised her hand for a high five. "Atta girl." The first high-five anyone ever offered Cyn.

"They haven't won," Dee argued, "because it isn't a race. But anyway, I really have to leave for a couple of days. I got a message from HR this morning. They need me to return for out-processing. If I don't go, they'll cancel my airline ticket, and I won't ever leave here." She chuckled. "Wouldn't that delight Wilburn?"

Cyn opened the refrigerator and peeked inside. "How about breakfast first? I have bacon, eggs—"

"Tell you what, let's go out to eat. I saw this neat little place on the corner yesterday—"

"I can't, sweetheart."

"Why in the world not?"

Cyn closed the refrigerator, grabbed a broom, and started sweeping the floor.

"Stop that. Look at me. It is Wilburn isn't it? He controls the money."

Cyn continued sweeping.

"Is your name even on the checkbook—the credit cards?"

"Of course it is, but—"

"But you have to ask him before you spend anything.

Okay, that settles it. I planned to treat you to breakfast, but instead, you're going to treat me. Where's your checkbook?"

"I'm in enough trouble as it is, Dee. Please don't push this."

Dee's shoulders drooped. "Okay, I give up. It's up to you, sweetheart. I'm heading upstairs to dress, and then I'm walking to the café for breakfast. From there, I'll call a taxi to take me to the airport."

"What about your suitcase?"

"No biggie. It has rollers, and there's a sidewalk between here and the café." After a final swig, she rinsed the empty cup, put it in the drain rack, and headed upstairs.

Caught between Wilburn's pull on one leg, and Dee's pull on the other, Cyn stood in the middle of the kitchen feeling like the baby King Solomon ordered cut in half and distributed to the two women who both claimed him as their son.

"Okay, okay, I'm coming," Cyn called out to Dee's retreating footsteps.

CHAPTER FOUR

Cyn entered the small neighborhood restaurant ahead of Dee, and the two scanned the room for an empty table.

"Hey, girlfriends," a sugary voice said. "I thought that was you two coming in the door."

Cyn and Dee both turned towards the familiar voice. Ginger stood with her car keys in her hand and an oversized bright orange handbag over her shoulder.

"Ginger, you don't live in this neighborhood, what are you doing here?" Cyn looked from Ginger to Dee and back again. "You already dropped Miller at school?"

"Girl, he loves school so much we have to hold him back until they unlock the doors." She signaled the hostess and asked Cyn if she could join them.

With little choice, other than to be rude, Cyn agreed.

They spotted an empty table and the three headed

that way.

Meanwhile, Ginger hadn't come up for air. "Stephen came into the kitchen this morning and asked what I thought about him calling Wilburn and offering the two of you tickets for the Chamber's charity ball. Told him I thought about calling you anyway, especially after the fiasco last night. Thought you might need a diversion. By the way, Dee, I wouldn't have missed that look on Hazel's face for anything in this world."

The waitress came, took their breakfast orders, and left.

"Doubt Wilburn got as much pleasure out of it as we did." Dee glanced at Cyn.

So Dee had heard Wilburn in the kitchen talking to Cyn earlier that morning. Cyn had hoped otherwise.

Ginger snickered behind her napkin then turned to Cyn. "I say we change the subject. So what do you think about attending the charity ball?"

"I don't need to think about it. Wilburn won't go. We don't dance."

"It isn't a dance per se. It's an event for charity. Maybe Stephen can talk Wilburn into it."

"Maybe. Stephen can more likely convince him easier than I could, but I'll be surprised if he's successful."

The waitress interrupted their conversation when she came to the table with a carryout bag. "Mrs. Goodman, here is the chicken casserole you ordered. It's frozen, so be sure you refrigerate it a soon as you get home. And, if you want, I can add it to your breakfast tab."

Ginger flushed but kept talking, almost as if she were embarrassed that they knew about the take-out order. She grabbed the bag, gave the server a curt nod, and shoved the order under the table. "I think you and Wilburn need a night out. As I told Stephen, you're such a neat person. I hate to see you put up with those busybodies at church. One of these days I hope you tell them off, but good."

"Only if Cyn wants to get Wilburn fired." Dee smirked.

"Cyn? You called her Cyn," Ginger cried. "Wouldn't Wilburn have a fit?"

"Why should he? That's her name."

"No, it isn't." Ginger looked from Dee to Cyn. "Is it? Is she telling the truth?"

"More like stretching it." Cyn shot daggers at her sister while she explained her nickname and Wilburn's refusal to call her that. All these years she'd kept the nickname a secret. Leave it to her troublemaker sister. Cyn grabbed Ginger's hand and squeezed. "Promise you won't call me that. Promise."

"You better not," Dee said, laughing. "Wilburn would kill us both."

The waitress brought their food, and the three sat in awkward silence until she went back to the kitchen.

"Not to worry, Cynthia," Ginger whispered. "I can keep secrets. By the way, Dee, I thought I'd die laughing when Stephen told me about Hazel and her entourage barging into the inner sanctum and giving Pastor a blast about you."

Cyn swallowed hard. The last thing she wanted was for Dee to get into that conversation with Ginger.

After another awkward silence, Dee shrugged. "Guess I didn't make any friends last night."

"You made a big impression on me." Ginger reached

across the table and rested her hand on Dee's. "I haven't had a good laugh in a long time. I guess you've heard the rumors that bitch, Hazel was the one who told stories about me and the last pastor."

Cyn's silverware clattered to the table.

Dee hooted. "Really? No, what?" A smile spread across Dee's face.

"Absolutely not," Cyn said, louder than intended. "I won't talk about Hazel. I can't. Wilburn would kill me."

Conversation stopped, not only at their table but also at the one closest to theirs. The couple rose in a hurry. The man tossed a couple of bills on the table and ushered the woman to the front.

Dee looked from Cyn to Ginger, and then back again. "Okay, I guess we better behave. But there's one question I'd like to ask you, Ginger."

"What's that?"

Cyn held her breath. What in God's name was Dee going to ask?

"Is your red hair natural?"

"Sure it is. If you call Clairol's Natural Red natural. It gets me lots of attention, that's for sure. I know people see me as ditsy. But you know what? I'm not as ditsy as they think. It's my cover. If no one takes me seriously, I can fly under the radar."

"I've heard of women like you." Dee chuckled and gave a quick glance Cyn's way.

"I've got the drill down to an art form," Ginger continued. "That's how I get what I want. How about you, Dee? Is yours?"

"Natural red? Afraid so. Led to all kinds of teasing in school. But that's behind me."

Relieved when Ginger's cell phone rang, Cyn fiddled with her food while Ginger stepped away from the table to take the call.

When she returned, she excused herself and hurried off, but not before she grabbed the take-out chicken casserole.

"Well, that's a relief." Dee added a packet of sugar to her reheated cup of coffee and then finished off a biscuit smothered in butter and jelly. "That woman makes me nervous. There's something about her I don't trust."

"What makes me nervous is how you stay so tiny, Dee, and eat like you do."

Dee smiled. "It's because I never worry about anything."

"Are you saying if I stop worrying—"

"I'm just sayin'..." Dee opened another packet of jelly.

"It's not fair," Cyn whined, winking at her sister.

"Not to change the subject," Dee said, changing the subject, "but is it just me, or did you get the idea Ginger didn't want us to know she was buying a take-out meal?"

"I thought the same thing." Cyn watched out the window as Ginger drove off.

"Okay, then I'm not going crazy. But that doesn't make sense. Why would she want to hide a foil pan full of King Ranch Chicken?"

"Beats me, but how did you know it was King Ranch?"

"Read it on her ticket."

They finished their meal, and when the waitress brought the check, Cyn dumped a handful of quarters on the little black tray, quarters she'd raided from the family piggy. Hopefully, Wilburn wouldn't notice them gone as easily as a check stub made out to the café.

Cyn looked up to see Dee glaring at the quarters. "Don't judge me, Dee. You never had a husband. When you're married, you work as a team. One doesn't go off and spend money without the other one's approval."

"Does he?" Dee shoved her plate aside.

"Does he what?" Cyn asked, as if innocent to Dee's meaning.

"Call you every time he wants to spend money."

"No, but that's different."

"How?"

"He makes the money and manages the budget. He knows if we can afford it."

Outside, a yellow cab pulled up and stopped.

"That's my cab." Dee plopped a couple of tens on the tray and slid out of the booth. "Pick up your dang quarters and save them for a day when you're more desperate. Sounds to me like you have one coming. I love you dearly, sweet sister, but I give up. If your life works for you, fine. I've said all I'm going to say."

She kissed Cyn on the forehead, collected her suitcase, and hurried out.

Stunned at Dee's sharp departure, Cyn watched her climb into the taxi and speed away.

Not ready to face the rest of her day, Cyn motioned to the waitress to refill her coffee cup, then leaned back and allowed her thoughts to wander. What happened to her perfect world? Or did it ever exist? If it didn't, it certainly wasn't for her lack of trying.

Then it hit her, perhaps there lay the fallacy.

At times, she'd flirted with the idea of leaving

Wilburn. But preachers' wives could not leave their husbands, because if they did, their husbands lost their jobs—at least in their denomination. A job God called them to perform. If she caused that, wouldn't that put her in league with the devil?

She'd slept in her bed, nothing else to do but wash the sheets.

The breakfast gang had emptied out by the time Cyn's mind returned to the present. Embarrassed, she grabbed her wallet and hurried home.

Soon as she stepped on the porch she heard the phone ringing like crazy.

Once inside, she hurried to answer, then wished she'd let it go to voice mail. Wilburn's irritated voice asked, "What took you so long to answer?"

"I do take showers you know."

"This time of day? Well, anyway, I called to tell you I can't make it home for lunch, and also to let you know we're going to the big charity ball the Chamber of Commerce sponsors every year."

Her jaw dropped. Her world spun faster. Why couldn't she keep up? And why could Stephen get things out of Wilburn that she couldn't—and never had. She wasn't surprised Stephen had asked, because at the café, Ginger said he had two extra tickets. What surprised her was Wilburn's willingness to attend.

"Each chamber member is expected to fill a table of ten," Wilburn explained. "Stephen still has two empty seats at his table. It wouldn't look good if he didn't get those filled, so I told him we'd go."

"That's formal, isn't it?"

"Tux and tails, yes. You did get my tux dry cleaned

after the Porter's wedding, didn't you?"

Cyn's mind rummaged through her closet, but it needn't have bothered. Years ago, she donated the only formal she owned—her wedding dress—to a charitable organization.

"Didn't you? Please tell me you did."

"What?"

"The tux, Cynthia, the tux. Did you get it cleaned?"

"Oh, uh...yes, sure. But what do I wear?"

"Don't you have something in your closet?"

"Not for a formal affair, Wilburn. You know I don't."

"Call Ginger. Stephen said she has a closet full, and he's sure you can borrow one of hers."

Dead silence.

"Are you there?" he asked. "Did I lose you?"

Much to Cyn's shock, Dee's words popped out of her mouth. "I'm not going."

Wilburn stuttered, then, "What did you say?"

"I said I'm not going if I have to wear a borrowed dress that everyone has seen before. It isn't like we are broke."

Cyn held the phone, waiting for a scream that did not come.

"Okay. Go get a dress," he said. "But don't spend much. I don't know how I'm going to pay the bills we have now, much less...and use the credit card. Don't write a check."

"I don't even know where to start looking. When is it? How much time do I have?"

"Saturday night."

"This Saturday? Wow. Not much time to shop, and I

don't have a clue where to look for a formal gown."

"Make sure you don't spend a lot of money."

Yeah, yeah, yeah. "When have I ever spent a lot of money on my clothes?" *Jerk.* She slammed the receiver on the base. Soon as she did, it rang again.

What's he want now?

Instead of Wilburn, Ginger's voice bubbled over the line.

"Oh good, I'm glad you're home. Stephen called and said you and Pastor are attending the ball and sitting at our table. I'm so excited. I've got this gorgeous new emerald-colored dress I'm wearing."

"With that red hair, you'll knock the men's eyes out."

"That's the plan, honey, that's the plan." Ginger gave a colluding laugh. "What about your dress? Got it all picked out?"

"Fancy you should ask. I planned to call you in a couple of minutes. Afraid my wardrobe does not include a formal gown. You know the stores at the mall much better than I do. I was hoping you'd go with me. Help me pick out something."

"Oh, girlfriend, I'm always ready to go shopping. I've wanted us to have a day out anyway. You know me. Say the word shop and I'm ready." Ginger giggled.

"Wilburn said the ball is this Saturday night, is that right?"

"Yep, seven o'clock. How about we go today? We can have lunch in the food court at the mall."

Cyn figured since Wilburn approved her purchasing a dress perhaps he wouldn't make a federal case out of her buying lunch. Besides, she had the handful of quarters in her pocket she hadn't used for breakfast.

They agreed to meet at the food court. With the smaller weekday crowd, and no waiting lines, they grabbed a slice of pizza and a soft drink and located a booth.

Before taking a single bite of food, Ginger returned to the one topic Cyn did not want to talk about ever again. "Girl, I'm sure I don't speak for you, but I wouldn't have missed this month's women's meeting for anything. You never told me about your sister. What a hoot."

"She's something, all right. I figure she's the topic of church gossip right now."

"You figured right," Ginger said. "I've already had five or six calls this morning. You know how these church biddies talk."

"That's funny. None of them called me." Cyn snorted at her own joke. She long suspected they thought her too dumb to know they talked about her behind her back.

"One thing I like about your sister is she's her own person. Women need to be." Ginger snickered. "And for me, the way I do that is to go shopping."

"Well, since I'm not a shopper, I don't have a clue what you're talking about. How does shopping—"

"Folks won't take you for granted, honey. Especially your husband." Ginger fiddled with her straw and smiled. "See, they never know what you'll buy or how much money you'll spend. Be unpredictable—that's my motto."

The word predictable described Cyn better than any other. Wilburn held her in such a vise she couldn't take a step without his approval, from her hairdo, to the length of her skirts, to the color of her nails—demure—befitting the wife of a pastor. Not just how she looked, but what she said, and to the extent possible, what she thought.

"So what's he going to say when he sees you in the gown we choose?" Ginger raised one eyebrow. "You know I believe in dressing to impress."

"Stephen doesn't mind you wearing those tight jeans and plunging necklines?"

"Plunging?" Ginger scoffed and pointed a long red fingernail at her cleavage. "You call this plunging?"

"I may not, but Wilburn would."

"Stephen says he likes me to look nice. Eye candy on the arm sort of thing, I guess."

Cyn wiped a drop of water off the table with a corner of her napkin. "I'm eye candy all right, but not the kind anyone wants to taste. And if shopping makes you your own person, then I guess I'm not that either. I bet I can count on one hand the times I visited this mall. And never without Wilburn."

"I tell you, Cynthia, you've got to get out more. Get a manicure, pedicure, facial—everything."

In her mind's eye, Cyn witnessed Wilburn's fury over her having such a conversation with a church member. She grabbed her glass and took one last swig of lemonade.

"As a matter of fact, after we find your dress, let's stop at that beauty shop at the other end of the mall and get a manicure."

Cyn shook her head. "Better not."

The two left the booth and tossed their trash in the bin.

"I get a manicure every week." Ginger said, wriggling her long red nails in Cyn's face. "You should too. Their prices are cheaper on weekdays. Besides, if you have a standing appointment, you get a discount."

Ginger wrapped her arm around Cyn's waist, and the two strolled the mall. "I know the best store to find your outfit," Ginger said. "I get all my gowns there. Fabulous prices and gorgeous fabric."

Once inside the dress shop, Ginger led Cyn to the rack of formals and began sweeping through them. "You wear a twelve?"

Cyn nodded. "Nothing too bold and definitely not revealing. Wilburn would have a fit."

"What color, let's see, how about this canary yellow?" Ginger snatched the indicated gown, held it up to Cyn, then tossed it over her shoulder and kept going.

After collecting several gowns, the two headed to a large, elegant-looking dressing room.

Discouraged at how one fit, how another made her look fat, how one bunched over her hips, Cyn almost gave up. Then she slipped into the yellow gown. Ginger gave the body-fitting, floor-length outfit a quick zip and both women looked in the mirror, their mouths agape. The soft fabric clung to her in ways only seen when wrapped around movie stars.

"That's the dress," Ginger said. "You look fantastic in it. Wow, what's Pastor going to say about this one? It fits you like a seamstress cut and sewed it to your measurements."

Cyn laughed, pleased at the woman in the mirror. "That's a cliché if I ever heard one, but it does look good. I love the cap sleeves, and the cowl neckline isn't too low."

"Hell's bells no. You should see mine. It plunges,

but not in front." Ginger's laughter filled the dressing room.

Cyn hadn't looked at the price tag. When she did, she wished she hadn't. But, the decision made, she paid for it and expected to take her licks later.

That task completed, the two left the store and turned down another wing of the shopping center. Meanwhile, Ginger continued to hone in on the women's meeting. "Guess you heard what Hazel Harrison said as you left."

Cyn hated to discuss their private life with church members, but always found herself saying more to Ginger than she should. Something about the woman encouraged confidentiality.

"No, but I can imagine."

"Said she knew Pastor wanted to be a big shot in the convention, but he'd never make it with such a marshmallow wife."

Marshmallow. The word stung. Condemned if she did, and condemned if she didn't.

"Before I could say a word in your defense, they abruptly ended the meeting and gathered in gossip groups. Didn't have the program. Said Jesus understood."

"Understood, what? That I'm a...a...white, sweet puff of air?" Tears formed. Cyn swiped her eyes on her sleeve.

"They make me so mad." Ginger huffed out her chest. "What do they expect you to do? I wouldn't give them the time of day. All they want to do is gossip. They said some awful things about the last pastor's wife."

"Not last night. The bigger they pumped her up, the more incompetent I felt."

"Forget those old biddies." Ginger grabbed Cyn's arm and led her into the nail spa, turned in their names, and the two went to the shelf to pick out a color of polish.

"Here, use this one."

"Yellow fingernails? Are you sure?"

"Look." Ginger held the lacquer up to the gown, now on a hanger and encased in a protective plastic bag.

"Perfect match okay, but yellow fingernails? That's for teenagers."

"Trust me."

Cyn snatched the bottle out of Ginger's hands, and the two sat to wait their turn.

With barely a breath, Ginger went on. "Guess you've heard some of the awful things Hazel says about the last pastor."

"Not really." Cyn hated to admit she had, since Ginger's name always accompanied the gossip. "I did hear the deacons asked them to leave." Cyn figured Ginger should know, since Stephen was one of the deacons.

"That part is true. Someday I'll tell you what really happened. Right now, I'm going to treat you to a facial." Before Cyn opened her mouth to decline, Ginger marched to the appointment desk. After talking to the receptionist, she turned to Cyn. "They can fit you in after the mani and pedi, but you'll have to wait a few minutes."

What the heck, Cyn thought. Go for it. She had the dinner she prepared yesterday. Wouldn't take but a few minutes to heat. And she didn't have to tell Wilburn she had a facial, and the wife of his deacon chairman talked her into it—and paid for it.

CHAPTER FIVE

At first, the idea of attending a charity ball excited Cyn, but when the day arrived, she wished Wilburn hadn't accepted the invitation. What if the dress didn't look as good on her as she thought? Maybe she should have cut her hair, or colored it. What if she tripped on the hem of her gown?

Even if none of those catastrophes happened, what would she talk about? If she possessed the gift of gab like Wilburn, her confidence might equal his. The charm he displayed at church seemed to win over almost everyone—they loved him. But somehow she never seemed to pull it off. Instead, she drew a blank when someone asked her a question. Either that or tripped over her words.

The day she brought the yellow dress home, Wilburn

asked the price and nothing else. She rounded it down and didn't include what she spent at the nail spa, but he raised his eyebrows and whistled anyway. "That's a lot of money. I don't know why women can't wear the same dress over and over like men do with tuxes."

"That wouldn't have worked anyway, since I didn't have a formal dress to begin with."

"Well, you do now."

Yes, and the way you think, I won't need another formal dress the rest of my life.

She'd waited for him to ask to see the dress. He hadn't, and she didn't volunteer to show it to him, certain he'd tell her to return it.

So ended that conversation until now, two hours before time to leave for the ball.

She half-expected him to disapprove her wearing it, saying it revealed too much, or fit too tightly, or— whatever. Then, what would she do?

They rarely went out on Saturday nights. Instead, Wilburn preferred a quiet evening at home putting the finishing touches on his sermon for the next day. Anticipating a late evening, he dressed before her and went downstairs to work on his sermon for the next morning.

With the bedroom and bath all to herself, nervousness battled excitement for first place.

She tossed her slacks and blouse into the hamper and eased into the steaming hot bubble bath, feeling somewhat like Cinderella. While soaking, she envisioned that enchanting moment when the perfect dress eased over her head and twittering bluebirds zipped it up the back. Ah, wouldn't it be nice if her fairy godmother showed up.

The bath did its magic, and afterward she wrapped an over-sized towel around her, sat at the dressing table and stared in the mirror.

"Cyn, you are going to a ball," she said to her flushed reflection.

She reveled in taking a little more care with her hair, even pinned up a few curls like Julia Roberts wore in Pretty Woman. Next, she chose a brighter lipstick and blush to help compensate for the lights in the ballroom.

At last, with every reason to stall extinguished, the time arrived, the donning of the gown—the gown that made Cyn beautiful—at least she hoped it would.

In case she felt disappointed after she put it on, she turned her back to the mirror as she slipped the dress over her head, straightened it, and zipped.

Holding her breath, she took slow, deliberate steps, rotated a half turn, and stared at the stranger in the mirror.

Wow. The sunshine color looked perfect next to her skin. She smoothed her hands down the front of the dress and viewed her figure from other angles.

She didn't look that fat—maybe a few extra pounds, but at least she had curves.

Her spirits soared.

"It's time to go, Cynthia," Wilburn called up the stairs. "We're already running late."

A quick, light spray of cologne completed the transformation. She held her breath as she headed downstairs hoping she looked as elegant as she felt.

He stood at the door, holding her jacket out to her. "Nice dress," he said as he opened the front door. "Now hurry." He ushered her to the car.

Conversation on the ride to the event lagged until

Cyn brought up what Ginger had shared on their shopping spree. "What have you heard about the last pastor and why he left?"

"Not anything, really. Only that he left sudden-like. Kind of makes me curious, and I guess a little nervous."

"Nervous? What do you mean? His leaving has nothing to do with you."

"You never can tell."

"Tell what? I don't understand."

Wilburn glanced her way and cleared his throat. "You always ask me what I'm thinking. Well, for one thing, on Sundays when I'm sitting on the platform looking out over the congregation, I wonder which one of those church members in the audience might stab me in the back."

Dumfounded, Cyn realized her mouth dropped open. Unaccustomed to Wilburn sharing anything personal, she couldn't think of a response.

"If they stab one pastor, there is no reason to think they won't stab another."

"That must feel awful," she said, surprised at the softness in her voice.

"It is. To tell the truth, that's why I like you on the front row—shows you support me. At least one person protects my back."

Silent for a mile or two, each lost in their own thoughts Wilburn broke the silence and again lifted the veil on his soul.

"It all goes back to my teenage years. You know what kind of home life I had. No one cared whether I came home or not. In fact, they preferred I didn't. Made life easier for them. So I started going to the neighborhood church. People there cared about me, especially the pastor—Brother Whitaker. He knew I wanted to pastor my own church when I grew up, so he took me under his wing—mentored me. Then, one day something happened—I never knew what—and the deacons got all up in arms over it. They accused him of...well...all kinds of things. The guy had to resign in shame. He never pastored again. I keep thinking that could happen to me. If it did, that throws us both out in the street and Justice out of college."

Cyn stole a glimpse at Wilburn. He stared straight ahead, jaws clenched.

Exhaust fumes from a passing truck filled the car. She covered her nose and punched the recirculation button on the dash.

Unsure what to say, she felt she must say something. "I'm really sorry about that. I can tell it still hurts to talk about it." Without thinking, and wanting to comfort him, she laid her hand on his thigh.

He jumped as if her hand felt like she'd dipped it in the flames of hell.

"Bygones," he said, pulling the veil back down as he turned into the event center parking lot, opened his car door, and shut the door to his soul.

Her eager anticipation of the evening somewhat abated, she mulled over Wilburn's revelation as they walked from the parking lot to the ballroom. However, when they stepped inside, excitement flamed behind her eyes.

Overhead, huge crystal chandeliers sparkled like ten million stars, each determined to outshine the other. Beneath them, large round tables covered with long white tablecloths dotted the room. In the center of each table, multicolored flowers in crystal vases bloomed their hearts out. Topping off the décor, gold place settings glistened atop solid black napkins.

Heady from the beauty of the evening, Cyn felt relieved when Wilburn steadied her with his hand on her elbow. They wended through the crowd in search of their table. At first glance, she didn't see a single familiar face. Evidently, Wilburn didn't either, until their banker greeted them, and later, the owner of the men's clothing store, who showed them to Stephen's table.

Ginger and Stephen already sat, chatting with the others. As soon as Stephen spotted them coming, he jumped up and took Wilburn's hand. "Oh, good, I'm glad Peter found you. Your place cards are at those two empty chairs." He pointed. "The committee wanted to separate couples in order for everyone to get acquainted with people they may not know."

Cyn moved around the table to one of the two empty chairs, relieved to see her place next to Ginger, who looked resplendent in the emerald-colored gown.

Stephen introduced the others at the table. Cyn smiled and nodded while Wilburn, ever the politician, moved around the table to shake the men's hands and bow to the women.

"I got here early and switched place cards to make sure we got to sit beside each other," Ginger whispered in her ear.

Cyn mouthed her thanks, relieved to have Ginger nearby. The man in the chair on the other side of her introduced himself as Mr. Cooper of Anderson, Cooper & Taylor, local homebuilders. Nice looking in a rugged sort of way. Maybe forties or fifties.

Ginger grabbed her hand and in a low tone said, "Girl, you look fantastic. What did Wilburn say?"

Cyn mouthed "nothing," and shrugged.

"Okay, that means we go shopping again Monday."

Cyn frowned, shook her head.

"Miller's got ball practice that afternoon, so I'll meet you in the food court at three. Be there, girlfriend."

How in the world would she explain another shopping excursion to Wilburn, and so soon after the last extravagant trip?

"I'm not so sure about that," Cyn whispered. "We'll talk later."

Mr. Cooper cleared his throat and fiddled with his silverware. "So, Mrs. Carter, tell me a little about yourself. What type of work do you do?"

His question stopped her like it did every time anyone asked where she worked. She did not give her usual answer—I don't work. This time, her words surprised even her. "Actually, I'm looking to change careers."

"Really? To what?"

Now get yourself out of this mess, Missy, her shaming-self whispered.

Make up something, fast, pride argued from the other side.

Cyn grabbed the first answer that floated through her head, unsure which voice offered it as an option. "New Home Sales interests me." Okay, that's not a lie.

Mr. Cooper smiled. "Oh, really? You have experience in that field, I suppose."

"Zero," she confessed. "I do know what women want

in a new home, though."

"Like what?"

She thought a moment. "Well—for instance—to me, at least, it seems builders always locate sink faucets too far back for short women, or even those of average height. I have to lean forward to reach the faucets. After a couple of hours working in the kitchen, the muscles in my back go into spasms. Why can't they put the faucets along the sides instead of at the backs of the sinks? That way, both short and tall people can reach them comfortably."

"Good question. I'll look into that. Anything else?"

"Yes, clothes racks in closets are often so high many women can't reach them."

"Another good point," he said, laughing. "You might fit better working with the architects and designers than in sales. Got any more?"

"Peepholes on doors. A giant installed the one on my front door. I have to stand on tiptoes to look through it. And our toilets—my feet can't touch the floor. Know what it's like to go your whole life feeling like a toddler who can't reach or see anything?" She looked at his size and chuckled. "No, I guess you don't."

"Sounds to me like we might need to talk." He pulled out a business card and handed it to her. "When you're ready, give me a call and let's put our heads together."

"I might do that." She tucked his card into her clutch bag while a world of new possibilities flashed through her thoughts—that is until the self-esteem sucker inside her head barged in uninvited. *What in the world are you doing*, it admonished. *Who do you think you are?*

"By the way," Mr. Cooper added, "you look beautiful in that yellow dress. Magnificent."

The compliment stole Cyn's breath. Ripped it right out of her chest and flung it to the ceiling. By the time her autonomic nervous system kicked in again, an elderly woman on the other side of Cooper held him hostage with a long tale about something. Disappointed, but desperate to not look ill at ease or dismissed, she turned to others at the table. One of the women looked a little familiar, but from where? Other than Ginger and Stephen, Cyn didn't know a soul. Regardless of how hard she tried, she found herself unable to interject anything meaningful into the conversation. She looked at Wilburn, of course in deep conversation with those around him.

She felt beautiful when she left home, but despite Mr. Cooper's compliment, she now felt awkward and out of place.

Relief came with dinner. While servers rested plates in front of each, another young man stood behind the servers and gave an elaborate description of the food.

"Our chef wrapped tender breasts of quail in apple-smoked bacon, grilled it to perfection, then smothered it in a tangy lemon tequila sauce. Next, she sautéed garden-fresh spears of asparagus in olive oil and crushed garlic and sprinkled them with Parmesan cheese. Last, she topped all that off with a pair of savory spaghetti squash fritters."

The banter soon changed to rave compliments of the food.

Guests at her table finished their main course, and servers brought large slices of pecan pie with a dollop of whipped cream. Later they cleared the tables and served steaming coffee in white china cups.

The master of ceremonies told a few jokes, made a

pitch for the Chamber, and then invited folks to dance. Soon, the soft background music changed to a foot-tapping beat. Couples headed to the dance floor. Cyn had never danced before and neither had Wilburn. All her life, she'd been taught dancing was a sin. Evidently, everyone else at the table missed that lesson, because soon, Cyn and Wilburn sat alone sipping coffee and pretending they belonged there. At least she did.

Head down, and without a glance her way, Wilburn scooted his chair back and stood, saying, "I won't be long. I see someone I need to talk to," and walked off.

There she sat in all her newfound beauty, feeling like the proverbial bump—or frump—on a Yule log. Overcome by the many strangers and the elegant surroundings, she scanned the room, hoping no one noticed her. Or realized how miserable she felt.

That hope dashed to the floor when she unintentionally made eye contact with a tall, blond man making his way toward her.

"Good evening, ma'am. Had to come over and say how lovely you look in that gorgeous gown."

Cyn's cheeks grew hot. "Thank you," she said, wracking her brain for small-talk topics.

"If you don't mind my saying so, I don't know of a better shade and hue to compliment that curly brown hair."

"You think?" She pushed a sprig of hair behind her ear.

"I don't think, I know—I'm a colorologist." He put his hand out. "Hi, my name is Thomas."

She clasped it. "Cynthia Carter—actually, Cyn, for short." Why on earth did she tell him her nickname?

Wilburn would be livid.

"I don't mean to sound dumb, but what's a colorologist?" she asked, hoping to change the subject.

"Forgive me, but the time isn't right for us to talk about that. I promise you we will soon. Right now, I want to talk about your name. Cyn. I like that." He winked at her and laughed while pulling her to her feet.

She grabbed her clutch bag with her right hand while Thomas held onto the other. When she turned towards him, she noticed a look of disappointment cross his face.

"So you're married." He fingered the wedding ring on her finger. "Drat. Some men have all the luck."

Not really, she almost said.

He put his hand at the small of her back and led her to the dance floor, but not before she wailed, "Wait, I don't dance."

"I'll teach you, my dear."

"You don't understand. My husband is..."

"What? Jealous? He should be. Actually, I'm glad he's not dancing with you so I can."

"He's a pastor of a local church. They don't believe in dancing."

"They might not, but what about you?"

"I...I..."

"A lot of these people go to church," he said. "If none of them danced, this floor would be mostly empty." Ignoring her refusal, he swept her into an embrace and waltzed around the floor.

"So tell me, why doesn't your church dance?" His eyes twinkled.

"Don't know about all of them, but I remember our youth pastor giving us this sheet of paper that listed fifteen reasons why a Christian won't dance."

"Really? Like what? Or do you not remember them?"

"Oh, yes." Cyn tossed her head back, laughing. "I could probably recount all of them."

"Give me one." He pulled her tighter and made a couple of fast twirls.

After her head stopped spinning, she thought a moment. "Okay, one of them went something like this: The dance is the only place where the vilest of men can embrace the purest of girls in the closest familiarity with the approval of society."

Thomas laughed so loud all the other dancers looked at him and chuckled.

"You gotta be joking."

"I kid you not. And the list does not get any better."

"Okay, I guess that must describe me, because you certainly fit the description of the purest of girls, well, women. Quite a woman at that."

By now, her head swam.

The song ended, but he didn't let her go. Instead, he tightened his grip, waited until the music started again and off they whirled. The room spun, she had no idea where to put her feet, but he led with such power, it didn't matter. She floated.

Until Wilburn stormed up, tapped Thomas on the shoulder, and grabbed Cyn's hand.

Startled, too embarrassed to resist, she allowed Wilburn to drag her off the floor. With her still in tow, he headed straight out the door, down the steps, and out to the car.

She'd crossed his line—and she knew it.

Without saying a word, he opened her car door, bustled her inside, got behind the wheel, and sped off.

"What do you think you're doing, Cynthia, trying to ruin me? Evidently you forgot, pastors' wives set the example for the world."

"But—"

"No buts about it. I knew something like this would happen when you bought that slutty-looking dress, put on all that makeup, and worst of all, painted your fingernails yellow," he yelled. "You humiliated me. Combine that with Dee's behavior, and I don't know if I can survive this embarrassment. If I lose my job, you'll have to go to work washing dishes or something."

"Or designing new homes."

"What?"

"Nothing."

They rode in silence for a few minutes until he picked up where he left off. "And who was that man, anyway? Never seen him before."

"Me, either." She crossed her arms over her chest and stared straight ahead. "His name's Thomas something or the other, that's all I know. And for your information, when he asked me to dance, I told him no. He pulled me on the dance floor anyway. I thought about screaming for help, but you'd have been even more upset if I'd done that. Good lord, the police might have shown up and arrested him. That would have made a bigger scene than the one you made."

Neither one spoke for a few seconds, then she added, "Besides, I figured no one would notice."

"I noticed."

"So did it bother you to see me in the arms of

another man? Or worried someone might think bad about you?"

"Don't be ridiculous."

They finished the ride home in silence.

Cyn wasn't silent on the inside though. This steam she felt—did Wilburn's behavior generate it, or did dancing with a good-looking man named Thomas?

CHAPTER SIX

Wilburn arose early, irritated at the morning's arrival before his body felt ready for the day ahead of him. He disliked events on Saturday nights because it always meant he got to bed late. He felt rushed now and hated that. Hated stepping into the pulpit without full confidence of his readiness. Every time he did, and struggled with the message, he promised himself he would never accept another Saturday night engagement.

However, last night he needed to support Stephen and the Chamber of Commerce. After all, Stephen's connection with the church and his leadership in the community didn't hurt Wilburn's status one bit. Besides…

Cynthia still slept while he eased into the bathroom to shower and shave. His heavy beard always required extra effort. He lathered his face and started scraping.

Meanwhile, worry burrowed into his brain. He hated to admit it, but seeing Cynthia in the arms of that man the previous night unnerved him. He'd said some awful things to her, and now he regretted them. Truthfully, that yellow gown looked delicious on her, and it obviously lifted her spirits. Maybe if he encouraged her to go shopping more often, to buy something new to wear, that would lift her spirits. She always wanted to look nice. Maybe he needed to tell her more often that she did. He wrote a mental sticky note and pressed it to his brain.

That worry taken care of, he picked up the problems with the deacons. Seems they had dug in their heels and refused to budge on the building proposal. That left him little choice but to slow down on the project and build a stronger support base. Later today, he would call Randy Del Rey and tell him to hang onto the plans, along with the bids. For now, he had enough to fret about.

Dressed for the day, he tiptoed downstairs, slid a gospel CD into the player, and lowered the volume so as not to awaken Cynthia. Next, he headed for the coffee pot. At least Cynthia prepared and set the pot the night before even though she said not another word to Wilburn after they got home.

Taking the steaming cup with him, he went to his study, sat at his desk, and pulled out his sermon notes. By the time Cynthia came downstairs, he felt halfway ready for the worship service

After a quick breakfast, he grabbed his Bible and sermon notes and headed for the door. The two went in separate vehicles because Cynthia preferred to go late and leave early, but he needed to hang around and greet his parishioners. They always wanted to talk to him about his sermon, and although he hated to admit it, their compliments fed his soul as nothing else. They reassured him he made the right decision years ago. No turning back, no turning back.

"I'm leaving now," he called up the stairs. "See you there in a few minutes, okay? You are coming aren't you?"

He left, not sure if she answered or not, but decided now wasn't the time to push it.

The full parking lot made him happy—a sign of good attendance. As soon as he opened his car door, parishioners swarmed up with questions and comments about his sermon the week before. Several sympathized with him over what happened at the deacon's meeting, claiming Hazel Harrison's behavior abhorrent and, of course, they welcomed his wife's sister.

As usual, that gossip traveled fast, but so far, it seemed he'd survive Dee's behavior, that was unless or until she came back into town and caused more trouble.

He didn't know why, but he felt uncomfortable last night at the ball associating with non-believers, or at least people who didn't believe like he did. This morning, back on his turf, he felt lighter—safer perhaps. He buttoned his jacket and marched inside.

The Sunday School hour progressed without too many unplanned teacher absences. Several people asked about Cynthia and whether or not she planned to attend.

"Yes, she's around here somewhere." He smiled, hoping he showed a sense of confidence. In truth, he couldn't swear to her presence, or even if she intended to come.

He knew members talked about how often Cynthia missed church. Baptists expected to see the pastor's wife every time the doors opened, looking perfect, and loving everybody. Cynthia often complained they wanted two for the price of one. Perhaps they did, but he could do little to change that long-held expectation. After Dee's shenanigans, he needed Cynthia to step up to her responsibilities like never before.

When time for the worship service approached, Wilburn escaped to the pastor's study to catch his breath.

A few minutes later, the organist started the prelude—his cue. He exited his study and stepped onto the sanctuary platform, checking to see whether or not Cynthia sat on the front pew.

She did.

The tenseness in his shoulders softened. She resented sitting there, he knew that, but did she feel any different about doing so today? The fact that he had confessed the reason why he wanted her there every Sunday surprised him. He seldom opened up about himself. He preferred that his private pain stay private.

However, he didn't reveal the whole story of that past event. He stopped short of telling her.

He rammed a proverbial rod down his back, and along with the rod, the memory. The organist finished the Prelude and gave Wilburn the nod. He cleared his throat, moved to the podium, and read the Call to Worship. Afterward, the music minister led the song service while Wilburn returned to the pastor's bench and perused the audience.

Stern faces, smiling faces, bored faces, faces of contempt, friendly-looking faces, whispering faces, children's intent faces, focused on coloring inside the lines of pictures from Sunday School. Teenagers passed notes back and forth while mouthing the words of the current hymn. What thoughts occupied the parishioners' minds? Would his sermon hit home? Or would they not hear a word he said?

Hazel and Harris sat on the last row. What might they be cooking up against him?

A couple of people nodded off in the middle of his sermon. He wondered if he bored them. Did others view him as ineffective? What about the two women near the stained glass windows on the right, whispering to each other? They looked bored. What did they talk about? Him? His sermon?

He spoke louder, slammed his hand on the pulpit for emphasis. At least that got their attention.

After the service, he stood in the vestibule shaking hands, wondering why he didn't see several faithful members. What kind of activity superseded faithful church attendance? Why would anyone ever put something like a ballgame ahead of going to church? What did he do wrong, why didn't more people attend service today? Hopefully, even though they didn't come, they sent in their tithe. The deacons blamed the in-the-red budget on Wilburn. So much so, they refused any opportunity for expansion—a factor critical to the church's future.

Even though he tried not to take it personally, he could always count on a couple of members to make sure he did. You've got to be a stronger leader, Pastor. Or, you need to do more Bible-based preaching, Pastor, not so much about money.

Damned if he did and damned if he didn't. Production and attendance—all performance driven. If he didn't get the attendance up, he wouldn't ever get a bigger church. If he didn't get contributions up, he might as well forget the former.

If only he could get a little notice from the denominational office, be invited to speak at the convention, get recognized somehow.

He put every ounce of energy and attention into creating an attitude of worship. At times like this, he wondered why he bothered. Even then, all that paled in the shadow of his biggest fear. If folks learned about that, and they would someday, it would all be over. Not to mention what that would do to Cynthia.

By the time he got home, Cynthia had Sunday dinner on the table. He spent the afternoon sitting with his feet up and the newspaper in front of his face. His thoughts centered on anything but the news.

Wilburn awoke the next morning wanting to pull the blanket over his head and shut out the world. But he dare not miss a church member's operation scheduled for eight o'clock. If he failed to have prayer with her and the family before the attendants rolled her into surgery, he'd never hear the end of it.

"Up and at 'em." He nudged Cynthia. If she got up now and started breakfast while he showered, he'd have time to eat and get to the hospital before they sedated Mrs. Nelson. If he missed seeing her before she went into surgery...well, that couldn't happen.

Wilburn reached the hospital in time, and the surgery went well. When they moved Mrs. Nelson to her private room and he had a chance to visit with her a couple of minutes, he excused himself and headed to the church.

On the drive across town, his overriding thoughts circled the now-defunct expansion project. He and the committee spent countless hours hashing and rehashing every nickel and dime of the proposal, but he'd take another look when he got to his office. Maybe they'd missed something.

He walked into his office and straight to the phone to tell Cynthia he'd pick up fast food and work through lunch. Instead of talking to her, however, he talked to the stupid answering machine. "I guess it's just as well I'm not coming home for lunch," he said. "Looks like you're out running the roads anyway." He hung up, ambled over to the window, and stared out at nothing. Some days he felt like walking away from everything. Get on a Greyhound Bus and ride to its last stop.

He turned and stared at the proposal on the corner of his desk. If he didn't know better, he'd swear the stupid thing mocked him. He sighed, walked over to his desk, and opened the file folder.

Wrapped in the minutia of the project, he ended up missing lunch altogether. By the time he got home that evening, exhausted, and expecting supper to be on the table, his stomach felt smashed flat and wrapped around his backbone.

Instead of Cynthia having dinner ready, however, he found a note taped to the refrigerator. It read; Lunch in the fridge. Help yourself. Ginger called, and we've gone shopping. Don't know when I'll be home.

He crumpled the note and pitched it in the trashcan. Days like this, he wished he drank. A couple glasses of whiskey and he'd forget Dee's behavior. A couple more shots and the failure of the expansion plan might fade— but he doubted it.

Halfway up the stairs to change clothes, the doorbell rang. He turned and leaned over the banister to look out the window, but saw only his car. He trotted downstairs and without bothering to check the peephole, threw open the front door.

"Hi, Pastor," Ginger sang in her lilting voice.

"Hello, Ginger." He looked around her. "Where's your car?"

"Oh, I parked down the street," she said, her face turning red. "Didn't want to take up all the room in front of your house." She danced from one foot to the other, her mitted hands holding a dish. "I know Cynthia hasn't felt well lately, so I brought this casserole over for your supper. Thought it might help."

"Why, that's awfully nice." Wilburn stiffened. "But you should know Cynthia isn't home right now. Her note said the two of you had gone shopping again."

"We did, but in the middle of it, I got a call from Miller. He needed me to go pick him up at school. So, I thought while I had a few minutes I..." She looked from Wilburn to the casserole, sucking through her teeth as if the dish burned her fingers.

"I'm sorry for my rude behavior. Here, let me take that." He reached around the door for the dish. The last thing he needed was to invite Ginger inside without Cynthia. He'd heard the stories about Ginger and the last pastor. Seminary professors drilled thou shall not into the heads of pastoral students over and over again. A pastor should never allow himself to be in questionable circumstances with another woman.

"Oh, that's okay, it's fresh out of the oven," Ginger said. "What kind of church member lets their pastor grab a hot dish? No sense in both of us getting burned. Here, I'll take it to the kitchen." She gave a nervous laugh as she charged past him and headed down the hall, spike heels pinging on the tile floor.

Wilburn stood with the door wide open, waiting, listening to the furnace kick on, picturing the whirling numbers on the electric meter and the growing suspicions of nosy neighbors.

"Ginger?"

When she didn't answer, he had little choice but to leave the door open while he headed down the hall in search of her. Certain she'd entered the kitchen he rounded the corner only to find the room empty.

"I'm in here, Pastor," Ginger called out, honeysuckle charm dripping from her voice.

Leery, but without a clue what else to do other than run out the front door, he stepped into the family room.

There stood Ginger.

Naked.

CHAPTER SEVEN

Still irritated that Ginger abandoned her in the middle of the shopping trip, Cyn decided to continue trying on dresses anyway. She found a blood-red dress, wriggled it over her hips and stared at her figure in the dressing room mirror.

Pretty dang good.

But dare she buy it so soon after the yellow gown, and without Wilburn's approval?

Turning sideways, she sucked in her stomach and turned to face the mirror again, finger-combed her hair and pinched her cheeks.

She gave another turn and looked. "This dress comes with me."

When she got home, she'd tuck it away where Wilburn wouldn't look. Eternal optimist, she hoped he wouldn't notice the credit card bill until he saw how good she looked wearing it.

The dress paid and packaged; she headed back to the house with a plan to hide the frock at the back of her closet before Wilburn arrived.

She didn't make it.

Soon as she stepped through the front door, she caught the aroma of chicken casserole with a hint of Ginger's cologne. But she hadn't seen Ginger's car in the driveway, only Wilburn's.

"Wilburn?" she called out, checked the living room and den, and then went to the kitchen. True to her bloodhound nose, a King Ranch Casserole, prepared and baked in an aluminum pan lay on the counter—and it looked like the same casserole Ginger purchased and hid under the table at the café down the street.

Confused when she couldn't find Wilburn or Ginger downstairs she eased upstairs, a knot forming in her gut.

On the way to their bedroom, she stopped and stashed the red dress in the guest room closet. No sense in complicating things. If he and Ginger were upstairs doing something they shouldn't, she certainly didn't want to make it any easier for Wilburn to throw a smoke screen at her.

Back out in the hall, she went to their bedroom and eased the door open to an empty room, but with the shower going full blast.

The bed looked mussed, and Wilburn's clothes lay in a pile on the floor. She stared at them for a second, then walked over and picked up the white shirt.

Red lipstick on the collar and a distinctive aroma of Ginger's cologne told Cyn she didn't like where this headed.

The shower stopped.

She held her breath and waited, listening.

The shower door opened and banged shut.

Of all the fears she ever entertained, Wilburn's unfaithfulness never entered her mind. But perhaps Dee knew Wilburn better than Cyn did. Surely, however, he wasn't stupid enough to have an affair with Ginger, and especially in his own house. With her feet stuck to the floor as if she'd stepped in super glue she waited for him—them—to come out.

Wilburn came out first, a towel wrapped around his waist. He stopped at the door and gawked at her. Guilt creased his forehead. But instead of defending himself, he went on the attack. "So, what did you buy now, and how much did you spend?"

"Not this time, Wilburn. This is not about me." She shoved the shirt with the lipstick-stained collar at him. "Where did you hide Ginger?"

"Ginger?"

"Don't tell me I'm wrong. I smelled her cologne soon as I walked in the front door. That and the fact that she left her take-out casserole in the kitchen."

"Well, it's a good thing she came. Otherwise, I wouldn't have any dinner since my wife ran the roads spending money we don't have."

"Don't change the subject, you bastard."

She'd never used the word in her life—at least not since she married Wilburn—and when it shot out of her mouth, she stopped, shocked at herself.

Wilburn's face turned purple. He came towards her. "Don't you back talk, especially with that kind of language."

Reflex led her back a step. He had never struck her before, but something about the look in his eyes told her he'd stepped over the line into darkness and her odds ended now. He came faster than her mind cognized. In one swift instant, his hot-as-a-branding-iron hand slammed into her face.

Knocked to her knees, horrified, her hand cradled her fiery cheek. Tears stung her eyes.

"Oh no, oh no," Wilburn cried, falling to his knees beside her. "I'm so sorry, I didn't mean to...I didn't...do that. It'll never happen again. I promise, I promise, I promise."

She cringed when he reached out, but he only pulled her hand away to see the damage. "Oh, Cynthia, please forgive me. I promised myself I'd never hit my family. I had enough of that as a kid. I know what it feels like." He helped her up, led her to the bathroom, and applied a cold compress to her face, while apologizing, over and over.

Cyn pushed her shoulders back. "I still need to know whose lipstick that is, and where you hid Ginger?"

"Ginger's not here. And the lipstick, I told you the truth, I don't know. I meet upset women all the time. At the hospital—"

"Nope, don't give me that. You won't sleep with me so why did you sleep with her?" Cyn knew she pushed it, especially after he struck her, but figured she better not waste his improved mood.

"Sleep with her? No. When I got home, I lay down to rest awhile. And yes, she came inside for a few minutes when she brought the hot casserole in." He threw his hands in the air. "That's it. Nothing else happened. I refuse to dignify your sick mind. If you think I'd sleep with her, you don't know me at all."

"Are you telling me the truth?"

"Cynthia, if you don't know me by now, you never will."

Refusing to let him pull her off the topic, she said, "Okay, say you didn't sleep with her. Then how did the lipstick get on your collar?"

"I already told you. You know how women are, they're always wanting to hug the preacher."

"So you admit the two of you hugged."

"I didn't admit..." He pulled off the towel and pulled on a pair of lounge pants and robe, then slid his feet into slippers. "I didn't hug her. She hugged me."

"She hugged you? You mean like needing comfort or—"

"Yeah, yeah, something like that. Take my word for it, nothing happened. Nothing."

"Wilburn, I know you think I'm stupid, but I saw her buy that casserole the other day at—" Uh-oh, he didn't know she and Dee ran into Ginger at the café. Relieved when Wilburn didn't seem to notice her slip-up, she clammed shut and refused to talk about the topic anymore.

On the way downstairs to prepare dinner, Cyn mused at Ginger's skill in timing her visit here to make a move on Wilburn when she knew for certain Cyn wasn't home.

She headed downstairs to toss a salad and set the table for dinner. The chicken casserole glared at her. She touched it. Cold. Ginger certainly didn't leave the mall in time to prepare and cook it. She planned and set up the event.

Cyn popped the pan in the oven and poured them both a glass of iced tea.

Neither of them said anything while they ate—or rather while Wilburn ate. Cyn couldn't force down a single bite of the casserole. She sipped tea and nibbled on the green salad.

After dinner, Wilburn locked himself in his study. Cyn flipped on the television and watched the last half of a Tommy Lee Jones movie, then roamed the house, wondering what really happened when Ginger came.

Wilburn's story didn't fit.

Regardless, she had little recourse other than to accept what Wilburn said and act like nothing happened—else he'd raise hell.

Her preacher's wife mask felt tighter, as if at any minute, it might cut off her breath.

Desperate for fresh air, she walked outside. The cicadas lost their hold on summer a while ago—along with the shells on their backs—and the early fall evenings, quieter now, felt peaceful. A cool softness wafted in with the breeze. She eased her weary body onto the porch swing, nudging its movement with her feet, loneliness enveloping her like a fog.

Face it, she thought. Even if Wilburn lied about what happened between him and Ginger, that didn't change the fact that he and Cyn barely tolerated living in the same house with each other. Night after night, she lay in bed, her body longing for a man's touch—a touch that never came. He stopped trying so many years ago, she'd lost track. How long could she stay in a marriage without it—without intimacy at least at some level?

Cyn closed her eyes and let the swing carry her to

memories of the movie she watched earlier. Tommy Lee Jones—a strong man, stood on his own two feet. He didn't need the woman for support. He wanted her, oh boy how he wanted her, but need? No. He had a healthy ego, thank you very much.

Indulging herself, she wondered about life married to him. One thing for sure, she could decide for herself whether she went to church or not—and if she chose not to, Tommy Lee wouldn't make her feel guilty.

He'd touch her, running his finger lightly up her arm, raising chill bumps. In her mind's eye, she shivered and snuggled into him. He'd write notes like; *You were great last night.* Draw a smiley and sign it at the bottom with a Chévere then tuck the piece of yellow legal paper underneath her windshield wiper.

He'd not expect her to be a submissive wife. Rather he'd want her as his equal, having a voice, an opinion different from his. He wouldn't feel threatened if she disagreed with his views on life, death, sin, goodness, right, and wrong. And he'd make love to her. Mad, passionate love, not mechanical or perfunctory, as though she had a button to push if he could only find it.

And he'd call her Cyn.

CHAPTER EIGHT

The soft chirp of birds settling in the sprawling live oak near the porch and the easy movement of the swing added to the magic of the evening. Cyn pulled her sweater tighter and allowed herself to drift from thoughts of Tommy Lee to events of the last few days. She must have dozed because the creak of the front door opening roused her. She looked up to see Wilburn striding out, the old boards creaking under his feet.

"You'll never guess who called." His smile grew bigger with each step.

"No, but from the look on your face, the news is good."

"Let's say they need a keynote speaker for the annual state convention, and someone put my name in the hopper."

"Oh, my." Cyn fought to clear the cobwebs from her thoughts. "Really? Wow, that's quite an honor to be nominated..." Her words reminded her of the Oscars. It's an honor to be nominated; the actors always said, knowing full well they wanted to win.

Regardless, an opportunity to present such a message never failed to boost a pastor's status in the convention. Wilburn had worked long and hard for this prize.

For an instant, Cyn felt the heavy tug between doubt and knowing—discomfort and comfort. Despite the lingering questions about Wilburn and Ginger, Cyn shoved them deeper into the black void vacated by her soul. When, or at what point that void occurred, she hadn't a clue—only the reality of its existence.

She felt the mask grow even tighter as she slid to the other side of the swing and patted the seat beside her. "That's great, Wilburn. I'm excited for you. Did they offer a formal invitation?" She tried to sound excited—put passion in her words—but knew she didn't make it. At the moment, all she felt was a growing sense of disillusionment with Wilburn and everything he stood for.

"Not yet. The chairman of the Committee on Order of Business, the man in charge of the selection process, called to ask me a few questions."

He sat next to her, fidgeting like an excited child.

"When does the convention meet?" She nudged the porch with her foot. The swing responded, creaking as it moved.

"November 12th, next year I think. I got so excited the exact date slipped my mind." He squeezed her hand. "I've waited so long for this, Cynthia. What a huge opportunity. If I can wow that group, no telling where I can go in the convention. Think about it."

Cyn's fantasies about finding someone like Tommy Lee dissipated into the evening breeze, leaving behind...nothing.

A man might exist who would love Cyn unconditionally, but Wilburn's status in the convention would be a train wreck without her. Their denomination might forgive one of their ordained ministers for committing murder, theft, even having an affair, but divorce? No way.

Besides, if she did leave, what would that make her—in cahoots with the devil? How did a pastor's wife leave her husband when to do so meant she deprived her husband of his ability to follow God's calling for his life?

She'd never seen Wilburn so excited.

Or felt so miserably trapped.

"This guy, Dr. Powell, pastors the big church in Montgomery," Wilburn said. "He said he would call to set up a time for us to meet. If that goes well, he will issue me an official invitation. I emailed him my vitae before I came outside."

"Did someone put your name before the committee or what?"

"Seems this year they plan a focus on the backbone of the convention, the mid-sized churches, which are the majority, of course. The leaders felt the time had come to honor the grassroots of the denomination. So, as a part of that effort, they are highlighting these churches that often get overlooked. Somehow, my name surfaced as a possible speaker."

Cyn's mind raced. "So, how do I fit into this? Am I expected to go?"

"Of course. Might even need to get you a new outfit—a suit maybe." He chuckled. "That yellow dress might be a little over the top, so don't take Ginger with you to pick it out."

Cyn stiffened.

He paused a moment, then added, "Come to think about it, I'm not sure you should spend much time with Ginger."

"Why is that, Wilburn?" She made no attempt to disguise the sarcasm.

"She brought the casserole over like I told you, but she knew you weren't here."

"That's what I said," she cried. "She had to have known. She left me shopping at the mall."

"Cynthia..." he stopped, looked at her before he continued. "She did try to get me into bed."

Cyn nudged the swing faster. Meanwhile, her mind raced to keep up. "Wait. Would you go flip off the porch light?" she said, stalling. She knew she'd not feel any better after he confessed the happenings with Ginger that day, but regardless of what he said, she wanted to hear it in the dark.

For the longest, they both sat without speaking. She didn't know about Wilburn, but the sense of betrayal and innocence-lost squashed any words. When at last she spoke, she asked, "So that was her lipstick on your collar."

"Afraid so. Nothing happened though. Believe me, nothing happened. I told her to put her clothes back on and leave."

Cyn choked. "Put her clothes back on?" She jumped out of the swing and hurried the length of the porch.

Wilburn remained seated, staring straight ahead. "She looked so humiliated after I said that, and begged me not to tell you—and especially not to tell Stephen."

He paused a minute, then continued. "You knew her actions ran off the last pastor, didn't you?"

Overwhelmed at the direction the conversation had taken, Cyn couldn't get another word out of her mouth. Dee warned her not to trust Ginger, but Cyn didn't listen. Even though she, too, had heard the rumors about Ginger.

Wilburn continued. "We sat and talked for the longest."

"After she put her clothes back on, I hope." Cyn's words sounded mocking, flippant.

"No, Cynthia. We sat there with her naked, talking. Of course she'd dressed by then. What do you take me for, some kind of sicko?"

"The thought crossed my mind."

"I should've known you'd think the worst of me."

"Don't you go there, you...you..." She stopped, caught her breath then changed directions. "I'm not thinking the worst of you. Maybe Ginger, and maybe of myself for trusting her, but right now, I'm trying to get the full picture. I thought I had it earlier, and now I learn you lied about it. I don't know what to believe."

Wilburn planted his feet on the porch, which brought the swing to an abrupt halt. He took a deep breath, and then another before he spoke. "I'm trying to tell you the whole story, Cynthia. Let me finish."

"Finish then."

"Ginger ended up telling me about her affair with the last pastor and said that's why he left."

"Affair? So she did sleep with him?"

"That's what she said. However, she never admitted it to anyone before now."

"Does Stephen know?"

"Seems the whole church knows. Although, as I said, she has always denied that they actually slept together."

"Yet Stephen stayed with her anyway? The two of them always put out this perfect marriage image."

"My guess is that it isn't as perfect as it seems."

"Like ours." Her words tasted bitter on her tongue. Perennially happy people made Cyn suspicious.

"No one else can know about Ginger's visit here, Cynthia. You know what folks say, where there is smoke...I hated to even tell you about it, but..."

"Then why did you? Could it be you were tempted, even a little bit?" Her back grew rigid, bracing for another slap, but determined to get an answer.

"Tempted not to tell you? Of course I was."

"To sleep with her, stupid."

"How could you even ask me that?" Wilburn's eyebrows arched high.

"You are a man, and—"

"Put that thought out of your mind. Listen to me. I tried to gracefully get myself out of the situation without ruining my calling from God. She begged me to forgive her."

"Did you?"

"Of course, that's what God calls us to do. She also begged me not to tell you."

"But you did. Why? To relieve your own guilt?"

"I told you because for me to get anywhere in the convention, I need a spotless record. So far, I have that. Plus, you must take care what you say to her about us.

She indicated one of the reasons she thought I might be interested in her was because we...you and me—"

"What? Don't have sex anymore? That I'm miserable?"

"She might have hinted as much, yes."

"Might have. I wonder what else she might have said. Well, I know one thing. You won't have to worry about me buddying around with her anymore. I had one friend in this church—one. Or thought I did, but...I can't imagine I'll have anything to do with her again, or anyone else, for that matter. She betrayed our friendship. I can't imagine forgiving her of that."

"Then that's something you're going to have to pray about."

Yeah, right. She wanted to slap that smug look off of his face.

The landline rang inside, ending the conversation. Wilburn hurried in to catch it before the caller hung up.

Meanwhile, images of Ginger naked, in the parsonage, kept flashing through Cyn's mind. How could Ginger do that to her, to any woman? What had Cyn missed that Dee hadn't? Well, not anymore. She wouldn't trust anyone. From now on, she'd draw deeper into herself—shut out the world.

Tears blurred her vision. She swiped them away with the backs of her hand.

Wilburn cleared his conscience by dumping this on her. Now, what did she do with her anger? And how in the world did she handle Ginger the next time she called, or ran into her at church?

What a mess. The feeling of stop-the-world-I-want-to-get-off rocked her thoughts. Without consciously deciding to do so, she grabbed her cell phone and called her sister.

Dee answered with, "Hey, Sis, what's going on?" like she was psychic or something.

"I...I..."

"What?"

"You were right about Ginger. She betrayed me."

"Talk to me."

Cyn recounted Wilburn's story, and Dee laughed. "Well, I'll be a damn monkey's uncle. The guy surprises me. Wouldn't have thought he'd handle something like that so well."

"So well? What did you think he'd do?"

"I figured he'd have taken her up on the offer—after all, he's a man, and when a woman puts it out there—you sure he didn't?"

"Said he didn't. That's all I know."

"But he didn't plan to tell you about it until this guy calls from the convention, right? Wilburn figured you wouldn't say anything about it to anyone, but it would stop you from hanging out with that Ginger woman. That makes him feel safer because he knows she's dangerous. Remember, I told you that."

"You did, and you can say I told you so. But now, his confession, and obvious forgiveness of Ginger's actions, dumps the whole thing on me."

Dee laughed. "So you're not so up on this forgiveness thing, eh?"

"I saw her as my friend, Dee. Friends don't betray each other."

"Honey, if she's your friend, you need more enemies."

"That's for sure, anyway, enough about that. Thanks for helping keep me sane. Where are you?"

"The movers came today and moved my stuff into storage. Tonight, I sent out resumes. Tomorrow, I move into one of those extended-stay hotels until I know what I'm going to do next. I'm hoping my old boss calls me back. He said he had something up his sleeve for me."

"Why don't you come stay with us until then, sweetheart? There's no need to spend money on a hotel when we've got a perfectly nice guest room upstairs."

"You sure? Sounds like it might not be the best time to have a guest in your home. Especially me." She laughed.

"Listen, you and I are the only family we have left. Besides, Wilburn owes me one. You come. I'll deal with Wilburn if you can overlook his behavior at times. Of course he might not want you going to church."

They both laughed at the likelihood of that happening again.

"Well, if you're sure I won't cause a problem."

"Can't swear to that, and knowing you, I wouldn't bet on it even if I could, but I sure need you."

"Guess you know me better than most. But I promise to be on my best behavior—whatever that means."

"Then load that suitcase in your car and get going. I'll keep the light on for you."

"Okay, great. I didn't want to live off of my savings if I didn't have to. I have a couple of errands to do here before I leave town though, and I promised a friend I'd come by for a visit. So it might be four or five days before I get there. I'll call and let you know when to expect me. You sure you're going to be okay until then?"

"I'll deal with it. But I'm glad you're coming. Gives me an excuse not to spend time with Ginger. Still don't know how I'm going to face her."

"Don't you mean how she is going to face you? And as far as she knows, Wilburn hasn't told you she tried to get him into bed."

"That's true, and I doubt he does. Not in his best interest, and mine doesn't count." Cyn heard a noise inside and lowered her voice. "He's coming back. Let me know when you leave." Cyn's heart felt lighter by the time Wilburn exited the front door. "That was Dr. Powell, you know, the program chair. He's coming to town day after tomorrow to spend the morning with us."

"Us? As in you and me?"

"Of course. The stability of my marriage sets the example. They want to see how we interact with each other."

Holy shit. If ever a time to curse existed, it existed now, but she stopped the words before they left her mouth.

CHAPTER NINE

After a couple of restless, sleepless nights for both of them, Cyn and Wilburn rose early, ate breakfast, showered, and dressed by eight o'clock. They sat in the living room—Cyn's least favorite room—and waited.

Wilburn insisted on formal décor for the living room and chose rich browns, gold, blacks, and reds. The white French Provincial sofa and high-backed red velvet chair looked as new as they did the day they bought them—five years ago.

A round, marble-topped mahogany coffee table positioned in front of the sofa matched a drum-shaped end table and lamp. A massive dining table at the opposite end of the room seated ten without the leaf. With it, she often entertained twelve at one time. The heavy upholstered chairs looked beautiful, but moving them strained her back. A thick decorative rug covered the polished hardwood floor.

Wilburn paced the room, but despite acting like he had ants in his pants, he seemed in an unusually good mood. He was treating her as if she mattered.

She guessed she did, at least today.

Reverend Doctor Nathaniel Powell rang the doorbell at straight up ten.

At least Cyn hoped it was Dr. Powell. A sinking feeling that Dee might have forgotten to call in advance, clanged against the insides of Cyn's skull. She held her breath while Wilburn hurried to the door as if he feared the caller would leave if he had to wait a minute.

Relieved when she heard another man's voice instead of Dee's, Cyn stood on first one foot and then the other, waiting. She glanced at the freshly polished silver service set out on the dining room table the night before. After the men talked a few minutes, she'd fill the coffee pot and bring in the plate of chocolate macadamia biscotti she stayed up until midnight baking. Wilburn wanted them fresh.

"Reverend Wilburn Carter? Dr. Nathan Powell. Pleased to meet you."

She visualized the men shaking hands.

"Dr. Powell, thank you for coming. I think we met briefly at the state convention a year or so ago, but perhaps you don't—"

"I thought we had, of course."

Liar, liar, Cyn thought. The man doesn't have a clue.

The two rounded the corner and stepped into the living room before Cyn felt ready. Then again, would she have ever been?

Doctor Powell came into the room bearing a smile as wide as the Mississippi River. Tall and bald, except for a few long wisps swept over the top, she'd recognize him as a big shot even if she hadn't known that in advance. He carried an air of importance—superiority, maybe.

"Mrs. Carter, I presume. So pleased to meet you. Thank you for opening your home. I hope I'm not intruding on any plans you might have for the day." His damp hand clamped Cyn's so tight she almost went to the floor. When he finally let go, she tucked her arm behind her back to exercise her limp, aching fingers.

"I always appreciate godly women. They are so gracious and create such a warm, loving atmosphere in the home. Look here." He waved his arm towards the silver coffee service on the dining table. "How lovely."

Another man well versed in platitudes. And so effective in controlling their women—at least they seemed to think their banality did. She smiled, not at him, but at what he'd think if he knew a few days ago the wife of the chairman of deacons stood in the next room without a stitch of clothes on.

"Have a seat, Doctor." Wilburn cleared his throat. "Cynthia will serve us. I hope you drink coffee."

"I do. I do, indeed. And that would be lovely."

After a few minutes of light chitchat over coffee and pastry, Doctor Powell looked directly at Cyn. "Tell me, Mrs. Carter, what leadership roles do you offer your church?"

Startled by the inquisition directed at her, the coffee cup rattled in her saucer. She steadied it while scrambling for what to say. If she told the truth—that over the last few months she did as little as possible—Wilburn's chances would drop to zero.

Thank goodness he stepped in. "Oh, she's very active. She stays involved in the women's missionary circles, youth groups, teaches Sunday School and—"

"I always ask because we want to make sure our convention speakers represent a godly home." Doctor Powell rested his hands over his slight paunch and smiled. "And I'm sure you realize how important our wives are in that process."

"You won't find a wife who stands behind her man any more than mine." Wilburn cut his eyes to Cyn as if daring—praying—that she not challenge him.

She nodded and smiled, taking that opportunity to sip coffee, nibble, and wonder how many always the convention expected and how far behind that support must be.

"I hope you like macadamia nuts," Wilburn said. "Cynthia stayed up until midnight to make biscotti. She wanted them fresh this morning. You'll find she attends her wifely duties with a passion befitting Solomon's virtuous woman." He gave a chuckle that hinted of admiration.

Dr. Powell took another pastry, dunked it in his coffee, and took a bite. "Delicious. Now, Reverend Carter, should we decide to extend the invitation for you to speak at the state convention, we will invite you to come meet the board members in advance. Maybe when you do, Mrs. Carter here wouldn't mind sending some of these delicious goodies for the members to enjoy."

"It would thrill Cynthia to bake and have them ready for me to bring. Just let me know how many men you expect to attend. We wouldn't want to run short, would we, sweetheart?"

Cyn's coffee spoon clattered and fell to the floor.

"Now, getting right down to business," Doctor Powell said. "We have this new program where we invite pastors who aren't so well known in the state convention to be our keynote speakers. I've made an inquiry about you and hear good things about your sermons, your pulpit presence, your teaching of the Bible. From what I see and hear, it seems to me you fit that description very well."

Wilburn's smile reminded Cyn of Alice's Wonderland cat.

"This year our program focuses on marriage and the home. That's why I wanted to come visit yours. So you have one son in college?"

"Justice is a freshman this year, yes." Wilburn sat up straighter.

Cyn felt the urge to tell Doctor Powell what a neat, irreverent son they had, but the set of Wilburn's shoulders warned her off. Instead, she leaned back on the sofa and sat quietly—like a good wife should.

The two men carried on the conversation without apparent notice of her silence. An hour later, Doctor Powell thanked Cyn for acting the perfect hostess and excused himself.

After the front door closed, she and Wilburn watched the man cross the lawn to his car and drive off. Only then, did Wilburn let out a loud sigh. "Thank you, Cynthia. You were perfect."

She kept her mouth shut, he meant.

"This offers a huge opportunity for me—for us. If I can pull this off, and I will, there's no telling where my career will end up. Mobile is a stepping off point."

Without warning, Cyn's food came up in her throat. She raced to the bathroom and got there in the nick of time.

Afterward, she stripped off her Sunday-go-to-meeting clothes and stood in the shower while hot water pounded her head and ran down her body. Something about the effort felt like she washed away the taint she felt, but from what, she didn't know.

Wilburn stayed in a grand mood all evening. The two of them watched a televised re-run of a Billy Graham Crusade. Rather Wilburn watched it. Cyn knitted and thought.

Wilburn's good mood continued into the next day. He acted decently at breakfast, even shortening the length of his sermon/blessing, and gave her a peck on the cheek as he left for the church.

That's when she remembered she hadn't told him about Dee. Cyn hated breaking the news about her sister coming to live with them for a few weeks—months—just when he expected the biggest break in his career. Sure would put a damper on that.

Dee said she'd call in advance. Cyn hurried upstairs to the guest room, put fresh sheets on the queen-sized bed, laid out clean towels, double-checked the toiletries and ran the dust mop over the hardwood floors.

As she finished preparing Dee's room, the doorbell rang, and she trotted downstairs to answer the door.

A friendly mail carrier handed her an express delivery letter addressed to Wilburn. She signed for it, then closed the door, and studied the return address. The state convention office.

"The invitation," she whispered. "What he's waited

for, what kept him in such a good mood the last couple of days. She placed the conspicuous envelope on the hall table and waited for Wilburn to come home for lunch, where both good and bad news awaited him. That was if she told him about Dee.

Maybe she'd wait until evening to tell him, or even tomorrow morning. Then again maybe not till next Monday. If the envelope from the convention did contain Wilburn's invitation, certainly he planned to announce it this coming Sunday during the worship service. Until then, he'd float on a high-stepping cloud. How unkind of her to spoil that mood—and in her own self-interest not to.

Close to noon, she went into the kitchen to get Wilburn's lunch ready when the front door opened and closed. She heard him shuffle through the mail and knew the exact moment he read the return address of the mail from the convention. Ripped envelope, paper shuffling, and then a cheer. "Cynthia? It came. I'm in," he called out. "They want me as the keynote speaker."

He hurried into the kitchen waving the piece of paper. The jubilant expression on his face looked priceless. She couldn't help but celebrate with him.

"That's great. You've worked hard for something like this. Makes me proud."

"Thanks. I'm so excited, I feel like I'll explode."

"What's the topic they gave you?"

"I don't know, let me look. I got so excited I didn't pay attention to that detail." He scanned the letter. "Like Doctor Powell said, marriage and the family."

"Wonder how hard that will be for you," she said under her breath. Their marriage may look perfect to the outside world, but it certainly didn't take into account her heart, or the overwhelming emptiness inside it.

Pushing herself to be supportive, she smiled and said, "That's great. I'm excited for you." She said it like she meant it, and in a way, she did.

"For us, babe, for us. I've worked long and hard to get to this point. No telling where I'll go in the convention after people get to know me."

"Who are you?" Cyn didn't know anymore.

"What do you mean?" A startled look crossed his face.

"Nothing."

"What?" Wilburn asked, his voice sounding irritated. "You can't ask a stupid question like that and drop it."

"Sometimes I feel like I don't know who you are. Or for that matter, who I am anymore."

"Don't be ridiculous. Of course you know me." He chuckled. "I sure know you."

No, he didn't. Twenty years and not a clue. As long as she kept her true self tucked inside, he seemed happy. Meanwhile, she felt that self, withering, dying.

She wished he might push a little deeper, but truth be known, she figured he didn't want to know—or even know how to want to know.

Tempted to prick his bubble with her news of Dee's visit, she bit her tongue instead. Preoccupied with his success, he didn't notice, and took the conversation back to how he might get the most attention out of his upcoming opportunity.

To her, Wilburn always seemed the consummate actor and a mastermind of his brows. At one time their expression told Cyn everything, then at other times, they told her nothing.

She watched for a hint of his thoughts. At first, his brows arched, looked uncertain, questioning. Then, when he saw her looking at him, he brought the arch down hard, removing all doubt.

"They are all going to be so proud of their pastor." He elbowed her in the side. "And hey, maybe I'll even get a raise."

He hadn't said so, but she felt certain he planned to announce his invitation to speak at the state convention during next Sunday's service. News like that commanded sharing, particularly with those most likely to be impressed with the news. Else what the benefit?

CHAPTER TEN

Wilburn remained in high spirits the rest of the week. By the time Sunday morning came, he startled Cyn by singing in the shower and humming his way through his other morning rituals.

Seeing him so enthused rubbed off on Cyn. She'd do her best to support him.

Playing hooky from church did not support him, she decided. So she forced herself out of bed earlier than usual. By the time Wilburn grabbed his Bible and prepared to leave, she waited for him at the front door, her own Bible in hand.

"I've waited so long for a day like this. I'm glad you're going with me." He opened her car door. She knew the two of them arriving at the same time, and in the same vehicle, set the stage for his big announcement. He rewarded her with a big smile.

Neither spoke on the ride to the church, but as Wilburn pulled into the parking lot, he said, "I want you to know how much I appreciate this, Cynthia. I realize you like coming later, but this will make a big difference to folks. You know how they like to see you support their pastor."

She offered a half-hearted smile in return, wishing her whole heart participated in it. She couldn't will it. But she could pretend.

Then again, maybe the missing pieces did not include her heart after all. The void seemed deeper, more profound—like a chunk of her soul had broken off and vaporized into the ethers.

She exited the vehicle and the two parted, him to his appointed duties, and her, to her Sunday School class. She took the long way around, stopped in the fellowship hall for coffee and donuts, then headed upstairs.

Voices from inside her classroom stopped her before she rounded the door. Several women talked in loud whispers.

"I met Pastor on his way to the sanctuary a few minutes ago," one voice said.

Beverly.

"I'll tell you one thing, if we don't have a Pastor Search Committee visiting today, I'll be surprised."

Cyn stiffened. *From where? Wilburn hadn't put out any feelers to move to a different church—not that she knew.*

"I thought the same thing," another voice said, "and my husband agreed with me."

Nora.

"For sure, I've never seen Pastor look so eager and excited."

"My heart would hurt if he left us," one of the women gushed.

"Me, too. He's the best we've ever had."

"Best looking, you mean."

Who said that?

Never mind. The lot of them left her cold, anyway. Cyn rounded the doorway and stopped.

When one of the women looked up, saw Cyn, and elbowed her neighbor, the other closed her eyes as if she hoped doing so might make Cyn disappear.

Martha, the class president, cleared her throat and held her pen up like a stop sign. "Ladies, our pastor's wife came today. Perhaps you'd like to ask her your questions."

Cyn forced a sweet smile and moved to one of the empty chairs. "No need to repeat it. I heard the question."

Bold Nora cleared her throat and said, "Pastor's always friendly to everyone, but today, he seems extra bubbly. Made some of us wonder if..." She stared down at her hands clasped in her lap, but didn't finish her sentence.

Another one did. "We want to know if he expects a pastor search committee today?"

"Not that I know of, no."

A collective sigh filled the room.

"That's a relief. We said Pastor Wilburn always looks happy here, but one never knows," Beverly said. "So when we ran into him out in the hallway and in such a happy mood..."

Cyn shrugged and smiled. "Go figure."

Martha nodded at Cyn. "Now that we've gotten that rumor out of the way, ladies, can we go on with our lesson?" Without waiting for a response, Martha started the discussion while Cyn's eyes wandered from one woman to the next.

Beverly, the one whose voice Cyn identified first, sat on the opposite side of the circle from Cyn. She wore a powder blue suit, the skirt hiked and her long legs crossed. Beverly carried more than her share of grief, evident by the numerous lines crossing her forehead. Cyn knew much of the grief came from self-inflicted wounds.

To Beverly's left, Nora carried no grief or pain on her face. She'd had work done.

Forcing herself to tune into the lesson, Cyn tried hard to participate in the discussion, but every time she opened her mouth, Beverly interrupted. Soon, Cyn stopped trying.

After the class ended, she headed to the sanctuary while sensing an air of excitement dancing off the walls. Evidently, Wilburn's good mood flavored everything and everyone.

Except Harris Harrison, who sailed by with barely a nod.

She approached the area outside the church office where Wilburn stood, straight and tall, deep in conversation with a gaggle of female admirers.

So easily entertained—the lot of them. However, she had to admit, Wilburn—when in his element—exuded magnetism. And today, magnetism raged.

Not wanting to attract attention from the star, she turned off before she reached them, entered the sanctuary, and took her seat on the front row.

The organist played while folks wandered in, greeted

each other and found their seats. In the background, an occasional child complained. A parent whispered for them to settle down and behave.

Cyn alone knew the cause for Wilburn's excitement. When would he break the news—before the sermon, or afterward?

As it turned out, he waited until the very end—right before he offered the benediction.

He came down the platform steps, stood on the plush burgundy carpeted sanctuary floor, and looked out over the congregation as if prepared to give the final blessing.

Thinking the service had ended, folks started gathering their belongings. Children pulled on their parent's hands, eager to escape to the outdoors and freedom, or video games. Women picked up their handbags and slung them over their shoulders. Men rolled their programs and tapped them on the palms of their hands.

When it became obvious Pastor hadn't finished, one by one, the people settled down to wait. A few retook their seats. Parents shushed their children.

Meanwhile, Wilburn stood smiling, his hands steepled at his chest.

One would have thought he'd received his personal copy of the key to Heaven's pearly gates—delivered by St. Peter himself, with copies for everyone else.

"Folks, I have an announcement to make," he finally said.

Her heart raced.

"Ladies and gentlemen, it pleases me to announce that your pastor received an invitation to give the keynote speech at the next state convention."

First, the audience looked stunned. It took a minute for the news to seep in, that their church, their pastor, was moving on up to the east side.

Then, questions came at him from every direction.

Instead of answering, he raised his hands, and had he not walked out while he pronounced the benediction, he wouldn't have made it through the crowd. As it happened, folks swarmed him in ways envied by any queen bee.

Cyn thought he'd have wanted her by his side, half-expected him to hold out his hand to her before he started down the aisle, but he hadn't glanced her way much less invited her.

Stunned, she wondered why. He always swore her presence at church mattered to him, but evidently he lied, or at the very least exaggerated the truth.

Childlike feelings of insignificance overtook rational thought. She wanted to hide, run home and get under the bedcovers like she'd done as a child when other children excluded her from play.

Instead, squeezed by the throng that emptied into the vestibule, she soon found herself pressed into a tight corner, feeling invisible.

Through the mob, Cyn caught a glimpse of Ginger at the forefront of the entourage, pawing at Wilburn, hanging onto his every word.

So, Ginger wasn't as through with Wilburn as he seemed to think.

Not far away, Hazel Harrison pulled in her coterie with snide comments like, "I thought sure a pulpit committee sat in the audience this morning. Now, with this, we'll never get him to stop pushing that building program."

Harris stood beside his wife, pouting. When another man walked up and started a conversation, Cyn couldn't hear what the two men said, but from the tightened grief muscles between their eyes she guessed they didn't feel celebratory.

Insignificant–that's how she felt, insignificant, isolated, and alone. Regardless of what Wilburn always said about the importance of her role to him and to the parishioners, today belied that statement. She mattered not, to any of them. She didn't even exist.

The week before, Wilburn insisted she listen to him read a decades-old article given at the national convention many years ago. He'd loved the piece and read it word for word.

Decalogue for a Preacher's Wife, written in the biblical verbiage of the original Ten Commandments gave the article more authority than it rightly deserved. A few of the commandments now echoed in her thoughts, made her want to scream.

A preacher's wife shouldn't care about public praise but care only about her role as the preacher's wife.

Guess that didn't hold true for pastors—not the way Wilburn luxuriated in the attention of his parishioners.

A preacher's wife should remember her husband and his needs first and above all others.

A preacher's wife must always provide stimulus to her husband in order for him to continue to study and remain fresh and clear in his thinking.

Then, the one that forbade the preacher's wife from committing adultery with another denomination; but to stay true to the state, national conventions, and local church ideals, implying of course, that none of these ideals fit the category of questionable.

A preacher's wife never felt jealous of the attention her husband received from the congregation. She never did anything to cause him to falter, or steal time that he needed for study, exercise, and rest.

Most of all, a preacher's wife must love, feed, and care for her husband all the days of his life in order that he may accomplish his primary task in the world—serving the Lord.

That wasn't all ten, but enough to send her into the same revulsions she'd felt the day he'd read them to her. Pushed beyond caring if anyone saw her, she stormed out the side door, got in the car, and sped home. After Wilburn milked all the proverbial cows dry, he could walk home for all she cared.

Unless he got a better offer.

CHAPTER ELEVEN

By the time Wilburn opened the front door and banged it against the wall, Cyn had Sunday dinner on the table.

"Well, if you wanted to humiliate me in front of our church members, you certainly succeeded this time," he said as he stormed down the hall towards the kitchen, fury in his voice.

Cyn's heart skipped a couple of beats while she waited for him to round the corner. When he did, she finished filling their glasses with ice, and then poured fresh-brewed tea. The cubes crackled and popped.

"I had everyone in the church looking for you. We almost called the police, until this kid came up and said he'd seen you speeding off towards home without a backward glance. One of the members had to bring me home. Do you have any idea how humiliated I felt?"

She set the glasses on the kitchen table. "Dinner's ready."

"I'm not hungry. Besides, if I have to look at you one more minute, I'll likely say something I'll regret." He turned and marched upstairs.

That night, he went to evening services alone. He didn't even bother to ask if she planned to come later.

She didn't.

As the evening passed, she began to feel ashamed of her childish behavior that morning. When Wilburn got home, she would apologize. Ask what she might do to make it up to him. Tell the church members she'd gotten deathly sick or something.

The time he normally got home after Sunday night church came and went—still no Wilburn. She waited a couple of hours longer, thinking at least she needed to explain how left out she'd felt that morning, how hurt she'd been, how the dang ten commandments exploded in her thoughts, how isolated and alone she'd felt.

But when the clock struck midnight, she gave up and went to bed in the guest room. Sometime after that, she heard him come in and head to the kitchen.

Over the next couple of days, neither of them spoke to the other unless necessary. She tried several times to share her pain, how she'd felt. Caught in his own, he refused to listen, just kept his head buried in the newspaper or his Bible.

By Wednesday noon, he'd cooled off enough to remind her to attend the Fellowship Dinner that evening at church. Would she please bring a dish of food to share?

After he finished lunch and left to make hospital visits, Cyn cleaned the kitchen and headed to the grocery store for brownie mix to bake and take to the fellowship dinner.

As usual, once she got in the store, she remembered several other items she needed. Brownies didn't take long to bake, so she indulged herself and browsed the aisles adding things to her cart. Several times, she remembered something she'd missed on a prior aisle. Rather than push the laden cart, she parked it to the side, reversed her path, and collected the needed items and continued her shopping.

She'd done that two or three times—left her cart, retraced her steps, collected what she'd missed, then returned to her cart and kept going, when a man's voice stopped her.

"Excuse me, ma'am, you have my basket."

"No, I don't." That's when she noticed the two bottles of wine in the basket she pushed. "Oh, I'm sorry, I guess I do." She turned to see a man dressed in a big smile, blue jeans, western shirt, and work boots.

"Isn't your name Carter? Aren't you—?"

"Cynthia Carter, yes. You look familiar, but I'm afraid I can't..." She racked her brain, but came up with nothing.

"Paul Cooper." He stuck his hand out.

She shook it, but her confusion still hadn't cleared.

"Cooper. Remember—of Anderson, Cooper and Taylor? We sat next to each other at the charity ball."

"Oh, yes. I didn't recognize you at first." Cyn wished she'd freshened up, at least put on lipstick and brushed her hair.

"That's not a problem. Tuxedos—or candy wrappers, as my son calls them—make a man look like someone other than himself, anyway."

"So do evening gowns."

"Not at all. Besides, I never forget a woman with ideas rolling off her tongue. You impressed me with your suggestions for homebuilders. I wanted to talk more to you that evening, but I couldn't get away from the woman on the other side of me. Then, when I did get loose, I couldn't find you." He chuckled. "I bet I asked every person there if they had seen you, or if they knew how I might contact you."

"I—we left early." Cyn didn't explain that her husband dragged her home when he found her on the dance floor. She assumed Paul knew the man who provided the tickets for their table. She wondered why he hadn't called Stephen and asked him her name.

"Earlier this morning I realized I'd asked everyone but Stephen," Paul said to her unasked question. "I planned to call him soon as I got home from the grocery. Figured he'd know how I could get in touch with you." He scooted his basket over to let a woman pass.

"Why? What did you want to talk about?"

"First, I wanted to compliment your spunk."

No one had ever accused her of having spunk—at least not since she married Wilburn.

"Besides, I'm always looking for fresh ideas, and you sounded like you are full of them. They roll off your tongue like you've stored them so long you're ready to explode. I like that."

"Me?" She worried the strap on her handbag.

"You. I wanted to pick your brain and see how you might fit into our organization. I have no idea what type of experience you have, but I sure would like it if we sat down and chatted about possibilities."

"Wow."

He laughed. "So you're one of those people who talk in one-word sentences?

"Not always."

"Two words. Now we're getting somewhere. I know you have lots more where those came from, because you used them the night of the party." His eyes crinkled when he smiled.

"I apologize for that. I promise I won't make a habit of talking your ear off." She put her cool palms against her warm cheeks then lowered them fast.

"No, no. I didn't mean to embarrass you. What I'm trying to say is, I like a woman who says what she thinks."

Cyn did a double take, but hoped he didn't notice.

He did.

"What? You never met a man that liked a woman who speaks her mind?"

She waved him off, afraid to go there.

"As I said, I've wanted to talk to you. Or rather wanted you to talk to me. There's a coffee shop at the rear of the store. Can I buy you a cup? After you find your basket, of course."

"There's my basket right behind you, so there," she said, joining the man's sense of humor. "But I don't have much time." Cyn checked the clock on her cell phone, reminding herself she still had to bake brownies.

"Fifteen minutes?"

"Sure." She shrugged. "Why not?" She parked her basket out of the way, and they wended their way to the coffee shop.

She sat at one of the small round tables while Paul Cooper went to the counter and ordered coffee. Something about sitting there, waiting for a strange man to serve her, felt like cheating on Wilburn.

Ridiculous. They only talked about her opinion on houses, so why did she feel guilty?

"Here you go. I took the liberty of adding sugar and milk. I forgot to ask, so I hope that's okay."

"Perfect."

"By the way, what do you know about cooking?" He placed his cup on the table and pulled out his chair.

"I know I've done a lot of it over the years. Why?"

"My son's convinced me to enroll in cooking school."

"Cooking school?"

"Yeah, I know. I don't look the type."

"No, it isn't that. It's that I imagine your development business takes most of your time."

"That's the truth." He chuckled.

"Okay, maybe I stretched it a little, but all kinds of people cook. Watch those channels on T.V. and you'll see."

"And truthfully, I don't have a lot of free time, but I decided I wanted to do something a little more, shall we say—domestic? Besides, since my wife died, I'm getting tired of eating dinner from a box."

She glanced at his bare ring finger. "Cooking school might be fun, then. Good luck. Let me know how it goes."

"That's one reason why I wanted to chat with you. I wondered if you'd like to work with the folks who design our homes, particularly the kitchens. Most of us are big galoots. We don't know what it's like to not reach something in a cabinet. I thought maybe you could start as a consultant and let's see how it goes. We could pay you by the project or by the hour—whichever worked out best for you. Who knows what might open up after that? Listening to you at the charity ball, it's evident we need a woman's voice from start to finish."

"Oh."

"There you go, those one-word sentences again." He laughed.

"I'm stunned."

"Moving to two."

She fiddled with her paper cup. "I don't know if I can. I'll have to think about it. I'm not sure..." *my husband will let me*, she almost said, but stopped short of such a 1950s sounding admission.

"Take your time. I know you didn't expect this. But I saw something—heard something the other night that I'd like to tap into. I'd like to mentor you because I think you have potential—not to mention filling a gap in our business. We have all these men who think they know what a home should be, but they have no clue what a woman's needs are."

Her cheeks felt hot again.

"Excuse me, that didn't come out right. I'm talking about—"

"That's okay. I know what you meant. Thing is, I thought more and more women were entering that field these days."

"Oh, yes, they are. But most of them think more like men—book learning, that kind of stuff." He opened another packet of sugar, dumped it into his coffee, and stirred. "They know the design business, but many of them don't cook. They graduate and go right to work, same as men."

"Thing is, it isn't just an average-sized woman that a kitchen needs to fit," Cyn said. "There are a lot of men who cook, and they aren't all big like you."

"See? That's what I'm talking about." He reached into his pocket and handed her his card.

Now she had two of them.

"Think it over, and give me a call."

The thought she'd have to ask her husband sprinted through her head and out the other side. Perhaps she needed to make her own decisions from now on.

"How about if I come by your office tomorrow morning?" She grabbed a napkin and wiped a small coffee spill. "I want to find out what you have in mind. Sounds fascinating."

She felt taller, smarter, and more confident already.

CHAPTER TWELVE

On the way home from the grocery, Cyn's mind constructed all kinds of ways to tell Wilburn about her job offer and an appointment to discuss it further. He'd have a fit. He still held to the same rules as his dad—a wife's place was in the home to support her husband and his career. Her decision and his response to it might well make the decision—did she stay or did she go?

Later, when the phone rang, and Cyn saw Ginger's name on the ID, she wondered, should she answer, and if she did, what would she say. What did one say to a best friend who, in truth, wanted one's husband? Especially when that friend belonged to her husband's flock.

She answered on the sixth ring.

"Oh, Cynthia, honey, glad I caught you. I'd about decided you weren't home." Her voice sounded rushed, nervous. "I'm calling to see if you could come to prayer meeting a little earlier tonight and help me get things set up for the potluck dinner."

Cyn's mind raced. She dare not push Wilburn into a bad mood before she announced her job offer. Him in a good mood worked in her favor much better than the alternative—and helping with church dinner always added points toward that end.

"Uh, sure, I guess I can do that. What time should I arrive?" Not wanting to reveal she knew about Ginger's attempt to seduce Wilburn, Cyn pushed friendly. "And I'm glad you called. I still need to cook something to bring." She considered mentioning a leftover chicken casserole, but reconsidered. Instead, she said, "I'm planning to bring brownies. What do you think?"

"Are you kidding? Everyone eats chocolate. Anyway, since we start eating at six, maybe get there around five? By the time people start arriving with their potluck dishes, we should have everything ready. I hate to ask, but I'm getting desperate."

"No problem. I can help."

After they hung up, Cyn finished putting away the groceries, except for the box of brownies and a bag of walnut pieces.

Dee. Oh lord. Just Cyn's luck for Dee to arrive before she left for church and insist on going with Cyn to spite Hazel Harrison and her entourage. If it were possible, Cyn would hold her breath to make that not happen.

She poured the brownie mix into the bowl, added an egg, oil, water, and stirred.

Dee's presence might dump ice water on Wilburn's

good mood.

What a crock. Of course it would, and then no telling how he might react.

Ever since the convention letter had arrived, he spent every waking minute planning his opportunity of a lifetime, the chance to advance his career with a presentation intended to impact the lives of everyone attending the convention. A speech that might well gain him national recognition—but most certainly where it counted—within their denomination.

Cyn came out of her fog and realized she'd gone way over the prescribed number of beats the mix required. She stopped, collected a pair of scissors, and cut open the bag of nuts. "If Dee gets here tonight, Cyn Carter, you must not allow her to attend prayer service. Let Wilburn enjoy this time. Let him gloat and strut all he wants to. Get yourself under control and support him like a good pastor's wife should—like he trained you to do."

She poured in the nuts and stirred faster.

Of course when Wilburn spoke at the convention, she'd be expected to attend. Sit on stage all prim and proper, look up at him, adoration on her face.

Torn between Wilburn's opportunity and hers, honesty built in her gut, slow, deliberate, and more forceful with each beat of the thick mixture. Dare she relinquish her long-held belief that she must mold herself into the person Wilburn wanted—demanded?

Or dare she save herself—discover a world outside the one prescribed for her? A few days ago, she thought that might happen, but the more successful Wilburn became, the less possible her chances for escape.

Until today.

The image of an acorn flashed in her mind, planted in the ground and swelling to the point of breaking through its shell, reaching for the sun. Then again, look at the price an acorn paid, losing its shiny, smooth, hard shell of glorious greens and browns.

She had to do it—but when? Now? With Wilburn on the verge of the biggest day of his life, and with Dee coming for an extended visit? Perhaps not, but then would there ever be the perfect time? Surely it wouldn't hurt if she just went and talked to Paul Cooper.

If Cyn took a job, her mother would rise from the dead to haunt her nights. Her mother always adhered to a code of morals that did more to induce guilt in a pig for being dirty, than it did to save anybody's soul. She bore her cross and put up with a husband who had more important things to do than help care for Cyn and Dee. As a result, the cross became her mother's excuse to never attempt anything. "I have these kids to take care of," she said more times than anyone wanted to hear. Cyn grew up feeling more a burden than a blessing.

Meaningless clichés accompanied her mother's strong set of beliefs. Clichés that Cyn grew up believing came straight from the Bible. Clichés like, a woman's place is in the home. A good wife always puts her husband's needs before her own. When she met Wilburn and learned he used the same clichés that sealed the deal. He always called Cyn smart, but only when she agreed with him—which by default, meant her mother, as well.

Wow. Dee had been right. Cyn still lived in the 50s.

After shoving the brownie pan in the oven, she set the timer and switched on the radio—of course set on the local Christian station. Amazing Grace played. She immediately switched it off. Although the song had always been one of her favorites, now Cyn cried every time she heard the thing. It all started when she learned the songwriter wrote the words while sitting on the deck of his slave ship bound for the new world. While in the bowels below, hundreds of men, women, and children lay naked in their own filth, many dying, others shackled and starving. Not a world of amazing love and grace, but of slavery, misery—of anything but grace. Some people argue that times were different then.

She didn't buy it.

Since then, every time she heard the music, her mind carried her straight to the innards of that deep dark hold of the slave ship. How could one human being write such magnificent, hopeful words, and at the same time, be responsible for the horrendous, inhuman conditions of the people below—people also worthy of God's grace?

Conviction hit her square in the forehead. Others weren't the only ones who glibly handed out pat answers to some of life's most complicated questions. She did the same thing. Sincere intent aside, she felt like a phony. The answers she gave weren't hers at all. When it got right down to it, she had no answers. Not a single solitary one. Only questions.

Her only way out? Leave the world she knew, leave everything she believed in—or at least tried to believe. So many times, she ignored the nag in her gut when something didn't ring true.

But what would that do to their son, Justice—her leaving his dad?

That won't surprise Justice. A still small voice whispered.

The kitchen timer went off.

Cyn grabbed a potholder and removed the hot, sweet-smelling brownies from the oven. There was truth, and then there was truth—nothing smelled as good as fudge brownies.

While they cooled, Wilburn called and said he wouldn't come home beforehand—he'd meet Cyn at the church dinner. Relieved, she wondered why, until it hit her. She'd made the decision to leave him, but she hadn't made a decision to follow through. If she had, wouldn't she know how to tell him? Maybe the time to do so would be after his speech at the convention.

The remainder of the afternoon passed quicker than Cyn expected. She dressed in a hurry, grabbed the plate of brownies and drove the few miles to church. A number of cars already filled the parking lot. Of course, Wilburn always parked in his reserved parking space. The church provided one for the pastor, but not his wife.

She found an empty spot at the rear of the lot, stuck her wallet in the glove compartment, and grabbed the brownies. Once out, she closed and locked the car, tucked her keys in her pants pocket, and hurried into the building, dreading the fact that Ginger waited inside.

However, she'd given her word she'd help serve. Still, it hurt that the one church member she trusted had betrayed her. It hurt even more that Dee had seen it coming and Cyn hadn't.

She trudged downstairs and stepped into the musty-smelling Fellowship Hall, pleased to see the tables and chairs up and ready.

Surprised that Wilburn hadn't called to remind her how important it was that she attend, she assumed he must be in the building somewhere, likely still floating on a cloud of importance.

Cyn heard Ginger talking in the kitchen. Why hadn't Cyn realized before how crass the woman's voice sounded?

She headed that way, albeit with reluctance.

Did Ginger know Wilburn told Cyn about Ginger's betrayal? He ordered Cyn not to say anything about it to Ginger, to not rock the boat, but had he followed his own advice? He said nothing happened, Ginger acted repentant, and all seemed well—but still, Cyn doubted that. These days, she doubted anything, everything, and everyone.

At first Cyn didn't see the betrayer, but then noticed a red head poking above the stainless steel worktable. Ginger busied herself pulling out stacks of plates and stacking them on top.

Cyn saw no one else in the room.

"Who were you talking to?" Cyn asked.

Ginger looked up. "Oh, Hi, Cynthia. Talking to myself, I guess. I'm so glad you're here. A couple of other women promised to help. I don't know why they aren't here yet." She gave a nervous giggle as she stood and tucked her bright green shirttail into her navy slacks.

"I think we're okay, though, even if they don't come. The janitor helped set up the tables. I made the tea, so we're close to ready. We need the glasses filled with ice. I guess that's about it. Thank goodness the ice machine works today. Last week everyone complained, saying they needed more."

"Where do you want the desserts?" Cyn indicated her brownies.

"I'm thinking the desserts seem too close to the main course table, and the line gets backed up. See that table over there against the wall on your right?" She pointed. "Let's put them there this week. I think it'll flow better that way. Of course, when we change things folks complain, so when they do, ignore it."

Ginger looked around the room. "Also, several dishes in the fridge need to come out and go in the oven." She added another little laugh. "A couple of women dropped them off earlier and asked us to warm them."

Cyn wondered if Ginger's nervous laugh resulted from guilt. Or did she know Wilburn told Cyn about Ginger's betrayal? The woman couldn't stand still or be quiet.

Act normal, Cyn, act normal. Be patient, this will be over soon, and you can go home and curl in a ball.

Her admonition didn't work, so when other women arrived to help get things ready in the kitchen, Cyn walked out and didn't return. Instead, she made sure she looked busy at the drinks table. She filled glasses with crushed ice and poured tea or water.

Soon, families started pouring into the hall bearing a multitude of covered dishes. Before long, the serving table overflowed with food.

When the time came to begin, and Wilburn had not arrived, one of the deacons led the group in a prayer of thanks for the food and lines formed at the head of the main table. For the next hour, families filed past, filled their plates, and then sat at the long tables. The room bustled with neighbors visiting with neighbors. Most of the children sat with their parents and behaved, but as usual a couple of children gobbled their food, and then ran around the tables playing tag.

Cyn still hadn't seen Wilburn, but she did have her eye on Ginger, so nothing to worry about there.

The line grew shorter and still Wilburn hadn't arrived. He liked for her to wait and eat with him, thereby setting the example of a united front, but everyone kept encouraging her to go ahead and eat. So, she filled a paper plate with fried chicken, potato salad, and baked beans then found an empty chair next to a new family and made friendly conversation.

Time passed, and soon most everyone had finished eating and sat waiting for the service to begin. In time, the crowd grew restless.

Still no Wilburn.

Several leaders looked at her in question. She shrugged, indicating that she, too, had no idea, and also wondered about him.

A few got up and left.

Larry Porter, the music director, came over and tapped her on the shoulder. "Know where the preacher is, Mrs. Carter? It's time for us to start the program."

Cyn glanced around the room. "I haven't seen him this evening, but I know he's here, his car's parked outside. He must have gotten tied up with someone. He should be here any minute."

"I'm thinking the same thing. Should I go ahead and start the singing?"

Wow. Catch-22. Whichever way she answered that question, she'd be wrong—at least to Wilburn. She hesitated, cleared her throat. "I guess so. I'm sure he's here in the building somewhere and lost track of time. Give him another five minutes, and then start the song service. I'll go check and see if I can find him."

"Never remember him late for service before." Larry looked at the crowd. "But okay, I'll wait five minutes, then start. Folks want to get going. The small groups that meet after this will already start late and tomorrow's a school day."

Ginger walked up behind Cyn. "Don't worry, Larry, we'll go find him. I haven't seen Stephen either, so I'll bet they're tied up in some committee meeting somewhere and haven't noticed the time."

"That's okay," Cyn said, shuddering at the idea of needing Ginger's help—for anything. "I can do it by myself."

"Nonsense." Ginger grabbed Cyn's arm. "Come on, let's go."

"Whatever," Cyn said under her breath. Her fingers itched to slap Ginger's face. Instead, she headed up the stairs, and down the halls, double-checking each room she passed.

Ginger followed close behind. The sound of their shoes echoing off the empty tile hallways sounded like random rifle shots—first, in step, then out, then in again.

Why couldn't Ginger leave well enough alone? Cyn felt prickles every time the woman touched her. Tears lay right below the surface, and she dang sure wanted them to stay there. How dare Ginger act like nothing had happened. Had she no shame?

She hadn't intended it, but the words came without Cyn's foreknowledge. "Wilburn told me what you did, you know." She increased her pace.

"What...I..." Ginger slowed then hurried to catch up. An invisible but powerful tension encased them, yanking each forward and then backward while Cyn tried to maintain her balance.

"I'm so sorry about that, Cynthia. I don't know what came over me. I certainly—"

Hazel Harrison walked up and gave them an odd, questioning look, and then ducked her head. "Cynthia, Ginger," she mumbled as she hurried past.

Cyn turned to Ginger, but out of the corner of her eye, caught Mrs. Harrison glancing over her shoulder at the two of them.

"You betrayed our friendship, you—"

"No, I...I didn't mean to, I—"

"You didn't mean to? For Christ's sake, you sure can't call what you did an accident."

Ginger stammered, looked out the window at the children's playground. Miller, Ginger's young son, waved at her. Ginger waved back, then turned and plucked a hair off of Cyn's white sweater.

"Don't touch me." Cyn slapped her hand away. "Wilburn said you did the same thing to the previous pastor and his wife—even ran them out of town. Well, you don't have to worry about me, because..." Cyn turned and hurried down the hall toward Wilburn's office. Ginger, hot on her trail, begging forgiveness.

They stepped into the church office. Evidently the secretary, along with everyone else, still waited in the Fellowship Hall for the service to begin.

"Stephen said some of the deacons are pretty upset about the plans for a building program." Ginger bumped into Cyn's back. "You don't think something happened, do you?"

"Like what?" Clueless as to where Wilburn might be,

Cyn felt the pressure of time and the heat of Ginger's breath on her neck.

The door to Wilburn's office appeared closed tight. No need to look there, because if he counseled someone, he'd be furious if Cyn intruded. She turned, and almost ran into her adversary who tilted her head and listened.

"Is that Stephen's voice? Maybe he's in there with Pastor."

Cyn listened a little longer. "Sounds like it. I can't tell what they're saying, but it doesn't sound..."

"Should we interrupt them?"

"No, don't. He'll get mad at me if we do." A drum pounded in Cyn's chest.

A faint groan came from behind the door. Cyn looked at Ginger, who grabbed Cyn's arm and stared back, the pupils of her eyes growing larger.

Was Wilburn hurt? Could someone have gone in and blasted the room with fire from an automatic weapon—maybe someone angry about the new expansion program?

"They're in pain; that's for sure." Ginger charged the short distance across the outer office, gave a quick rap on the door, and stormed in.

Cyn stood frozen in place until Ginger screamed.

CHAPTER THIRTEEN

Chaotic thoughts rushed through Cyn's head as she ran in behind Ginger. Her plan to leave Wilburn flashed through her thoughts. She didn't want to live with him, but she didn't want him dead.

Items normally atop Wilburn's desk lay scattered around the room like someone's arm swiped across it in one fell swoop. Ginger stood stock still, frozen with fear, horror—something.

Cyn grabbed Ginger's arms from behind and looked over her shoulder.

At the end of Wilburn's desk, Stephen stood leaning across the top, his pants around his ankles, while Wilburn, similarly clad—or unclad—stood behind him—in him. Frozen in the act of passion, both men stared at Cyn and Ginger.

"We can explain; it was only this one—" they both said.

A voice coming from behind Cyn yelled, "What the hell's going on in here?"

Cyn whirled to see Bud Harvey, the chairman of finance, who had taken in the scene.

He rounded Cyn, gawked at the half-dressed men, then turned, and stormed out, yelling, "Put your damn clothes back on and get out of this church." He slammed the door shut behind him.

He needn't have bothered. Cyn opened it and hurried behind him, leaving the two men and Ginger to deal with the impending chaos.

Bud Harvey, a building contractor, owned his own business. He came up through the ranks of the construction industry. A hard, no-nonsense person, he tolerated neither man nor woman who didn't fit his model of right and wrong.

She hurried up behind him. "Where are you going, Bud? What are you going to do?"

"I'm going down to the prayer meeting and tell everyone what I just saw with my own eyes."

"Oh, please don't. Not like that. Not blasted out to everyone. Can't we—"

He shoved her away. "No, missy. These church members deserve to know what's going on back there between our so-called pastor and deacon chairman. I've never seen anything like that in my life." He tromped downstairs, glancing back over his shoulder as he went. "I'd think you'd feel the same way. That's your husband up there, or don't you care?"

"Horrified. But wait—"

"I'm doing what you should do—if you weren't such a patty cake."

She stopped mid stride.

He continued down.

The minute he stepped into the hall, he yelled above the singing. "Wait, hold up. I've got an announcement to make."

Her heart pounded, she couldn't catch her breath, but she forced herself down the few remaining steps and stood against the back wall as Bud Harvey stomped down the aisle to the platform.

"I've got an announcement to make. First, will the teachers of the children's programs take the kids out of the room? Go on to your classes. Our children don't need to hear this."

Members looked at the persons sitting around them, then to those at other tables. The air in the room changed from holy celebration to unholy fear. An ominous, and growing cloud covered them all. Should a hair from anyone's head have chosen that moment to fall, everyone would have heard the air move aside as the single hair floated to the floor.

Larry Porter held his hand out to the pianist to stop playing and relinquished the podium as Bud Harvey stormed up and gave him a don't ask look.

"Again," Mr. Harvey said in the microphone, "teachers, please take your students to their classes. I take responsibility for cancelling this part of our prayer service."

The pianist had stopped playing, but her hands still hovered above the keyboard, and her mouth dropped open.

A couple of teachers, with children in tow, passed Cyn, who crammed herself against the pale green wall, a light switch digging into her shoulder. The women looked at her, questions in their eyes, but they didn't stop to ask, just hurried the children along.

Hazel Harrison led her small group of young girls by Cyn, but averted her eyes as if she knew whatever happened, Cyn caused it.

Thoughts and disconnected questions raced through Cyn's mind while people exited the fellowship hall. What was happening upstairs in Wilburn's study? What were the men saying to Ginger? Were they trying to excuse their behavior? To explain? Had Wilburn told Stephen about Ginger's trip to the parsonage? Had anyone else come in and discovered them?

All her life, she'd heard the adage that the wife always knows last. Before Ginger's escapade, Cyn never suspected Wilburn of sleeping with another woman, much less a man. The thought of that, however, seemed to answer more questions than it caused. But Stephen of all men—the deacon chairman. How long had it gone on? With all those late-night committee meetings—why hadn't she guessed? Then, all those nights in bed, when she approached him, only to hear how long his day had been and how tired he felt.

Was this Wilburn's first affair with a man? What about before Justice's birth? Afterwards? Or had he always known he preferred same sex relationships?

At last, the bustle of children leaving, accompanied by teachers who looked like they'd rather stay and listen settled. The room took on the pall of a funeral home. Anticipated dread hung heavy in the air. A boneyard would have made more noise.

Bud Harvey cleared his throat, looked out over his audience, and seemed to reconsider whether or not to continue. She knew the instant he made his decision, for he threw his shoulders back and stepped closer to the microphone.

"I...I have just come from..." He choked, the words sounding like they caught in tears at the back of his throat. After a couple of seconds, he started over. "I've just come from the pastor's study, and..."

Silence fell over the room. Cyn knew it could not grow quieter.

It did.

Wasn't anyone breathing? She sucked in a load of oxygen, unsure how long it would last. Meanwhile, her life flashed behind her eyes. Ready or not, the end of her world stood only seconds away.

"We no longer have a pastor or a deacon chairman." This time, the tears rolled down Harvey's cheeks, darkened from years of working outside in the sun. Deep lines crinkled his forehead.

Someone from the audience called out, "What happened, Harvey? A car accident? What?"

Mrs. Harvey scraped her chair on the tile floor and while everyone watched, made her way between tables until she stepped up on the platform. With great tenderness, she took her husband's arm, stood on tiptoe, and whispered in his ear. He shook his head and with his wife still at his side, again looked out over the crowd.

"I've just come from the pastor's study and..." His voice broke again.

"Good god, Harvey, spit it out," a man called from

the crowd. "If you don't, I'm going to go check for myself. Is he dead? Did someone shoot them?"

Cyn couldn't see who spoke, nor did she care. Regardless of who it was, the results remained the same. Wilburn would not professionally survive this.

A sudden lightheadedness overtook her. She placed her palms flat against the wall behind her, using every ounce of willpower available not to sink to the floor.

"Might as well have," Harvey bellowed out. "They're dead to us."

Someone gasped. Others stared at their neighbors, questions in their eyes, while couples whispered in the ears of husband or wife.

"I found them...they...they're fags, that's what they are." Fury overtook Harvey's grief. "It's sick, sick I tell you. I...I caught them...doing...it...on Pastor's desk, of all places."

"That's a lie," someone yelled. "Pastor wouldn't do that, he..."

Again, Cyn couldn't see who spoke. Again, she didn't care, for it made no difference.

"I do not lie; I tell you. I saw it with my own eyes." Harvey pounded the podium with his fist, his voice loud, strident. "I know what I saw, and no one can convince me I didn't." He looked over the room until he found Cyn leaning against the back wall.

She knew what came next, but her legs refused to let her run. If only she had the ability to vaporize.

"Ask Mrs. Carter." He pointed. "There she is, standing right there against the wall. She saw it, too. So did Ginger. They got there right before me. If I hadn't seen it, we probably never would know the depravity of those men."

Over a hundred pairs of eyes turned to glare at Cyn. Even if she wanted to deny it, she couldn't open her mouth. She lacked the strength to flee, much less the energy it would take to tell a convincing lie.

A middle-aged woman standing halfway across the room, her back to Cyn, looked like she almost convulsed. "How horrible," she screamed. "Why, I would never...Surely this is against the law. I say we call the authorities—have these men arrested."

The whole room exploded in yelling, pointing fingers, each blaming the other for getting them into this mess.

"How come the deacons didn't know about this a long time ago? It's their business to know," someone yelled.

"Who served on that pastor search committee?"

"How could we have known that? He's been here over five years now, so get over it."

"Maybe we should give Pastor a chance to explain. Maybe there's more to the story than we've heard."

"What about Stephen? He fits into this equation, too. I'll bet he's the one who talked Pastor into this."

"Every man's responsible for his own behavior," another yelled.

"The Bible says they'll burn in hell; that's for sure. Same as those in Sodom and Gomorrah."

"That's a crock of bull."

Cyn's knees wobbled from the weight of the responses. She willed her eyes open, when they begged to shut out the world. Marcus Harvey, Bud, and Lorene's son, fled past her, tears streaming down his face.

Need to go after him, want to see...help...him, must, must...

Icy cold, Cyn shivered, pulled up the covers.

What covers?

She blinked a couple of times, then forced her eyes open. Disoriented, she looked around for a minute or two before she recognized she lay on one of the sofas in the church parlor, now empty except for her.

Hands. Someone must have grabbed her as her knees buckled. Who...and why had she...oh, yes. But how'd she get to the parlor?

She heard someone out in the hall yell something about tar and feathers.

Then it all came back. She pulled the afghan over her head.

Wilburn? What happened to him? Where had he gone? Had he run? Stephen? Ginger? Dear God, what did she do now? She certainly didn't want to face anyone.

Home. She'd go home. But home would never be home again.

CHAPTER FOURTEEN

The loud voices outside the church parlor grew faint. Cyn threw off the coverlet and eased to her feet. At first, she felt woozy, but when her head cleared, she tiptoed to the doorway and peeked out into a now-empty hall.

She hurried to the closest exit and out into a blinding rainstorm. Darting between buildings, posts, and automobiles, she finally reached her car.

By the time she crawled into the driver's seat, her clothes dripped with rainwater, and her breath came in short, hard gasps. She grabbed an old cloth diaper she kept under the front seat, wiped her face and hands, and then started the motor. Within seconds, the engine roared. She sped off, wheels spinning, and rear end fishtailing. For the first time in her life, she didn't care if she made a fool of herself or not. Besides, Wilburn had already done that.

Cloud to ground lightning slashed the night sky. The rain fell heavier, eliminating any sight of the yellow line down the middle of the street. Cars passed, their drivers heading to a world that made sense to them, while her world continued its avalanche into oblivion. She swiped her face again, uncertain whether the wet came from rain dripping off her hair or tears running down her cheeks.

Wilburn? Was he still at church and now under attack? Had she abandoned him to an angry mob? Or had he abandoned her to save his own skin?

The idea that he might have reached the parsonage before her didn't cross her mind until she turned on their street and saw his car in their driveway.

Unsure what hell awaited her, she made a dash through the rain, opened the front door, and hurried inside.

Nothing. Not a sound anywhere.

She slipped into the laundry room for a towel, dried off as well as she could, and then started her search, uncertain whether she wanted to find him or not.

Downstairs, she went room by room, but found no evidence of Wilburn. Nothing.

Was it only a couple of hours? Or a lifetime?

The thought that Stephen might have followed Wilburn to drop off his car, and then the two of them leave together crossed her mind.

Moving to the stairs, she realized the carpet looked wet, like someone stood there for a few minutes, their clothes dripping.

She glanced at the front door and saw a trail of wet footprints in the carpet from the front door, through the entry and to where she stood at the foot of the stairway.

Wilburn must have come in and gone upstairs. She followed the trail up the steps, down the hall to Wilburn's sopping wet shoes on the floor in the middle of their bedroom. She tiptoed in and checked the bathroom.

Nothing.

She moved to his closet to see if perhaps he'd gotten a dry pair of shoes and left again.

But he hadn't.

Instead, he sat cross-legged on the closet floor, soaking wet and shivering. Eyes fixed, he stared off into nothing.

"Wilburn? Wilburn? Look at me. Where is Stephen?"

He gave an almost imperceptible shrug, but didn't raise his eyes to hers.

"Who the hell are you?" she shouted. "I gave you everything—including my so-called soul—and that's what you've been doing. For how long?"

No response.

"Answer me, damn it. Is that who you are—why you never made love to me?"

He nodded, his eyes vacant, hollow.

"How long have you known?"

No answer.

"Since you met Stephen?"

He shook his head.

"All your damn life?"

He shrugged again, tears rolling down his cheeks.

"I can't believe this—wait, on second thought, I sure as hell can. If you knew that, though, why did you marry me? Why have you lied about it all these years—to me, to your son, to everyone?" Her voice grew shrill. Her thoughts roared like a tornado ripped through her soul. Wilburn always held the morality whip over her. For the first time, she felt it transferring to her hands—if she wanted it.

Right now, she damn well did.

Wilburn broke into sobs, struggled to speak. "Because God called me to the ministry, that's why. What church would call a man as pastor who is...you know...a...if I told the truth, how far do you think I would have gotten as a Baptist preacher? I needed you to—"

"To what? Cover for you? I get that." Cyn sat on the side of the bed, hands in her lap, beaten, and with no idea what to say.

Thunder rumbled, and a flash of lightning lit the room.

The phone rang. And rang. When it wouldn't stop, she walked to the bedside table, yanked up the receiver and yelled, "Hello."

A man whose voice she didn't recognize said, "Is this, Mrs. Carter? No offense against you, ma'am, but tell that faggot husband of yours, he better watch his back."

Slamming the phone on its cradle, she shook her head, then turned, and looked at Wilburn. "Now, you're getting death threats."

He looked up, but his expression didn't change. She got the idea he no longer cared about death or anything else.

Clueless what to do next, she stood in the middle of the room and did nothing until the doorbell rang.

Relieved and scared at the same time, she wondered whether she should answer it. Perhaps whoever it was might help her. Blinded by tears, she stumbled downstairs, looked through the peephole, and saw nothing.

Fear squeezed her chest. She couldn't breathe.

Desperate, heart racing, she flipped on the porch light and looked again.

Stephen stood with his head down, shoulders slumped, sopping wet. The last person she wanted to see, and likely the only person Wilburn did. Anger renewed, she turned, and marched down the hall toward the kitchen.

The doorbell rang again, and again, and again.

When she didn't open the door, he pounded on it with his fists.

"Cynthia, let me in," he yelled. "Please. I'm worried about Wilburn."

She ran to the door and swung it open. "You're worried?" she screamed. "Seems to me you should be a lot more than worried." She knew she'd lost control, but powerless to stop; she didn't even try. "None of this will cause you to lose your job, but it certainly will his. Not to mention what it's done to me. We'll soon live on the street. Don't you think you've done enough?"

"Please, Cynthia, can I see him?"

"My name is Cyn, damn it. Since you two can go behind my back and do whatever the hell you want, then you can damn well call me by my name. It's Cyn. Always has been—or was, until I married Wilburn. Guess it reminded him too much of his own sin."

Stephen looked at her, confused, like he didn't recognize the woman standing in front of him yelling like a banshee. He wasn't the only one. She didn't recognize herself. She turned away. "Never mind. Do whatever you want. I'm getting the hell out of here." She grabbed her handbag and car keys and ran outside.

"Where're you going?" Stephen called after her.

"I'm leaving this nightmare," she yelled through the deafening rain. "Next stop can't be worse."

She raced to the car, and then sat staring through the windshield at their bedroom window, visualizing what might be going on upstairs. "Who fucking cares?" she screamed.

Never in her life had she used the F word, but at the moment, nothing else fit.

CHAPTER FIFTEEN

For the first time in her life, Cyn now understood why some women ran away, left everything behind. Yes, even preacher's wives like Cyn Carter.

Knowing nothing else to do but the same thing, Cyn ran.

In a blinding rainstorm, headed to nowhere but away—away from the chaos, the shock. Trying at some level to incorporate, no, perhaps separate, what she always believed to be true, to truth, as she knew it now.

Around midnight, the rain eased to a sprinkle and then stopped altogether. Still she drove, without direction, without destination.

Halfway to nowhere, Cyn remembered Dee and glanced at the clock on the dash. Likely Dee had called by now. One hand on the wheel and another fumbling in her bag, her fingers latched around the cold, hard cell phone and looked from it to the highway and back again. Yep. Three missed calls from Dee.

Right now, Cyn refused to talk to anybody—even her baby sister. She dropped the phone back inside her bag and shoved it onto the passenger seat. When she did, the bag tumbled over, spilling its contents on the floor, phone and all.

Her shredded heart dangled in her chest, each strand carrying its own separate pain—betrayal, humiliation, anger, and stupidity. All that time she struggled with whether to stay or go. Now she understood why.

She'd never known a homosexual. At least she didn't think so. As a result, she always bought into what people said about them—damned to hell. Which of course, was what Wilburn taught her to believe. Sinful. Abominable. Unclean. No hope for redemption—unless of course, they changed their spots.

Leopards couldn't, so she doubted homosexuals could either.

That part confused her the most. Why did Wilburn preach against gays, knowing all the while...

He even justified his position on the subject by reading—even quoting scripture. How could he do that, when he knew all the while...he and Stephen...How long had they...She had missed something for sure and right in front of her cotton-picking eyes. All those late-night committee meetings. Wilburn's disgust at Ginger's advances.

No wonder he turned the woman down—and no wonder he lost all interest in Cyn years ago. She blamed it on those few extra pounds she struggled to lose. Her hair.

Fighting to achieve the latest, most popular style.

And all along, it had little—nothing—absolutely nothing to do with her. It had to do with the fact that men turned Wilburn on—not women, and especially not her.

Now, their disastrous wedding night made sense.

Justice. Oh God, what would he say? What would this do to him? Did he have any idea? She glanced at the cell phone on the floor. Good thing she couldn't reach it. His first semester at college seemed the worst time to deal with something of this magnitude.

No, she had to handle this herself—at least for now.

Funny how she'd thought about leaving Wilburn—when she never had him in the first place—except his name. Of course, he would have to leave the church, and certainly no other Baptist church would hire him. She read of a few other denominations now accepting gays and lesbians, but not Baptists.

"God no," she said, and then smiled at the expression. Even if she wanted to, she couldn't live with him this way—nor would he want to. He wanted Stephen. Evidently, the two men really cared for each other. She recognized it in Stephen's eyes when she opened the front door to his pain shortly before she ran away.

Ginger—Wow. No wonder she reached for Wilburn. Her home life must be no better than Cyn's. What would she do? Of course, since Stephen made a better salary than Wilburn, she might not have to find a job like Cyn would.

Paul Cooper's offer might bring the best opportunity available. She had scheduled an appointment with him for the next day, but she couldn't talk to him in her current state of mind. Soon as she got her head on straight, she'd call, apologize, and see if he'd still talk with her. At least she wouldn't have to consult Wilburn. She could do whatever the hell she wanted.

Her mind jumped from Paul to Wilburn, and how he might respond to his parishioners. They must feel as betrayed as she did. The ultra-conservative members would want his hide. Only a pound of flesh might come close to satisfying them. The horror of what Wilburn faced brought her a small amount of pleasure, then guilt for the satisfaction.

Thankfully, by the time she used up a box of tissues, she ran out of tears—but then she couldn't breathe. Exhaustion begged her to stop and get a hotel room. Shock refused the request. Thoughts kept up their onslaught, batting her back and forth. Unaware of how long she drove, she stopped a couple of times for gas, but her car had a bigger appetite than she did. She topped off the tank, left without buying any food, and kept driving— as fast as the law allowed—sometimes faster. Perhaps, if she went far enough fast enough...

Sanity returned with sunrise, emerald waters, and white sand beaches.

She pulled off the road and parked, stunned that without paying attention to her directions, after an all-night drive, she ended up in Destin, Florida—a couple of hours from Mobile. Knowledge of the route she'd taken didn't exist. How had she survived the night without killing herself or someone else?

After a few minutes, she got out of the car and inhaled the fresh gulf air. Mesmerized, she stared out over the stark white sand and turquoise waters. Then, as the sun continued its rise, she pulled off her shoes, wandered to water's edge, and stepped into cool liquid turquoise.

Ripples played with her toes as the unbridled water soothed her soul. Some wounds, however, went far beyond Mother Nature's ability to ease—wounds from living in the shadow of a phony, manipulative man who handed out meaningless clichés and dogma like manna from heaven. What about the pain one suffered when they witnessed the pain of others—the parishioners who came undone with the discovery of Wilburn's imperfection.

She cast her gaze down the shoreline and surrendered to its pull.

Never much of an athlete, for the first time in years, she wanted to run—had to run.

She took off, racing along the water's edge. Tiny crabs scattered back into their wet holes as her feet pounded in the surf.

Her breath came in short puffs. Her heart pounded in her ears. How could she describe her pain? Did anyone care?

Physically, the demon of revenge drove her to run faster. Mentally, the demon drove her to get even.

Cool waves splashed her legs. A seagull flew alongside her for a few seconds, then squawked, and headed out to sea.

Breathless, exhausted, unable to run another step, she slowed to a stop and faced the horizon, panting for oxygen. As her breathing slowed, she became aware of the ancient smell of salt, carried by the wind, coating her skin. She licked her lips, unsure if the salty taste came from tears or the primal waters of birth.

The tide rolled out, unsettling the sand beneath her feet. She shifted, regained her balance, but soon the tide returned and repeated the process.

Water, nothing but life-giving—and sometimes life-taking—water.

She watched and waited, wanting nothing more than for a giant wave to swallow her and drag her into the deep.

She waited...and waited...and waited.

CHAPTER SIXTEEN

"I never knew it would hurt like this." Wilburn grabbed Stephen's hand and squeezed. Tears poured down his cheeks. "I didn't expect it would come to this. We've been so careful, and then, to get caught after all these years. I was just so discouraged over that last deacon's meeting…and you touched…It's my own…"

Stephen flopped to the closet floor beside Wilburn, his own shoulders heaving. He tried to speak but couldn't. After a few minutes, he composed himself long enough to choke out, "No, no it isn't. I refuse to let you…I'm equally—"

Wilburn leaned into Stephen, the man who helped him understand himself—who freed him to be Wilburn— to embrace who he'd always been, and to accept it as okay. "Have you talked to Ginger?"

"No, not yet," Stephen choked out. "Right now, I need...to be right here."

Wilburn nodded, but sat in silence—thinking. Guilt from his teenaged encounter with his pastor—and his pastor's banishment from church work after that left an overwhelming fear in Wilburn, and a determination to be something he wasn't. Which left him full of shame, of hiding, of acting phony—to Cynthia, to Justice, to his congregation—his father and mother.

"Now, what do we do?" Stephen finally asked.

Wilburn tried to look at Stephen, but his swollen eyes made it difficult, so he wiped them with his shirtsleeve and blinked several times. "At least your job isn't at stake like mine is." Wilburn gave a sarcastic laugh. "Correction—it isn't at stake, it's gone. Everything I've worked for, everything I felt God called me to do— up in flames—ashes."

"It will all work out. We've got each other—now more than ever, and that's likely all we've got."

"Think Ginger knows you're here?"

"She does. I told her we'd talk tomorrow—but you needed me more than she did at the moment, that I'd come home later and pack a bag."

"Had she guessed you were gay...that we—"

"I think she suspected for a long time."

"Even though, evidently she didn't know about me and you."

"No, no she didn't know that."

The phone kept ringing, but they ignored it until Wilburn finally got up and yanked the plug from the wall. "Maybe that'll give us some peace. I doubt anyone's coming to the door. Did Cynthia say where she went?

What time she planned to return home?"

Stephen got up, walked over to the window, and looked out. "She didn't. I'm sure she'll come home pretty soon. Likely she needed time to sort all this out. She looked pretty bad."

Wilburn nodded. "I imagine she did—and for good reason."

When the doorbell rang, Stephen moved first. "Stay here. I'll go get it."

"Tell them to go away, whoever it is."

He heard voices, one Stephen's, the other...Oh, dear God, Dee. The very last person in the whole world he wanted to see or deal with at the moment.

Regardless, Stephen shouldn't have to deal with her. Wilburn pulled his handkerchief out of his back pocket, and wiped his eyes, then blew his nose before heading downstairs.

Dee stood in the entryway holding a suitcase.

Stephen held empty palms up to Wilburn. "I told her this wasn't a good time, but she wouldn't leave."

"What's going on, Wilburn? Why isn't my sister here, and why hasn't she answered my calls? Is she hurt? In the hospital?"

Wilburn motioned for Dee to calm down. "Cynthia must have forgotten about you coming—I assume she knew."

Dee nodded. "Of course she knew." Uncertainty wrinkled the lines across her forehead. "What's going on? You're scaring me."

"Hold on a minute," Wilburn hurried to explain. "First, no, Cynthia is not sick, and she isn't hurt—well, not physically, anyway. She's...Well, she's..." *What the hell did he say? How could he explain—especially to Dee, of all people?*

"Want me to leave?" Stephen half-turned to go.

"No, no, no. You stay here. I...I've denied you long enough."

"Will someone tell me what's going on?" Dee shouted.

Wilburn ushered Dee into the living room and indicated the sofa. "Sit, please." He'd never done that before, and he understood the skeptical look on her face.

"It's okay. Please. Sit, and I'll explain."

She cut her gaze to Stephen, then took tentative steps across the room and perched on the edge of the sofa as if ready to bolt should the need arise.

Wilburn reached for her hand, but when she flinched, he yanked his away. "Dee, I know you think very little of me, and I can't blame you. Truth is, I don't think much of myself."

"Okay, this is getting weird. Where's Cyn?"

"She left. I have no idea where or when she's coming back." He gave a hopeless laugh. "I don't even know if she's coming back."

"What?"

"Hear me out, Dee."

"Believe me, I'm trying to, but you're not making any sense, and that's scaring the piss out of me."

"I'm gay, damn it." No sooner had the words left his mouth than it seemed a loud whoosh rushed in, lifted the weight of the world off his shoulders, and sped away.

Dee's eyes opened as wide as her mouth. "Gay? Did you say gay?"

"That's what I'm trying to tell you."

"And Cyn just found out?"

Wilburn nodded. "Along with about a hundred or so members of my church."

"Good Lord. How did that happen? When?"

"Tonight, or rather, last night now, at the Wednesday Prayer Service."

"How the hell did she find out at a prayer service? Who told her? How'd they find out? I know you didn't choose that location to..."

Wilburn glanced at Stephen. "Actually...we did, and lost track of time."

"Oh shit. You mean you two are lovers and got caught in the act at church? By whom, Cyn?"

"Afraid so. She and Stephen's wife, Ginger, came looking for us and barged into my study."

"Ginger, of all people? Oh my God."

Wilburn started to call her on the irreverent use of God's name, but for the first time in his sorry life he realized he had no right to call down anyone.

Dee fell back on the sofa, her face white, eyes wide. "I don't believe this. I should. I should believe any weird thing I hear about you, but in my wildest nightmares I never expected this."

She stared at the two men, then after a long pause, said, "I...I've got to find my sister. You have any clue where she went? Did she pack a bag?"

Wilburn tried to speak, but his voice broke.

Stephen had been standing in the background, but now moved forward. "Not that we know of. She grabbed her purse and car keys and the last thing we heard—"

"Sorry if I sound rude, Stephen, but haven't you caused enough problems?"

Wilburn shook his head at Dee. "Don't speak to Stephen like that, Dee. He's—"

"You can't tell me what to do or how to behave, you shithead. You've ruined my sister's life, and now we don't know where she is or what she might do."

"Dee, you know as well as I do that things weren't going well here."

"You're right, and I tried to talk her into leaving you, you idiot. She seemed on the verge."

Wilburn's mouth dropped open.

"Shocked, are you? Well, you're not the only one dissatisfied in this relationship. My sister was dying inside. Now, I fear she'll do something foolish—like—die for real. If she does something like that, I'll see that you go to jail, Wilburn Carter, if it's the last thing I ever do. You haven't heard the last of this, but right now, I'm going to a hotel."

Suitcase in hand, she fled, slamming the front door behind her.

CHAPTER SEVENTEEN

Cyn waited for some higher power, if there was one, to tell her what to do, but when the answer came, she rejected it. Instead, she left her cell phone inside one of her shoes and stomped in the wet sand, water splattering, crabs scampering, waves coursing. She never pretended perfection—not by any means. And she certainly didn't cause this problem, so how could she be the solution? Why did she have to be? Without a sliver of fight or energy or caring left in her DNA, she wanted only to walk out into the water and let it carry her away.

But then, there was Justice. She couldn't hurt her son on top of what his father had done. Nor could she become a homeless vagabond. If she did, she knew Dee would track her down and drag her home by the hair of her head.

Oh God. Dee. She must have shown up on their

doorstep last night in the midst of the chaos. Had Wilburn let her in? Did he tell her what happened? What did Dee say to him? On second thought, she already knew what Dee would have said. She grabbed her phone and checked the battery. Almost gone. But with enough to see that Dee had texted several urgent messages for Cyn to call her.

But Cyn couldn't. Not yet. She felt bad that her poor sister had to face Wilburn alone. Had he explained what happened? That he caused Cyn to run away.

She dropped the phone and walked back to water's edge, collapsed, and allowed the surf to wash over her. Arms at her sides, she dug her fingers into the wetness, sand grains burying underneath her nails. A pelican flew overhead, a fish in its beak. Like her, the fish lay limp, already surrendered to its fate.

Where had she gone wrong?

In all fairness, however, with little in her arsenal of healthy relationships—no plumb line at all—how could she have known the true issue? Even suspected such?

Alternately, she swore at her stupidity, her blindness. Visualizing the scene of him with Stephen, she gave a sarcastic laugh. And here she worried about Wilburn and Ginger—when all the time, Stephen was the one to worry about. What kind of woman doesn't sense her husband's infidelity? Doesn't question his lack of interest in his wife? She knew who didn't—an idiot like her; that's who.

Wilburn only cared that Cyn fill the role of a good pastor's wife. A convenience. She laughed. Certainly not eye candy, but at least she helped him succeed while he took everything, leaving her a shell.

She slapped the watery sand, and slapped, and slapped, and slapped.

Wilburn had taken everything she had to offer. Now what? What would he do for a living? That church certainly held no plans for him to stay, and they owned the literal roof over their heads.

And what about her? Yes, she'd call Paul Cooper—but not now. Not in this condition.

She certainly couldn't run to Dee. She didn't have a job either. Likely Dee sat at Cyn's house right now, waiting for her.

Well, Cyn certainly couldn't fix Wilburn, but she wanted answers, and to get such required her to return and ask the questions. She had to pack anyway, and maybe while she did that, God might come on a big white stallion and carry her off to glory. Yeah—right. When pennies rain from heaven.

Oh gosh. Wilburn's speech at the convention—surely his actions shot that to hell, as well as everything else. On the verge of soaring with eagles, he'd crashed big time.

All she'd been thinking about was how his actions impacted her, but in reality his world had fallen to pieces.

However, she hadn't caused his pain. He caused hers.

Odd she never suspected he preferred men, and even odder that she'd missed every sign. He'd used their marriage to hide behind, and had done a damn good job at it, too—until now. If he hadn't, he'd never have become an ordained minister, at least in his denomination.

However, good had come from the marriage. They had Justice.

Oh God, Justice. She needed to call him.

She lay in her misery until she visualized Dee

standing beside her, hands on her hips, ordering stop acting so melodramatic. You're not going to die. Get your lazy butt up and do something—even if it's wrong, do something—anything.

Cyn sat up, and the voice faded.

Hurrying across the beach to her car, she started the motor and plugged the battery charger to her cell phone.

Hands shaking, she dialed her son. When he answered, his voice sounded groggy.

"Hi, Justice, it's Mom. Did I wake you?"

"Oh, hi, Mom, yeah, I had a late night study group, and my first class today starts in the afternoon, so I slept...What is it? Has something happened?"

She chuffed. "I'll say. Have you heard from your dad?"

"No, not in a few days. What's going on, Mom?"

"Cutting to the chase, sweetheart, and I don't know any other way to say it."

"Say what, Mom? You're scaring me. Is Pops okay? Aunt Dee?"

After several interruptions, while Cyn choked up, she at last finished recounting the scene at church. During the telling, Justice said not a word—not a sound—nothing.

Emotionally spent, she grew quiet, heard her son sigh, then, "Mom, you mean all these years you never suspected Pops was gay?"

Too stunned to speak, Cyn fought to catch her breath.

"Mom? You there?"

"You mean you knew? About him and Stephen?"

"Not about Stephen, no. But I knew about Pops. I figured you did too. Sometimes the way you said things–"

"Said things? Like what?"

"I'm not sure exactly. It's just that—I got the idea you two had come to some type of agreement or something." He sounded uncomfortable, as if unsure he should continue.

"Go on, Justice. You know you can say anything to me. We've always—"

"Yeah, but this is different. This is...about...you know...It's—"

"What, Justice? Spit it out." She hadn't a clue what the kid thought.

"Sex, Mom, sex. It's kind of hard for a son to talk to his mom about—"

"Oh," Cyn choked out. "Okay, but I need to hear what you have to say. Please, I'm okay, go on."

"I always got the idea that, that...well, that you were more interested in it than Pops. He never has acted affectionate towards you. I don't know...it's difficult to describe. I guess I thought Pops wanted to stay in the closet so he could pastor churches and you just, well, accepted that and settled."

"Did you ever see him...see him do anything inappropriate?"

"No, nothing like that, it's—there's a couple of guys here at school that I'm pretty sure are gay—they try to hide it—they're still in the closet. It's like they hate who they are. One of them is this Jewish kid—the other is Catholic. Then, back in high school...Well, never mind. Anyway, there's something about them that reminds me of Pops."

"Can you be more specific?"

"I don't know...it's like Pops always seemed like...I

got the idea that—"

"What, Justice? Spit it out."

"Like he acted—like whatever he did was never good enough for people at church, and for, well, even God. I see that attitude in some of my gay friends—especially those still in the closet—particularly those with families who..."

He let the sentence drop. Like he couldn't bring himself to say the words.

"Like what? Now's not the time to hold anything back."

"Who think they know God's mind better than everyone else because they go to church and talk about God all the time."

"Oh."

"I don't mean to sound prejudiced, Mom, but certain religious parents aren't bothered so much about other people's kids. But when they learn their children are gay, they think the sky's falling. Sophie and I have talked about this a lot."

"Sophie? What's she got to do with this? Is she gay?"

"Mom," he said, "she's my girlfriend. Has been for a long time. We talk about everything."

"But she's going to college out of state. How...Oh, never mind—of course, social media."

"As I was saying, we've talked about this over the years, and both agree. These kids grow up feeling like God made them gay, then doomed them to a life without the love and acceptance they so desperately need from their families."

"The thought of that breaks my heart," Cyn said,

fighting back tears. "It's so sad."

"I know, Mom. It's hard to describe, but I always felt like Pops might be."

"You think that's why he preached against gays?"

"I must admit—that always bothered me. I wondered why he did. Pressure, I guess. Then, of course, if he didn't take that stand, he couldn't pastor. I always got the idea pastoring a church mattered more to him than anything in the world. Don't get me wrong, I know he loves me, but..."

When the line went quiet, Cyn nudged her son. "But what?"

"But I always felt like if he had to choose between me and his role as a preacher or his denomination, I'd lose out."

"Oh, Justice. You described how I've always felt. I don't mean to put your father down, but..." She let the sentence end itself.

"Anyway," Justice said after a couple of seconds, "him coming out of the closet doesn't bother me, except for the way he did it, and what that does to you. How are you coping?"

"By running."

"Running? What do you mean? Where are you?"

"Some beach on the northwest coast of Florida."

"Good God, Mom, you mean last night you just got in the car and took off driving?"

She didn't answer. Couldn't.

"You want me to come stay with you?" Justice asked, near panic in his voice.

"No. No. You stay right where you are. This is our mess. We'll...we'll...I'll call you in a couple of days."

"You sure?"

"I'm sure, yes. You take care, and make no decisions to leave school until I call you."

Cyn punched off the phone and exited the car. This time, she strolled the beach, but instead of the easier wet, hard packed surface near the water's edge, she chose the soft dry sand, forcing her legs and lungs to power up. The sun, now blazing, warmed her skin. She hadn't showered in more than a day. The smells of salt, sweat, and her own musky body odors reminded her of the stench coating her soul.

The image of Wilburn with Stephen kept forming behind her eyes. The more she tried to shove it aside, the larger it loomed.

She never would have guessed—but why not? Justice even suspected.

Largely, she supposed, because the thought never crossed her mind. Evidently, it should have. Wilburn certainly dropped plenty of clues.

Her thoughts slipped back home. What went on there now? What kind of chaos faced Wilburn? She didn't know much about homosexuals except what Wilburn always preached about it. Said it was Satan's way to take people's minds off of God and put it on erotica.

What might he have felt like all those years denying his sexuality, condemning everyone like him only to see the playing field leveled when events blasted him out of the closet?

She had no other choice. She must go back and face the remnants of her marriage. Regardless of how she felt, she could not dump all this on Justice. His father occupied an important place in his life. Even Justice was more accepting and understanding of homosexuals than his father.

Parents should teach their children, but she always felt like she learned so much more from her son. She wondered if he knew that. Someday soon, she'd tell him.

Dee must be at the parsonage, too. That must be a pretty sight; Cyn thought, smiling. Should she ring Dee and let her know to expect her later that day? No, on second thought, she'd better not. Dee had a way of overpowering Cyn to the point where she couldn't think clearly. First, she needed to get her head wrapped around what she'd do when she got there.

On second thought, the drive home might not be long enough to do that.

CHAPTER EIGHTEEN

A cool front had rolled in. Leaves scurried in front of her car, then scattered in the wind as Cyn turned on her street a little after three. Her leaden stomach had not allowed her to eat a bite since she left the night before. Now, she felt famished.

The street she lived on for the last five years looked strange—vaguely familiar, but definitely not home. In a little over twenty-four hours, home ceased to exist. The century-old house felt foreign, and she an intruder.

Should she knock, or just walk in? Then, once inside, what did she do? Hopefully she could slip in, take a shower, and rest before anyone knew she returned.

No such luck.

She found Wilburn and Dee in the kitchen. Dee faced Wilburn, her back to the door, her hands clenched into fists. Wilburn looked dejected—defeated, like he didn't care if she hit him or not. As furious as Cyn felt, a glimpse of the depth of his pain and what he had done to himself slid in around her anger, softened the edges a bit.

Engrossed in their argument, neither of them noticed Cyn.

"If any harm comes to my sister," Dee raged, "I'll hold you personally responsible, Wilburn Carter. You're at fault here. You and this Stephen guy think you can cavort at will, and everyone else be damned."

"It wasn't like that, Dee." Wilburn's hands went up as if to ward off an impending blow. If he had a tail, Cyn felt certain it would dangle between his legs.

"I'm okay, sweetheart," Cyn said, her voice barely a whisper. At the moment, she wondered if she'd ever feel okay again, but she knew she must fight this battle for herself.

Dee swung around, saw Cyn, and dashed to her. She swept Cyn up in her arms, crying, "Are you okay, honey? I've been worried sick about you. Have you slept? Eaten?"

For the first time in her life, Cyn could not put her arms around her sister regardless of how tight Dee squeezed. Cyn only nodded, for an abiding emptiness left her without words to express how she felt. It seemed her spirit had even taken flight, with no indication it would return, and if it did, no promise she'd ever feel anything again. Her eyes stayed fixed on Wilburn, who stood with his head down, staring at the floor. His shoulders shook, like he wept, but she saw no tears.

So he did care about her welfare. At times, she wondered.

He must have sensed her looking at him, for he glanced up, gave her a one-sided smile, then slipped around them, and went upstairs.

"Here, let me get you a cup of coffee. Have you eaten anything?" Dee, now the mother hen to her older sister, led Cyn to the table and sat her in a chair. "I'll fix you a couple of eggs and toast. Don't move."

Dee caring for Cyn's needs felt eerie—and so out of character. Regardless, Cyn sat and stared at her hands while Dee busied herself scrambling eggs and popping bread in the toaster. Once the coffee pot finished dripping, a steaming cup of the black brew appeared in Cyn's hands, clasped on the table in front of her.

She heard Wilburn opening and closing drawers upstairs, followed by the shower coming on. Her mind leapt to the image forever burned in her brain. Seeing her husband having sex with a man. That was the last thing she ever expected to see—so foreign, so degenerate—after all these years of holding her husband right next to God.

"It would be easier, I think, if Wilburn had died." She didn't realize she'd voiced her thoughts until Dee dropped the spatula, along with the eggs she tried to plate.

"Shit." Dee scooped the food from the floor and pitched it in the trash.

It sounded strange to hear that kind of language in her kitchen. Cyn cringed, thinking what Wilburn might say. Then she remembered how little she cared about anything he might say.

"I'm sorry I wasn't here when you arrived." Cyn's voice sounded flat, indifferent—even to her.

Dee took out another couple of eggs and broke them

into a dish. "You were a little busy, sweetheart."

"I guess you could call it that—busy." She played with the word on her tongue. Such a simple word to describe so much chaos. "I assume Wilburn told you what happened."

"Didn't have to go into too much detail. When I arrived, Stephen—I think that's his name—was here comforting him." Dee gave a derisive laugh. "And here I was warning you about the guy's wife. I left right away, checked into a hotel down the street."

"Well, I needed the warning, anyway. After all, she tried to seduce Wilburn in his own home."

"That's right, she did." Dee's mouth dropped to the floor, along with the second plate of eggs.

With that, both women laughed, easing the tension in the room.

"At this rate, I'm going to have to take you out to eat."

"Just the toast, Dee. That's enough. I doubt if I could get the eggs down, anyway."

"Well, at least with some butter and jelly." Dee put the saucer of toast in front of Cyn.

Neither of them spoke while Cyn nibbled on the food and almost inhaled the coffee. When she downed the last drop, Dee broke the silence.

"Okay, what next?"

"Beats me. I'm surprised the phone hasn't rung off the hook."

"It did until Wilburn unplugged it. I overheard Stephen telling Wilburn the church called a special meeting later this week to discuss where they go from here."

"I figured they already fired him."

"From what I can tell, it isn't that simple. Some folks are calling for blood. They want to strip Wilburn of his ordination, blackball him, so he never stands in a pulpit again, let alone, preach."

"And here he was on the verge of his big breakout presentation at the state convention."

"Do you know what happened? Did you never suspect—"

Cyn pushed the palm of her hand towards Dee. "Don't say it. I feel stupid enough. How could I have not known my husband of twenty years liked men instead of women? Thing is—I talked to Justice and guess what? He's not surprised."

"You mean Justice knew? How?"

"He didn't know," Cyn said. "But he suspected, and had for years. Kid's smarter than me, or more observant. It's like I never knew Wilburn. Here I made him God—or God's representative, with a straight line to the man upstairs. Now, I'm lost."

Cyn glanced Dee's way. "It might please you to know only a day or so before this happened, I made the final decision to leave him."

"You didn't. Really? I wondered if you had the ovaries."

"To follow through on that? I'll never know, but the thing is, I fought against leaving him for so long. When, all that time, I didn't have far to go—he was never with me in the first place."

"True. You don't just one day decide you're gay."

"I know. Justice said he always knew there was something different about his dad. Suspected he was gay, but thought I knew, and that we'd..."

She couldn't go on. Her words stuck in her throat.

"So what now?" Dee picked up the empty plate in front of Cyn.

"What I'm thinking is, I'll file for divorce, and you and I can bum around the world, both unemployed."

"What?"

Cyn chuckled. "Just teasing. To tell you the truth, I have no clue, but as devastated as I feel about all this, I can't get Wilburn off my mind."

"Give me a break, Cyn. Look at what he's done to you."

"I know, I know. But—"

"He's a phony, Cyn."

Cyn nodded, but something about the word didn't quite fit. Yes, she begged God to carry her off to glory, but what about Wilburn? In his deepest heart of hearts—beneath the phoniness, the church-ascribed façade, what gnawed at his core?

Yes, he acted arrogant, like he saw himself above her, superior in every way. Operative word—acted. He played the role so long he convinced himself. What must it feel like to keep life locked within one's soul? Did it ever beg to get out—to see the light of day?

She should feel livid, and indeed she felt every bit of fury anyone in a similar situation might feel—yet her pain made sense. Cheated and betrayed, not because of who she was—but because of who she wasn't—a man. What must his soul feel like right now? And why the hell did she care?

Dee interrupted Cyn's thoughts. "So, shall we both pack our bags and head off into the wild blue yonder?"

"Maybe so, but not yet. I know you'll be unhappy to hear it, but I can't leave until I see this through with Wilburn."

"Oh, sure, I know you need to file for divorce, and all that, but that can be done from a distance. Lawyers work that way all the time."

"I don't mean that. I mean I've got to understand this whole thing. I've got to understand Wilburn. I know what I feel. My reactions are rather expected—but I can't throw away twenty years and discard my son's father on an ash heap."

"Ah, sis, come on, he got himself into this mess, let him dig his own way out."

"I know you don't understand, but I've slept with this man for twenty years. We've made love—or rather tried to—all those years. I bore his son. That counts for something. Yes, he's driven me crazy with all his superior talk, acting so holy, acting like he had all the answers. Well, it's obvious he didn't. He didn't have an answer to anything."

"You should feel superior to him after all he's put you through."

Cyn thought about that—she'd felt inferior because he needed to make her feel that way. And she allowed him to do so because she didn't have the courage to stop him. Correction. At one time, she had the courage. Before she married the phony. That sure worked against her. When he couldn't be his authentic self—who could he be except a man who put others lower than his opinion of himself? By acting superior. Not just better than her, but better than everyone. She bought the dang myth.

Oh God, oh God. This hurt like hell. But how could

she explain this to Dee, who never felt inferior to anyone.

And there her sister sat across the table from her, eyes staring into Cyn's soul.

"You need time alone," Dee said. "And here I sit, butting my nose into your business. Well, as luck would have it, my old boss called last night and has a new assignment for me. He wants me on a plane as we speak, but I told him I couldn't leave until you got home. I hoped to carry you away with me, travel the world, you know, but I see the time isn't right. What if I save a spot for you and when you're ready, let me know?"

The two clasped hands across the table.

"And when you're ready to eat scrambled eggs, let me know." Dee smiled and winked.

"What time does your plane leave?"

"Nothing scheduled yet, but I told my boss I'd catch the first flight out soon as I found out you were okay."

"I'm not yet, but I will be."

"I don't envy what you face—either you or Wilburn. But you know my heart's always with my big sister." She stood. "I'll call the airlines and see if I can get a flight out today."

Dee dialed the airlines and booked a ticket.

"I can take you to the airport," Cyn said as soon as Dee hung up. "Please let me. I need a few more minutes before I'm ready to face Wilburn anyway."

The two stood, and Dee collected her bag. "In one day and out the next—story of my life."

Cyn called up the stairs to Wilburn that she'd return after she dropped Dee at the airport. He mumbled okay, and called out a goodbye to Dee.

CHAPTER NINETEEN

Cyn dropped Dee at the airport to catch a flight to New York and then on to parts unknown while she and her gut load of dread headed back to the parsonage. When she walked inside, home held an eerie quiet. Pushing discomfort aside, she headed straight upstairs. At the moment, the need for a long, hot shower superseded everything else.

That changed when she entered the bedroom and saw Wilburn sprawled across their bed sound asleep.

Their bed—what a joke.

Irritated that he slept so soundly while she hadn't slept a wink for more than twenty-four hours, she stomped over and shoved on his leg. "Get up, Wilburn. Wake up."

He didn't move.

"Wilburn, I said get up."

Still no reaction.

Anger swelled in her gut. How in the world could the man sleep so soundly when he'd crashed not only her world but his own and every parishioner's in the church? If nothing else worked, she'd splatter water on him. That would get his attention.

Then she spotted the open pill bottle in his hand. She snatched it and looked. "Oh no! Don't tell me you took...Wilburn...Did you take all these?"

She shook him again.

No response.

Without hesitation or stopping to consider other consequences, she dialed emergency, and ordered an ambulance. She didn't report the incident as a possible suicide attempt, rather an accidental overdose of sleeping medication.

Within minutes, the medics arrived, hustled him into the ambulance, and prepared for transport. Despite her reeking condition, she climbed in beside him hoping the medicinal smells inside would cover up her own not so medicinal odor.

The scream of the siren tore at her insides as she watched her comatose husband lying on the stretcher. Even with the oxygen mask and tubes, he still looked handsome. She could easily understand Stephen's attraction to Wilburn. Years ago, she fell victim to him herself. She'd thought she could handle his death easier than she could his betrayal—but she'd been wrong.

Emergency room staff stood ready as they pulled up to the hospital and bustled him behind closed doors. They allowed her to go with him, gathering information on the patient as they walked, then shuffled her off to a waiting room while they wheeled him deeper into the catacombs. "Someone will touch base with you as soon as they can, Mrs. Carter. For some reason we've been busier than usual—it's been an out of the ordinary week."

Out of the ordinary week—an understatement for sure. Without a doubt, she didn't need to call anyone to confirm Wilburn's absence at Sunday's worship service. Most likely, after Wednesday night they'd already found someone to fill in.

In the waiting room, a family huddled in a corner. One of them cried while others spoke in low, grief-stricken voices. Cyn picked up a magazine and flipped through the pages, more to keep her hands busy than anything else.

After what seemed an eternity, a nurse stepped into the room, empty now, except for Cyn.

"Mrs. Carter?"

"Yes." Cyn stood and stepped toward the nurse. "How is he?"

"Looks like, barring any complications, he'll be okay. We've pumped his stomach, but he'll sleep for a while still. It's a good thing you found him when you did. A few minutes later..." She shook her head. "He took a...a..."

"To put it bluntly, he took a buttload of pills," Cyn said, finishing the nurse's sentence.

The nurse smiled. "Exactly. We'll keep him in ICU until he awakes. You can visit him now, if you like, but he really needs to sleep it off. After we see he's out of danger, psychiatry will come visit with him."

"Psychiatry?"

"Standard procedure when someone overdoses. We can't prove he accidentally took too many pills, even if Reverend Carter swears he did."

"Suicide?"

"He took almost a whole bottle, Mrs. Carter. I'm afraid we can't report that as unintentional."

"Of course, of course."

"Wait here, and as soon as we get him set up in ICU, I'll come get you."

Cyn collapsed into a chair, although she preferred a cave—a deep, dark cave with no way out.

Should she call Justice? What about Stephen? She'd never felt so alone. Before, they always had a congregation keeping watch over them. None of them wanted that responsibility now. Not with Wilburn viewed as unclean. A reprobate.

How on God's good earth had her life and Wilburn's fallen to such depths?

Pain, indescribable, tore at her heart.

Time dragged. The more she considered calling someone, the stronger she felt led not to. She would wait until Wilburn stabilized, until he woke up. Should he change for the worse, she'd get Justice here right away.

The doctor said it would likely be several hours before he came around. In the meantime, she'd sit and wait. Despite her rage over his betrayal, she knew if she ran away again, she'd never heal from this. For some stupid reason, she must see this through.

As far as the church went, she saw no need to contact a single one of them. Yes, technically he still held the title as their pastor, but likely most of them would as soon he die and go to hell.

A familiar-looking nurse stepped into the waiting room as Cyn returned from the cafeteria where she'd gone to buy a sandwich and coffee. When she tried to eat, the food couldn't get past her throat, and she ended up tossing it in the trash.

"Mrs. Carter?"

"Yes?"

"Your husband's vital signs are all good, so we've moved him into a private room. You can see him now."

The identity of the familiar-looking nurse became clear. Emily Brownstone, a member of their church and a leader in the young adult department. Instant questions raced through Cyn's mind. Could this woman put aside any bias she might have? Could she keep this information confidential?

Emily extended a hand to Cyn. "Don't worry, Mrs. Carter. My job is confidential. I will not share any information about Pastor with anyone."

"Thank you." Cyn grabbed the nurse's arm as a wave of lightheadedness made the room spin.

"You look exhausted, Mrs. Carter. Please, let me help you." She held onto Cyn and led her down long halls and double doors.

"I don't know what all happened, but I want to assure you, Pastor will receive excellent care here, and if I can do anything—anything at all for you, Mrs. Carter, please let me know." They turned the corner, and Emily stopped at a room directly across from the nurse's station. "We have Reverend Carter here close to our station. That way we can keep a close eye on him."

She led Cyn into the darkened room. "We'll leave his door closed for now. That will give you a little privacy. We're right outside should you need us."

"How long can I stay with him?"

"He's sleeping now, but stay as long as you like. We'll come in every few minutes to monitor his vitals."

"Thank you, Emily. And thank you for not asking any questions."

The young woman put her arm around Cyn's shoulder. "You know we will have to ask in time, and psychiatry will come talk to you before we dismiss him." She looked at her pastor with a kind, caring look in her eyes. "For now, rest. How about I order you a food tray?"

"I don't think I could eat a bite."

"A cup of soup?"

Cyn nodded. "Maybe. That sounds good."

"Coming right up."

Cyn moved to the far side of Wilburn's bed. The lines around his eyes and mouth looked a little softer, making him appear younger, happier than he'd looked in a long time. When he woke, would he be upset with her for calling the ambulance? Maybe he preferred she let him die.

Of course, she couldn't do that.

Besides, no way in hell would she face all this by herself. He caused it—he could well face the consequences with her.

Moving to a small brown recliner, she sat with her feet up, her eyes closed, and allowed her mind to wander.

Where in the world did they go from here? For certain, they couldn't continue in the marriage like nothing happened. Without a clue what action the church would take—or the convention, she figured Wilburn would soon join the unemployment line. For all she knew, the deacons might have already taken such action.

Despite all the talk about forgiveness, Baptists excelled at shooting their wounded.

Evidently, some folks put limits to God's love. In all honesty, she guessed she had, too.

She heard a noise and opened her eyes.

Emily stood nearby with a Styrofoam cup. "Hope chicken noodle sounds good." She handed the container to Cyn, who inhaled the steam. "It not only sounds good, it smells good." She took a sip. "And tastes good too. I didn't realize how long it had been since I ate."

"Good. I ordered you a tray. When it comes, eat what you can. The night will likely be a long one."

Efficient and concerned, Emily walked over to Wilburn and lovingly held his hand for a couple of minutes, observing, and then checking his vitals. She turned to Cyn.

"I've put a No Visitors sign on his door so no one should disturb you. Stay as long as you like. I'll check on him in a few minutes."

Cyn couldn't help but believe the No Visitors sign might also have something to do with protecting Emily's pastor and Cyn's husband from any potential onslaught.

Weariness crept into her bones. She finished the soup then eased back in the chair, put her feet up again and dozed. Over the next few hours, she heard first one nurse and then another come in and check on Wilburn, then slip out without disturbing her.

The morning shift came on, and a new nurse came to see Wilburn, who still appeared in a deep sleep. "We've had dozens of calls inquiring about Reverend Carter," she said, a frown on her face.

"What did you tell them?"

"We won't say anything. Health information is protected."

"Guess that pissed a lot of them off," Cyn said, and then bit her tongue. "When do you think he might start to awaken? He's slept quite a while now."

"It's difficult to tell. It depends on how long the meds stayed in his system before we got to him. Could be another twenty-four hours or so. Why don't you run home, get a shower, and something to eat. You'll feel a lot better."

"Maybe I will. I'm stinking up the whole room." She laughed.

"Hey, no smell can supersede that of hospitals." The nurse said, joining in the laughter. "You go on, I'm right here. If we see any change, I'll call you personally."

The sun peeked over the horizon by the time the taxi she'd called pulled into her driveway. She crept up the stairs telling herself she'd shower first, then take a short nap before calling Justice. After that, she'd return to the hospital.

Instead, soon as she got near the bed, she collapsed across it.

Startled awake a couple of hours later, she looked at the bedside clock then checked her cell phone, relieved to see she hadn't missed a call from the hospital. She scrambled up, shed her clothes, and stepped into a steaming hot shower, letting the water do its magic as it pounded on her head.

By the time she'd dressed, the world didn't seem as full of doom and gloom as it had earlier. Perhaps hope existed after all.

Until she went downstairs and checked the answering machine. The ringer was in the off position, so the messages had piled up. She stiffened and punched the message button, then hit delete and went to the next message and repeated the process. The hatred in the voices of the callers startled her. How could a group of people who called themselves Christian sound like spawns of Satan? Several demanded everything but Wilburn's blood. Some even threatened that.

Overcome with emotion, she headed out the door and back to the hospital. Nowhere else seemed as safe.

She hurried down the long hall toward his room, hoping he'd awakened. She needed someone to talk to—even Wilburn.

He still slept.

A different nurse stood at his bedside checking his vitals.

"Has he roused at all?" Cyn moved to the opposite side of the bed.

"Not yet, but his vitals all look good. He probably won't sleep much longer." She straightened his sheets, and fluffed his pillow, then moved to the door. "We're right outside. Call us when he starts to waken."

Cyn wandered to the window and stared out, feeling more alone than she had in her life. More than ever, she wanted the comforting arms of her mother. Tears crept to the edges of her eyelids and tumbled down her cheeks. She couldn't remember ever feeling so alone, so...

Cyn heard movement. She wiped her eyes and turned to see who'd entered.

Stephen stood just inside the door. Unshaven, disheveled, he still wore the same clothes he wore the night she found them in Wilburn's office, the same night her world crashed and burned in an earth shattering ball of fire.

They stared at each other without either saying a word. Cyn noticed the swollen, red-rimmed, blank eyes.

Finally, Cyn broke the silence.

"What is it, Stephen? What do you want?"

She wanted to ask him hadn't he done enough? He ruined Wilburn, their marriage. Then it hit her. He did no such thing to their marriage. It didn't exist, except legally. She already planned to leave Wilburn before any of this happened. And Stephen looked like he hurt as much as she did, perhaps more.

"I know I'm the last person you want to see or talk to, Cynthia—"

"Cyn."

"What? Oh, that's right. Sorry. Cyn. I'd like to come in if I may?"

Cyn wanted to scream, not no, but hell no. The image of Wilburn stretched across their bed, comatose, a result of guilt enough to last a lifetime prevented her from doing so.

"Looks like you're already in."

Stephen moved to Wilburn and stared at him for the longest, not saying a word. He didn't need to. His body language said everything. Head down, shoulders slumped, he took Wilburn's hand. After the longest pause, he turned and sat in a side chair.

"I know I have no right to ask this, but would you please tell me what happened?"

Cyn perched on the foot of the bed. Thinking as she did, that Wilburn would chastise her had he been awake.

One of his pet peeves had always been people sitting on the edges of beds. Said it broke down the binding and over time, would make the bed lopsided. Suddenly she wanted to laugh. Their bed had been lopsided for years, and it had nothing to do with the framework.

"Please, believe me, neither of us wanted to hurt you—to hurt anyone."

For the first time in a long time, she felt like she heard truth.

"How long have the two of you been—"

"Together?"

"Yes. How long have you committed adultery? I guess that's what you call it. These days I don't know what to call anything."

"Since shortly after you moved here."

CHAPTER TWENTY

"That long?" Incredulity washed over her like a typhoon, sending everything she knew into the trash heap. She choked, caught her breath.

"I don't understand. You mean to tell me that Wilburn...That you..."

He looked from Cyn to Wilburn. "I fell in love with that man the first time I saw him. The day you came to the church in view of a call."

"So how long did it take you to seduce him?"

He cleared his throat and squirmed. "I don't recall, maybe a couple of months. Neither of us intended to. It just..."

"Just happened, I suppose."

He nodded.

"Didn't you know it would kill him?"

"What do you mean?" He looked up at her, fear on his face.

She stood and paced the room, ready for this tale to end.

"He attempted suicide," she said softly, when she really wanted to scream the words at him.

"Why didn't you call me—call somebody?"

"It's no one's business anymore."

"It damn sure is—you don't understand, Cynthia—Cyn. This man means everything to me. Tell me he will be okay." Worry coated his demands.

"Looks like he'll make it, no thanks to you—or him."

The nurse must have overheard the heated conversation because she poked her head in. "Everything okay?"

Cyn turned her back to Stephen. "He's on his way out."

Stephen kissed Wilburn on the lips and walked out. The nurse ducked her head and closed the door behind her.

"Stephen?" The word whispered in the softest of voices, Cyn swore came from Wilburn's direction. She moved to his bedside, wanting to clasp his hand, but also wanting to slap him in the face.

His eyelids fluttered.

"Stephen?" he called again, a little louder this time.

"No, it isn't Stephen. It's Cynth...Cyn—your wife, damn it. Answer me this—why in the hell did you marry me? That's what I want to know—now, right this very minute," she screamed. "Answer me."

"Oh-h, I thought I heard Stephen," Wilburn

mumbled. She could not deny what he thought—nor the person he wanted. To her dismay, his eyelids settled again, and he slept.

Cyn wondered why the pain of rejection felt so great—especially since she'd decided a long time ago that Wilburn only tolerated her—and she him.

Returning to the chair, she waited and finally dozed.

Late that afternoon, Wilburn opened his eyes and struggled to sit. Numb by now, Cyn watched him stir, then stuck her head out the door, and signaled a nurse who hurried in.

"Well, good day, Reverend. You've had quite a sleep. We're glad you're awake."

He said nothing, glanced around the room, past Cyn, and then back to the nurse.

"Are you hungry? Think you can eat something?" She checked the catheter, the IV, and straightened his bed sheets. "Lots of people calling to check on you."

He gave a half-smile.

"Your wife's here. Don't you want to talk to her?"

He didn't answer. Just blinked—a long slow blink.

The nurse left, promising to return with a food tray.

Cyn sat and watched him. Tried to read his mind. Tried to imagine him in love with Stephen—with anyone but himself. Over the last few hours so much had started making sense. All the late-night committee meetings, Wilburn's lack of interest in her, sexually or any other way, except the role she played as the preacher's wife.

Had he always been gay? Then why had he married her?

He always said he felt God's call to the ministry at an early age—to be a pastor. One couldn't do that in his denomination and be gay.

So he used her while living between two worlds.

"Cynthia?" He reached his hand out to her.

She stalled, waiting, wondering how in the world to respond. What would she say? Truthfully, she had no clue what hell he lived in all his life, but she certainly knew her own. Maybe she started there. She walked over to him but didn't take his hand.

"You look awful," he said. "I'm sorry."

"For what?"

"For everything, I guess. I figured if I died, then everyone's life would be easier."

"And what made you think that, Pops?"

Cyn swung around to the door. Justice stood there with his hands on his hips, and a dark curl lying against his forehead. "What I want to know is, don't I count in this family? Why didn't someone call and let me know about all this?" He waved his hands around to include the hospital and all its trappings.

He walked over, put his arm around Cyn's waist, and with the other hand, clasped that of his dad's.

"Don't you two know I love you? I'm a part of this family, and I don't care what happens, I want to be included. Sophie wanted to come, too, but couldn't get away."

Cyn put her head on Justice's chest and allowed the tears to flow. "I'm so glad you're here, baby. I need you something fierce."

"Well, it certainly doesn't look like it." Justice pulled Cyn tighter.

"I should've, I know, and I planned on doing so soon. It's that..."

"When neither of you answered your phones, I called Stephen. He told me. I caught the first bus headed this way."

Cyn felt like the world stood still, stopped in its path of turning. Stephen. Her enemy.

"He's not your enemy, Mom. Although I can understand why you might think so."

"So now, you've taken up mind-reading?" She laughed.

"After what you've gone through, it doesn't take mind reading. And Pops, how in the world could you have taken an overdose? You sure don't practice what you preach—that's for sure."

Wilburn gave a sarcastic snort. "Evidently in more ways than one."

"I meant to talk to you about that." Justice gave them both a squeeze.

"Now, someone is out in the hall going crazy to see you, Pops. Mom, think you can handle it?"

"Who is it?"

"Stephen. He picked me up at the bus station and brought me here."

Betrayal seeped into Cyn. She pulled away from her son's embrace, walked to the bathroom, and shut the door, but even that didn't shut out what she didn't want to hear. So she cracked the door and peeked out.

"You're asking too much, son," Wilburn said.

"Let's give her a couple of minutes. She's already talked with him."

"When?"

"Earlier, while you slept it off. Stephen told me."

"I'm so ashamed, son. I should have come out of the

closet a long time ago. I've really done you and your mom wrong. She's angry, and I don't blame her. She has a right to be."

"I told Mom when she called that I've waited a long time for you to come out of that proverbial closet."

Wilburn sat up, his eyes stretched wide.

"I've known you were gay since I attended junior high school, Pops."

Wilburn tried to swing his legs to the side of the bed, but he must have gotten dizzy, because Cyn saw him lie back in bed.

"I didn't know you cheated on Mom, though, or I'd have called you on it—never mind that you're my dad."

"It ate me alive, son."

"Humph. Well, forgiveness is a done deal as far as God is concerned—but Mom and your congregation, that's another matter. Not sure how you plan to handle that. They might forgive an affair, but you know how Baptists are about homosexuality."

Cyn could stay in the bathroom no longer. She'd never before heard her son talk like such a man. He always seemed like her little boy. Now, it sounded like he had more maturity than either of his parents.

She moved into the room. "Okay, you can invite Stephen in. I'll go get a bite to eat. I need more time than you two to deal with this. After all, Wilburn, you've preached against homosexuality—the sin of all you are—ever since I've known you. Now you expect me to switch my beliefs because you confess all this time you were wrong. At this point, I'm not sure if anything's true. I need more time."

She hugged Justice and walked out of the room and

into Stephen, who stood outside the door. She wondered if he heard their conversation.

"They want to talk to you," Cyn said, as unemotional as she could muster. Stephen gave a gracious bow and walked into Wilburn's room.

Unable not to, she stood listening. The room fell quiet for a couple of seconds; then she heard the heart-wrenching sobs of two men. She visualized them in each other's arms and fled down the hall, tears blinding her, rage filling her heart, and at the same time feeling lost and alone.

Then, strong arms wrapped around her—familiar arms—her son's.

"It's okay, Mom. Let it out. You have a right to cry, to scream, to be livid with Pops." He led her into the waiting room, now filled with another family. Once they saw Cyn's condition, they eased out into the hallway to give her and Justice privacy.

"Thank you," she heard Justice say to them. "Would you give us a couple of minutes?"

He led her to the sofa and held her ever so tight while she released hot, salty tears held in over a lifetime.

"Want me to call Aunt Dee, Mom?" Justice whispered in her ear.

She shook her head. "She left for a new assignment." She grabbed the tissues Justice handed her, and wiped her eyes and nose. She sniffed. "I'm okay, or I'm going to be. It's that I've held so much in for so long—and this is the last thing I expected."

"I know, I know."

"But you didn't know I planned to leave your dad."

Justice massaged her shoulder. "No, I didn't know

that. Want to tell me about it?"

"Not really." She laughed. "But I will. Give me a minute." She swallowed hard, struggling for words to explain the failure of his parents' marriage—at least her part of the failure. "To put it bluntly, when I married your dad, I lost myself. I became only the pastor's wife." She bracketed the last three words with her fingers. "I let your Dad—and others—define God for me. Your dad always needed reassurance in everything he did, his sermons, any speech he gave...I'm sorry, sweetheart. He's your father. You don't need to get caught in the middle here."

"It's okay, Mom."

She heard shuffling footsteps and looked up to see the last person she expected, or wanted to see—judgmental Hazel Harrison, standing in the doorway staring at Cyn. The elderly woman wore her usual floral print shirtwaist dress, stockings, and practical shoes.

CHAPTER TWENTY-ONE

Justice glanced at Cyn, up to Mrs. Harrison, and then to Cyn again. He whispered in Cyn's ear. "Are you okay with this, Mom? I can ask her to leave if you're not ready to talk to anyone from church."

Cyn patted his hand. "It's okay."

"You're sure, Mom?"

"Why don't you go check on your dad? Give us a few minutes."

He stood, released her hand as if that were the last thing he wanted to do, then left, giving her a thumbs up after he passed Mrs. Harrison.

"Come in, please." Cyn patted the chair Justice vacated. "You have a family member in the hospital?"

Mrs. Harrison sat, rested her purse on the floor then smoothed her skirt. "You might say that. I've come to see you, Cynthia."

Cyn tried not to appear shocked but doubted she made it.

"I don't know what to say...I...thank you for coming."

Mrs. Harrison slid over and took Cyn's hand. "You poor dear. I feel so sorry for you and everything you've gone through. I can tell you're devastated."

Cyn had no clue how to answer. So she didn't. She smiled and squeezed the woman's hand.

"How can I help you? What do you need? Can I bring you some food? Take you out for lunch?"

At first, Cyn shook her head and then, overcome with the sudden memory of her own mother, heard herself say, "You know, come to think of it, I'm starved. Can I change my mind? Might we go somewhere for lunch—or a late breakfast?"

Mrs. Harrison gave Cyn's hand another squeeze. "Of course we can, sweetheart. Come on, let's go."

The two walked to the elevator in silence and waited. When the doors opened, they stepped in, still without a word. The quiet felt awkward, but Cyn had no idea what to say.

Once outside, Mrs. Harrison led Cyn to her Chrysler New Yorker. After they settled in and buckled their seatbelts, Mrs. Harrison turned to Cyn.

"Where shall we go? I know this place along the beach. Does that sound okay to you? Their seafood is always nice and fresh."

"Sounds good to me."

A few minutes later, the two women walked into the restaurant and found a table near the window. A server came and took their order before the two settled into conversation.

"I love the water, don't you?" Hazel stared out the window, then, without waiting for Cyn to answer her question, added, "And by the way, Cynthia, would you please call me Hazel?"

Cyn felt herself smile, albeit weakly. "On one condition."

"What condition?"

"That you call me Cyn."

"Sin? S-I-N?"

"No, C-y-n, short for Cynthia. That's my childhood nickname, and I like it so much more than the more formal—"

"Of course. I like it, too. Why didn't I know that?"

"Well, Wilburn—"

"Say no more. I understand. Remember, I have a husband, too." Hazel blushed. "To tell you the truth, honey, I don't really know what to say to you. I just needed to come and..."

Cyn choked back tears.

"...and apologize for that instance with your sister the other night at our meeting. I felt so ashamed of myself afterward. I wanted to call and apologize, but I listened to others who convinced me—or tried to, that I had done nothing wrong. Sometimes I get to acting so high and mighty."

"Now, I'm the one who doesn't know what to say." Cyn wiped at her eyes again, sniffed.

"You don't have to say anything. I just wanted you to know I'm here for you because folks are saying Pastor tried to commit suicide, and if it weren't for you, he'd be...Is that true? Did he?"

Hazel appeared to hold her breath, as if doing so might make the answer she expected change by the time it reached her ears.

Cyn paused, unsure whether to tell the truth or lie about Wilburn's desperate attempt to escape what he knew headed his way as a result of his actions. "You want the truth?" She clasped Hazel's hands in hers.

"I don't know. Do I?"

"No, you don't. You want me to tell you what you want to hear. That all of this is one big nightmare, and nothing has changed. That we can go stick our heads back in that sandbox."

Tears broke through Hazel's resistance. "I don't know what's going to happen to our church now. The congregation is so fractured. Some of them still love Pastor and are trying to understand—to forgive him. The others are out for blood. They've even called the state office and asked for advice. They're yelling for financial audits—swearing he and Stephen took money from the offering plate. Others say Pastor has cheated the church because of his preoccupation with other things." Hazel wiped her eyes, caught her breath. "Here I am thinking about myself. What about you, sweetheart? What are you going to do?"

"I don't know what to say, much less what I'm going to do." Cyn's words sounded dull, passionless—spent. "Right now, I'm trying to keep breathing."

Hazel paused when the server brought plates of fried shrimp and baked potatoes. They spent the next several minutes eating.

Figuring they had each lived with enough secrets for

a lifetime, Cyn said, "Justice and Stephen are in Wilburn's room now—together."

Hazel's pale blue eyes crinkled at the corners. Heavy with compassion, they looked into Cyn's. "That must hurt. I'm an old woman, sweetheart. If I had to deal with what you have on your plate, I'm not sure I could. You know, I used to think I had all the answers, but these days...I'm thinking I'm too old for this world."

"Oh, don't say that. Please don't." Cyn broke down, the responsibility for everyone's welfare slamming into her chest.

"Oh, honey, I'm sorry. I didn't mean to add to your heartache. I'm such an old fool. We're going to get through this. I know we will. Our church will, too. It will look different than it has, but that's not always a bad thing."

"How does Mr. Harrison feel about all this?"

"Well, now, that's another matter." Hazel snorted. "To tell you the truth, I always let him make our decisions—who I voted for, what I believed, how I dressed."

"Sounds familiar."

"He swore homosexuals sinned against God, said Pastor preached the same thing. And now we learn Pastor is one. That throws everything I believe into the air."

Hazel stopped talking when the server came and refilled their tea glasses, and then continued after he left.

"I need to rethink all this. Right now, I don't know what's right and what's wrong. But you know what? I'm learning to trust myself more than I've done before. I'm tired of letting Harris decide what I believe. I figure I know God about as well as the next person."

"Atta girl. I'm learning that, too." Cyn laughed along with Hazel.

"Excuse me, let me check the time. I don't know how long Stephen planned to stay at the hospital." Legally Wilburn's wife—but not his life—she no longer knew the rules.

"Honey, I can see you want to go back up there to check on Pastor. I'm going to pay the check, and we can go, but you remember, I'm here for you."

At the hospital, Hazel pulled up to the front door and stopped. Cyn stepped out of the car then turned to Hazel. "Thank you. You don't know how much this has meant to me."

"You call me when you need me, okay?" Hazel looked more sincere than Cyn had ever seen her.

Cyn smiled and nodded, then headed inside and up the elevator.

Relieved when she peeked into Wilburn's room and saw Stephen not there, she felt more comfortable going in.

Wilburn's coloring looked better, and the room didn't smell as antiseptic.

Justice met her halfway across the room. "Mom, come on in. Pops and I have been talking about the impact of all this on you. I told him how furious I am at how he's treated you all these years. How I thought you knew and accepted who he was, like I did. Not Stephen, of course. I know I said that earlier, but to make sure he knows where I stand. You and his parishioners deserved better."

"Sounds like you've been pretty direct with your dad." Cyn glanced at Wilburn, but suppressed saying *I told you so.*

"If he chews out his future kids like he did me, whew, I feel sorry for them." Wilburn shook his head. He looked stronger, although a mite chastised. "I told Justice he is a lot smarter than his dad was at that age." Wilburn laughed, moved his gaze from Justice to Cyn. "You have no reason to believe me, but I almost told you about Stephen that night on our way to the charity ball—and then again when we drove home. Guilt ate me alive and grew worse, but I couldn't get it out."

Cyn felt like a zombie.

"What is it, Mom? Spit it out. It's obvious you want to say something."

She wanted to say she could fight her own battles. She'd slid down the slippery slope of helplessness long enough. She strolled to the window and stared out, building her nerve, figuring out how to tell her son. In the parking lot below, people came and went. She wondered if their world had fallen apart like hers.

"Sweetheart," she said, still looking out the window. "Don't think I'm not grateful for everything you've done, but this isn't your fight. It's ours. I hope you won't take this the wrong way, but you need to go back to school, take care of yourself."

She felt Justice come up behind her. Soon, his arms snaked around her waist, and he held her tight. "You sure?"

"I've grown up a lot over the last couple of days. I can handle whatever comes. This isn't about you—we both love you more than our own lives—and you need to trust us to deal with this." She grabbed his hand. "We'll be okay." She turned to face Wilburn. "Unless your dad does something stupid again, like taking too many—"

Wilburn put his hand up. "I know. I promise I won't do anything that brainless again. At the moment, everything seemed hopeless."

"And now?" Cyn forced herself to release Justice's hand that at the moment felt like a lifeline.

"I told Justice the same thing, that you and I need to talk." Wilburn shifted in the bed, straightened the blanket. "That we've got a hellacious journey ahead of us, but we'll work on it. Now that I can be honest with you—with everyone—well, at least it's a start. We will figure it out as we go."

Justice looked from Wilburn to Cyn, then back again. "Do you know how much I love the two of you? How proud you both make me? Pops, for your honesty for the first time in your life—and Mom, for coming home to deal with this."

Cyn smiled her thanks, but no words came. Truth was, if she acted on her feelings right now, she'd scream. Figure it out? What the hell do you mean, we'll figure it out? Here my life, everything I believed in, shattered, and you expect me to figure it out? But if she let go, Justice might feel like they still needed a caretaker.

The room fell silent except for the soft beep of hospital equipment and a leftover sniff or two, until Wilburn cleared his throat. "Well, now that we've got that settled, Cynthia, are you okay with Stephen taking Justice to the bus station, so you and I can talk?"

Cyn clenched her fists. "My name is Cyn."

"What?"

"It's either Cyn, or I'm out of here."

"You heard her, Pops." Justice tried to suppress a snicker. It didn't work.

Wilburn's shoulders dropped. "I deserved that. It may take me a while to break the habit, so be patient, and don't hesitate to remind me if I slip up."

"You can count on it. But until you do, don't expect me to respond."

Pressure on her chest eased ever so slightly.

Justice's cell phone rang, breaking the tension. He looked at the caller ID. "It's Stephen."

After Justice clicked off, he explained that Stephen bought Justice a ticket back to the university. The bus left in an hour. After hugs around, Justice gave them a thumbs up and left as a woman dressed in street clothes walked in.

"Hello. Reverend Carter?"

"Yes."

"Psychiatry sent me to see you. I'm the social worker."

CHAPTER TWENTY-TWO

Mid-afternoon the next day, doctors released Wilburn to Cyn's care with the promise Wilburn would keep his appointment with a mental health worker the following day.

By the time Cyn, Wilburn, and the attendant headed down the elevator, Cyn only wanted to get home and barricade herself inside—lock away the world. Later, she and Wilburn had time to deal with the fallout at church.

However, as soon as they stepped outside, an unexpected media circus pounced on them. Cameramen pointed cameras while reporters described in minuscule detail who and what they saw. A local news channel van with a satellite dish sat nearby.

"Today, Reverend Wilburn Carter, one of Mobile's most respected ministers leaves the hospital after a reported suicide attempt," one local TV personality said.

Another continued. "Reverend Carter is said to have overdosed on sleep medication after his wife barged in on him with another man last Wednesday night before the church's mid-week service."

A third chimed in. "Given the current fight for equality by the gay and lesbian community, this news has made national headlines. Reverend Carter built his reputation on what he called his biblically-justified stand against homosexuality."

Another stuck his microphone in Wilburn's face. "Reverend Carter, an inside source confirmed your name on the slate of speakers at your denominational convention this year." The journalist glanced at his notes, then back at Wilburn. "They gave you the topic of marriage and the family. Can you confirm or deny the withdrawal of that invitation?"

Wilburn covered his face with his jacket while the attendant pushed the wheelchair through the throng of curious people and tucked him inside the car.

Cyn wedged her way through the crowd, hating the rude questions reporters threw at her.

"Ms. Carter, did you suspect your husband was a homosexual?"

"What do you think the church will do to him?"

"Do you plan to divorce him?"

"What about your son? How is he—"

"Shut the hell up," she yelled and shoved her way around and into the car. Only then did she realize the cameraman filmed her, she'd be on the evening news—profanity and all—and she didn't give a rat's ass.

"Drive, drive." Wilburn yelled before she could get

her key in the ignition.

"I'm doing the best I can. If you don't like it, get someone else to drive you home."

The motor started, she eased the car through the throngs of people pounding their fists in the air, some in support, while others pounded the hood of her car and jeered. Others held posters that ranged from FAG to EQUALITY NOW.

Wilburn slumped in the seat and again tossed the jacket over his head.

"Hurry, Cynthia, hurry."

"I can't run over these people."

"Calm down, calm down."

"And don't tell me to calm down," she yelled.

Once out of the parking lot, the crowd thinned, and Cyn felt the pressure ease. "Wow, I didn't expect that. Where'd all those people come from? They weren't here a few minutes ago when I moved the car closer."

Wilburn said nothing. Stared straight ahead, his eyes glazed.

Even though they headed home, Cyn knew things would never be the same again. At the moment, she had no idea how bad the situation would get. But as soon as she turned into the driveway reality hit its mark.

Someone had spray painted the front of the white, two-storied parsonage with despicable words. FAG. COCKSUCKER. REPROBATE.

Both stared at the hateful words as if the slander would go away if they waited long enough.

"It doesn't matter," Wilburn said at last.

"What are you talking about? It does matter," Cyn cried. "That's our home. The church parsonage."

"Wouldn't surprise me if one of our parishioners did it. I told you they can turn on a dime, stab you in the back."

"No, I don't think so," Cyn argued. "A parishioner wouldn't use such hateful words about you, and they sure wouldn't paint it on their own building. That doesn't make sense."

"I said don't be surprised. Anyway, I'll call the building and grounds committee and see how soon they can get a painter out here."

"I doubt they'll listen to you. Folks are pretty upset." Cyn turned off the ignition and opened her car door while Wilburn punched numbers on his cell phone.

"Sure, they'll listen," he said and waited.

Evidently Wilburn didn't know his congregation as well as Cyn did. After he reported the problem to the head of the committee, he hung up. "Seems I'm the one that caused this, so I can try to find my own painter, and pay for it myself—they refuse to even report it to the insurance company."

Stunned, they exited the car as a vehicle marked Private Security drove up and parked at the curb.

"Wait here," Cyn said to Wilburn. "Let me see what this man wants."

The officer behind the wheel saw her coming and stepped out. "Good afternoon, ma'am. My name is Detective Patrick. My company has been hired to provide you home security."

"Hired? By whom?"

"Not right sure, ma'am. It's 24/7 though. They told me to stay until someone relieved me."

"I see. I wished you'd arrived in time to see who did

this." She pointed up to the house.

"Sorry, ma'am. I do, too. We just got the order."

She joined Wilburn to report her findings only to see him standing at the front door, staring at words typed on a piece of paper plastered on the porch wall. The neighborhood association ordered the Carter's to remove the slanderous words by the end of the day or suffer a fine.

Adding insult to injury, they went inside and found their answering machine full of nasty messages.

Cyn raced to the bathroom and threw up everything she'd eaten that day—and more. When she finished, Wilburn came in with a warm, wet washcloth. "Here, use this to wipe your face, then come sit and rest. I'll call around and see if I can find a painter."

After several calls, he finally located someone who agreed to do the work. Cyn supposed the man and his family must be hungry.

"He said he could get to it today." Wilburn sat beside Cyn. "At least start the job. With the size of the house, he thinks he might not finish until tomorrow. If that doesn't satisfy the neighbors, they'll have to fine us—that's all I can say."

He put his arm around Cyn's shoulder and squeezed. "I still can't believe you came back. Thank you. I don't deserve it, but I'm glad you did. There are no words...." Tears clouded his voice. He rubbed her back. At first, she stiffened, but then relaxed into his touch. The comfort felt good. Without an expectation of arousal, he seemed caring, compassionate. Who was this man, and what had he done with her husband?

After a couple of minutes, she got up and went to put

on coffee, surprised at how different she felt performing the simple task. Whereas she'd grown to resent his demands, now she felt free to welcome the process. Besides, keeping her hands busy took her mind off of her future.

"By the way, Hazel Harrison came to the hospital yesterday," she called out to Wilburn.

"She did? When? I don't remember seeing her."

"I don't think she tried to go into your hospital room. Stephen was visiting with you at that time."

"I'm surprised she even came. So you talked with her? What did she say? I can only imagine."

"Believe it or not, she came to support me. To see how she might help."

"That's a bombshell." Wilburn stepped into the kitchen.

"Actually, she seemed quite compassionate and non-judgmental." Cyn poured water into the coffee pot and clicked the switch. "Apologized for her reaction to Dee's behavior at the women's meeting."

"Really? That's a surprise. Evidently her husband doesn't feel the same. Stephen called and said they kicked him off the deacon board, and Harris took over. Sounds like they aren't done with him or me."

"I would hope not."

"What do you mean?" Wilburn looked confused.

"Folks can't drop this—act like nothing happened. Everyone's done enough of that. Besides, this is a big deal, Wilburn."

"I know it is. But I figured if they got me out of town they could live their lives like nothing ever happened. You know how good folks are at that." He paused, looked at the floor. "Me, too."

Cyn felt a twinge of pity, but although she knew Wilburn hit the nail on its proverbial head, she also knew she'd failed to speak up, too. She ignored, pushed down, and buried anything uncomfortable, but not anymore. "From what Hazel said, not everyone in the congregation pushes for tar and feathers. Seems some still support you—not the affair, of course, but they want to hear your side. I guess they—"

"How about you?"

"Me?" She handed him a cup of steaming coffee, collected hers and walked to the back door. "I need to sit in my garden for a while. Want to join me?"

He didn't say anything, but he followed her outside.

They walked the path that wound between her rose beds, the plants now turning inward for their winter rest. She stopped near the back fence and sat on the wooden bench that curved around the large, sweet-smelling pine tree—as green as ever. Pinecones lay scattered on the ground. She picked up one and inspected the marvel.

"I read this article the other day," she said. "Did you know that throughout recorded history, these little pinecones have symbolized enlightenment? The pineal gland between the two hemispheres of our brain gets its name from the pinecone because it's the same shape and serves the same purpose."

"No, I didn't know that." He sounded disinterested, like his mind centered on other things.

"See these spines here?" She pointed. "They spiral in a perfect Fibonacci sequence in either direction." She traced the patterns both ways for him to see. "That little gland at the center of our brain is directly connected with our ability to see light."

He stared at the pinecone. "I remember in one of my seminary classes on pastoral care, the professor talked about Sacred Geometry, and how we humans tend to repeat the same mistakes over and over again because we didn't learn the lessons the first time around."

They sat without talking for several minutes. Cyn waited for him, and evidently, he waited for her to begin.

She didn't.

"You're not the only one I lied to. I've lied to myself more than anyone. Told myself I wasn't gay. That the devil gave me those feelings for men."

Cyn wanted to talk about the pinecone, the gland. Anything other than what she knew headed her way. Instead, she placed the cone on the bench between them and forced her ears to hear.

"I remember, even as a teenager I felt different than other boys."

"Different how?"

When he didn't answer, she wondered if he'd heard her question. She shifted to where she could see him. His eyes revealed he'd gone somewhere else—way off. She settled in to listen.

CHAPTER TWENTY-THREE

Wilburn stared out over the garden as though his thoughts visited the past. "For years, I denied it. Convinced myself that God tempted me like he tempted Job. That my hometown pastor..."

"Go on—your hometown pastor what?"

Wilburn struggled, as if wondering if he had the courage to go on.

"You can tell me anything." Cyn stared down at the pinecone between them. "It's okay."

"I swore to myself I'd never tell anyone about that day. Swore to him, too, but he's dead now, so I guess it won't matter."

"Never tell what?" Cyn kept her voice soft, encouraging, for she suspected whatever Wilburn wanted to say likely revealed the root of his pain. She prayed that he would say it.

"My pastor—the one who got fired from my boyhood church?"

"Brother Whitaker?"

"That's the one. Remember I told you about the church putting him on trial?"

"Yes, you did. You said that experience had a lot to do with why you like me to sit on the front row."

"I loved him, and he loved me—I know he did."

"So are you saying the two of you had sex?"

Wilburn collapsed against her, sobs racking his body. She put her arm around him and held him tight until the sobs quieted and he sat up straight.

"Sorry about that." He wiped his eyes, pulled a Kleenex from his pocket, and blew his nose.

She wanted to say something, but feared if she did, he might shut down, so she sat quietly and listened.

"After his trial—"

"Your pastor's," she whispered.

He nodded. "After his trial, the poor man broke down. I went to comfort him. That's when...when..."

"Say it, sweetheart. It's time to say it out loud."

"You see..." he said, struggling to explain. "...I'd never had sex before—with anyone. I lost my virginity the day he and I made love. For some time, I fought my feelings for him—fought hard, because I didn't know...That all those years, he'd hidden in a closet like me—to keep his job—you know? God called him to be a minister. What else could he do?"

"Much like you, then."

Wilburn nodded. "Yeah, like me."

"So what happened after—"

"He had a church contact him with a job offer, and he and his wife left town. I never heard from him again. Years later—before we moved here to Mobile, I read where he'd died."

"Wow. That must have hurt. I'm sorry you never felt like you could tell me that—but of course if you had..."

"I never told anyone—not even Stephen. I felt so ashamed." Wilburn snorted. "All these years I figured God sent Stephen as another test to make sure I really trusted Him."

He stood, paced a minute, and then returned to the bench.

"In the dark recesses of my heart, I'd raise my fist and shout, 'You can't fool me, God. I'm not gay. I only did that one time.'" He sucked in a breath. "Then to top it off, in my first year of college, God called me into the ministry."

She had heard the term the ministry so many times she no longer knew what it meant. The cliché had overtaken reasoning.

"One night, while on my knees in my room, I pled for God to forgive me that one time, years ago. I swore I could master these feelings. That I could, I would be obedient."

"I can only imagine what that must have been like." Cyn wished she could think of something more to say that might ease the pain radiating from him.

"So I lied, over and over," Wilburn said. "As I finished college and prepared to attend seminary, I knew if God wanted me to pastor a church, I needed a wife to...So I lied again."

"Lied? You never told me you were heterosexual."

"Didn't need to. Like everything else, people who are, assume everyone else is."

"I guess you're right about that."

"Then, to carry it off successfully, I had to preach against it."

Cyn picked up the pinecone and inspected it, along with another one. Sure enough, the spirals looked the same, backward and forward—or maybe left to right, or right to left?

"I fooled everyone—no, not everyone—I didn't fool two people—two that I know of, that is. I didn't fool Justice. Somehow he knew. Maybe it's because young people these days are much more understanding and accepting of people's differences."

"You said two."

"I didn't fool Stephen."

Cyn cringed at the mention of Stephen's name and wondered if she felt that way because he had stolen the affection of her husband? Or that she'd never had it in the first place?

"I don't mean to hurt you, but..."

"Nothing you say can hurt me anymore than you already have." Cyn pounded her thigh with her fist. "I'm sick of lies, Wilburn, sick of them. Whatever the truth is—say it, for God's sake—and mine—say it."

"Stephen and I fell in love the first time we laid eyes on each other."

"When? The day the pulpit committee visited our last church to hear you preach?"

"Memorable day. It scared me so much I almost didn't accept their call to pastor here in Mobile. I told myself I could fight it, and at first, I did. Before long, it got too strong. I...we..."

"How long?"

"Did we resist? I don't remember exactly." He grabbed her hand and squeezed. "As much as I care about you, Cyn, this is different. If I've learned anything, it's that love isn't about how two bodies bump into each other, but about how their souls connect and interact. My love for Stephen connected at a level I never knew existed. In a way, I couldn't ignore, even though I tried. God knows I tried."

Time for her to also be honest. "I felt like you cared about me before we married, but then right after the wedding, it seemed like you didn't. That confused me. I didn't know what I'd done wrong."

He sighed, looked at the pinecones in her hands. "I know you didn't. But I did care. Just not the way heterosexual men love women."

"I know that now."

Silence hung between them until a man wearing painter's clothes hollered from the back gate. Wilburn left to show him what needed doing—not that the man hadn't seen the nasty words when he drove up. The whole world had been privy to the venomous attack.

Cyn waited, unable to move, unable to breathe, barely able to think. A sparrow flew up and lit on the seat Wilburn had vacated. It darted its head, chirped once, and flew to an overhead branch. She wondered if Wilburn would return, and thought about not waiting to see. But she did. For he described a connection with another person she had never experienced. She wanted to hear more.

"How humiliating," Wilburn said as he came through

the gate. "Having to face a stranger and pay him to remove this trash—this hatred painted on the house belonging to the church."

"Had he heard the news?" Cyn asked.

"Evidently. Otherwise, I figure he'd have asked questions. He didn't ask a single one."

Wilburn sat in the sparrow's place. He'd aged ten years since he walked to the front of the house and returned.

"Did you call Stephen and tell him about the slander?"

Arms on his thighs, hands dangling between his legs, he looked at the ground a minute before answering. "Yes, I called him after I met the painter out front."

"Figured you had. I don't know why it hurts me that you call him, but it does."

Neither spoke for a couple of minutes.

"I know it does. I'm sorry, Cyn, truly. I never meant to hurt you—still don't. Living in that stupid closet dries a man's soul in a most painful way. For years, I told myself I had a great wife and asked why I couldn't be happy with that. I knew you suffered too. I did. That's why I tried to force myself to...to..."

"Make love to me," she said, and then bit her tongue, wishing she hadn't finished his sentence. Giving voice to the memories intensified her pain.

"Exactly. I felt so ill at ease, so phony. Like going to a men's department and buying every size of clothes they made, thinking surely one of those sizes would fit me, but none ever did."

Cyn listened, knowing for the first time since she'd married this stranger sitting beside her that she heard the truth, for everything he said resonated with what she knew in her heart.

She toyed with the idea of whether or not to tell him her truth, that she'd recently made a big decision of her own, then decided she had nothing to lose. "Did you know, that right before all this happened, I planned to leave you?"

He turned and faced her. "Dee said something about it. Seriously? I knew you were depressed but—"

"Depressed? No. I felt like I'd lost my soul and if something didn't change, and change in a hurry, I'd never find it." She tucked another small pinecone in her pocket.

"Wow. I had no idea. I thought my actions only damaged my own soul. Now I see my lies damaged us both." He sat in silence for a minute then continued. "Thank you for telling me that."

"What does Ginger know?" Time to switch the subject off of her and onto someone else.

"Stephen says he thinks she suspected he might be having an affair, but not with a man—not with me, for sure."

"Evidently. Since she tried to get you in bed with her."

Wilburn ignored that comment. "He said she married him because she wanted the financial stability he offered—she and her mother grew up on the streets of New Orleans, so—"

"I can't feel sorry for her because of that."

"Stephen and Ginger live separate lives. Evidently the gossip about her and the last pastor caused him embarrassment, but..."

"Then you moved to town and took his mind off of

the rumors."

"Guess you could say that, yes, and much to my shame. Not for loving him, but for the deception and betrayal we perpetrated on everyone."

"Seems like you're the most popular man in town. Men and women alike are hot after your body." Soon as the words left her mouth, she regretted saying them. She snatched his hand. "I'm sorry. That sounded ugly, and totally uncalled for."

"It's okay. I have it coming." He shrugged, fiddled with a fingernail.

"So, what's next for you? With the church, I mean?"

"I don't have a clue," Wilburn said. "I'm waiting to see what their next move will be."

"Well, it's obvious we can't stay married. Ginger might put up with it, but I can't."

"So what are your plans?"

"Right now, my plan is to go to the kitchen. Mama always said when you don't know what else to do—cook dinner. Something—anything to get us to a more normal day."

"Can I help you?"

"With dinner?" She looked at him like he'd gone absolutely crazy. Never before had he offered to cook—even boil an egg, or put on the coffee pot. "Peel the potatoes?"

"You got it."

The two went into the kitchen and stared at a familiar room that now felt strange, like unknown territory. They had never worked on anything together as a team.

"Point me to the potatoes."

She did.

"And the knife?"

She pointed.

"So, do you cut them in cubes—boil in water, or what?"

"You're not as clueless in the kitchen as you've led me to believe."

The two laughed while she dug a couple of salmon steaks from the freezer, popped them in the microwave to defrost, and got out the makings for a green salad.

By the time they finished preparations, and the two sat at the table, Cyn wondered what to do next. Should she eat without waiting for him to say grace? Would he expect her to?

They waited, both lost without their usual ritual. He seemed uncertain as he picked up his fork and glanced at her.

"Would you like me to say grace?" she asked.

"I'd like that, yes."

This time, she followed her inclination—or was it a temptation? She focused her gaze on Wilburn and with tenderness and sincerity, opened her mouth, and said one word. "Grace."

Wilburn looked stupefied, like he didn't believe his ears. Then, he laughed and spread his napkin across his lap. "Thank you. I reckon I need more grace right now than most anyone else."

"Mazel tov." she raised her glass of iced tea to him. "Tomorrow's another day, a day when we face the onslaught we know heads our way."

As the sun set, the painter rapped on the front door ready to be paid. He reported he had wiped out—or at least painted a blanket of pigments over the ugly words underneath.

They walked outside to inspect. A paint gun had created a miracle on the house, but Cyn knew it would take more than paint to erase the vindictive hatred multiplied millions of times over the course of generations.

The two watched television for a couple of hours. Stephen called Wilburn on his cell phone a couple of times, but tonight, she didn't care. Tonight, she felt better than she had in a long time, and closer to Wilburn than ever.

CHAPTER TWENTY-FOUR

Rain pounded on the roof as Cyn crawled into bed close to midnight. She snuggled under the covers of the guestroom bed and tried to will away the thoughts rattling around in her head.

After what seemed like hours, she dozed, but soon awakened with the memory that she and Wilburn had another horrendous day to face—another day of hell.

She tossed and turned and ran her fingers through her matted hair.

Others hurt, too. She knew they did. Every parishioner must feel the pain of recent events. If not the same pain, at least similar. No doubt they loved Wilburn, some of them did—worshipped him, actually. The Wilburn they thought they knew.

How wrong they were—she was. She felt betrayed

for sure, but at least not by some trick of birth like Wilburn—born to be the type of person so many people despised, then called to preach to the very people who despised him. No wonder he'd denied his sexuality. No wonder he'd cheated.

Lightning flashed across the sky. Wind rattled the windows.

She pictured Wilburn and tried to imagine what kind of night he was having and what his life must have been like living with her all those years, knowing all the while he lived a lie. Feeling either tricked or betrayed by the very God he served, a God Wilburn had been taught, demanded he deny himself.

With dawn, she swung her feet to the floor, took a quick glance in the mirror, then went into the guest bathroom, and stepped into the shower.

Later, she heard the phone ring then stop. Evidently whoever called hung up, or Wilburn answered. She wrapped a robe around her, slipped to the head of the stairs and listened.

"I understand—well, actually, no, I don't understand, Doctor Powell, but you do what you think best." Wilburn's words sounded aloof and full of suppressed pain. His ache touched her heart, for he'd been so thrilled to receive the invitation originally—an invitation evidently withdrawn as a result of the happenings at church. For certain, the convention would want to distance itself from a situation like this. If it didn't, the sin of homosexuality tainted them—guilt by association.

Wilburn paused, then said, "Yes, I know. Yes, yes, I understand you feel like I made a fool of you. Trust me, I did not intend that."

Pause.

"I'll deal with it the best I can. I can't undo anything—and yes, I know you know that. On the other hand, I won't say something like this never happened before. It has, many times. In a way, except for the pain the behavior caused everyone, I feel relief. I don't have to keep it secret anymore. Over time, secrecy kills a person."

Pause.

"Believe what you want. Print what you want. Homosexuality is not a choice, and it isn't a lifestyle—but this one thing I know for sure, living life in the closet is certainly a death style."

Wilburn went silent again; then she heard the phone replaced in its base.

Doctor Powell, executive director of the state convention, the same one who visited and invited Wilburn to speak at the annual meeting. It sounded like the man was less understanding than one might think—oh, wait, why would anyone think that in the first place? Unforgiveable sin didn't count. She'd heard people talk about the unpardonable sin. Now, she knew the identity of that sin—at least to some people.

Homosexuality.

She took the steps slowly, listening, watching to see where Wilburn had gone. She found him in the family room on the sofa, face in his hands, shoulders heaving.

Aching for this man she'd given her own life to support, to see him destroyed, not only him, but also everything he'd spent a lifetime building, broke her heart. She eased over, sat next to him, and waited, then slipped an arm across his shoulders.

Unable to hold back, or perhaps not even trying to

restrain his grief any longer, he buried his head into her chest and wept. She should be livid, she told herself, have a smart come back, like he got what he deserved, but she couldn't. His pain became hers.

Perhaps if the affair involved Ginger or some other woman, she might separate her pain from his. But it didn't. This pain went much deeper than betrayal. It ripped out the taproot of all his hopes and dreams, his calling, his very being. His devastation struck a chord deep inside her, and for the first time she felt pity for him. Pity and pain.

In her heart, she wept, too.

Between gut wrenching sobs, Wilburn choked out, "I tried so hard to be a good husband and father, but it got harder and harder. Like my skin grew too tight, cut off my breath."

"I know that now."

He sucked in a deep breath. "Our marriage created a sham. I knew it then and hated myself for it. Knew I couldn't love you like a husband should love his wife. Over the next few years, I denied the slow, painful draining of my soul—the dry-up of everything that made life worthwhile."

"I don't know what to say, Wilburn. I always believed everything you told me—or tried to believe it. You taught me homosexuals sinned against God, but now I learn you didn't believe any of that."

He straightened and looked at her. "That's just it; I did believe it with all my heart, just not my soul, Cynthia. Sorry, I mean Cyn. Habit—you know."

They laughed, not funny, more bitter sounding.

"Seminary professors taught us that homosexuality

fits the category of a mortal sin. I've struggled with this until I can't struggle anymore. I must surrender to it. In a way, I feel born again. I've never been more vulnerable, but I've also never felt closer to God. I've never been more honest, more spiritually authentic."

She patted his hand. "But then you have the church to deal with."

He stood and paced the room. "I know that's coming. I just don't know when. Stephen says the wagons are circling. Thing is, there are two circles, he says. Half the people want to hear what I have to say, to understand why I lied all these years. They want to hear what I stand for—since they don't know anymore."

"And the other?"

He chuckled. "They've erected a stake and built a bonfire around it, waiting to set it ablaze."

"Wow."

"Newspaper folks are calling them. Since it made the local news, I rather suspect it will go national."

"So, I guess its hang on to the knot at the end of the rope." She sat deep in thought, then said, "You sure we shouldn't get Justice home? It isn't safe here, but maybe safer than a university campus."

"Actually, I'm thinking he's safer there."

Cyn's heart pounded in her throat. Her hands quivered. She'd never in her life faced anything so serious—so potentially life threatening.

"You sure you're up for this?" He stopped his pacing long enough to caress her shoulder. A caress that felt more genuine than any he'd ever given her. "Why are you doing this? I'd think you'd run and never look back. You don't have to put up with all this...this..."

"Prejudice and hatred?"

"That's about what it is."

"To tell you the truth, I don't know. I'm hoping I'll figure it out as I go, but I will stand beside you until we're done here."

Wilburn looked at her, his facial expression the closest to affection he'd ever given her.

"You want to know where I went when I ran away that night after I found you and Stephen?"

He looked her in the eyes, touching her soul with his sincerity. "I do, indeed." He sat beside her again, took her hand. "Tell me. Please. I didn't expect to ever see you again. What made you come back to face all this?"

"I drove and drove, with no destination in mind, until sunrise found me along the northwest coast of Florida."

"Wow. That far?"

"I cried, I yelled, I splashed in the surf, I watched the horizon, waiting for God to send some savior to carry me off to glory. At that moment, I welcomed death—welcomed anything to take away the pain."

"Sorry about that. Stephen and I should not have let that happen. It must have been awful—a tremendous shock."

"I stood in the cold water and waited and prayed, waited and prayed."

The trash truck pulled up outside and emptied their can, then drove on.

She laughed. "You know what? When you ask God to do something, you dang well better prepare for the answer."

"I don't know what you mean." He squeezed her hand tighter.

"The answer came, but not the one I expected—and the last one I wanted."

"What answer?"

"Go back."

"I don't understand."

"I don't either. But the waves blasted me with the words with such undeniable force, I gathered my shoes, got in the car and headed back the way I came—with no idea why, or what I would face when I got here."

"You know the marriage is over, sweetheart. I can't—"

"I know that. I'm not here to put it back together. As I said, I had decided to leave you the afternoon before I found you with Stephen."

He looked at her, eyes wide.

"That's the truth. I'm not just saying that to save face."

"You said that earlier, but I guess I didn't take you seriously."

"I could no longer handle your phoniness—your self-righteous, all-knowing attitude about everything. Your inability to understand—or give a rat's ass how I felt, or what I thought."

"Ouch."

"You asked."

"I did." Quiet for a couple of minutes, he patted his knee, as if nerves got the best of him. "Guess I didn't fake it as well as I thought."

"You always acted so holy. That throws a person's defenses up real quick. It creates an intimacy barrier."

"But you see, I needed that barrier for protection. Too bad my success caused you pain. I do indeed regret that, sweetheart. You are a great woman. It bothered me that you didn't know that about yourself."

How long had she waited for the slightest hint of affection from him, never understanding what kept him from giving it? Now, she knew she had expected the impossible—odd how much better that made her feel.

Silence.

"I'm so glad you came home—and I hope you don't regret it before it's all over."

"I just don't know what to expect or where we go from here," Cyn looked him in the eye, "but I do know I'll be sleeping in the guest bedroom. Once we get past this chaos, we can make more permanent arrangements."

"I'll help you move your things to the other room. I'm sure we'll both sleep better. If I sleep at all."

Cyn sucked in a long, deep breath and slowly exhaled. "I feel like we're waiting for an invasion."

"We are in a way."

"You know you soon won't have a job."

Wilburn nodded. "I plan to get another one—but right now, I figure no one will hire me. Plus, when this ends, Stephen and I will likely leave town."

Silence.

"You asked what I planned to do next. First, I plan to call Ginger."

"Ginger? Really? Why?" Wilburn looked surprised that she'd take it that far.

"When I chose to come back, I swore I would no longer stay quiet when I had something I needed to say. I need to speak to her—after all, she betrayed me, too."

"You really think it's the best time to do that?"

She stood. "No better."

Wilburn shrugged. "Guess now's as good a time as any. Neither one of us has anything to lose anymore. Truth is, we never did."

CHAPTER TWENTY-FIVE

When the telephone rang and the ID announced Stephen calling, Wilburn looked at Cyn. "Do you mind if I take it?"

"Go ahead. He's in this as much as me—more, really."

Wilburn picked up the phone and after a couple of minutes, said, "Hold on, let me check with Cyn," then turned to her.

"Stephen has news that we both need to hear. It affects my job and this house. Are you okay with him coming over?"

She shrugged. "I guess I don't have a choice."

"You do have a choice, but since this impacts you, I thought—"

"Go on, tell him yes."

"It's okay with her. We'll see you in a few minutes."

While they waited, Cyn went upstairs and changed into jeans and a T-shirt, then stood in front of the mirror brushing her hair. "Sometimes I wonder if I'm a dope." She stared at her reflection. How did she get herself in this situation? Even more, how did she not repeat the same poor decisions in the future?

Pay attention to the details. The words echoed in her head.

Details. Had she spent more time looking at the big picture than the more important elements that made up the reality of her world? Had she focused so much effort on avoiding pain that the effort paralyzed her, kept her from living life? It ended up making the pain greater. Fear of change so controlled her that she'd squatted along the edge of the fear, never stepping into it, never embracing it, and never walking through to the other side.

When the doorbell rang, she tossed the hairbrush on the dressing table and went down the hall toward the stairs.

She heard Stephen ask who hired the security guard outside, and Wilburn say he didn't have a clue. Then Stephen told him what he'd seen on local television.

"We're all over the news, buddy. They have our pictures and everything. I expect it will make the national broadcast. News media can get a lot of mileage out of a story like this. People eat it up—makes their troubles seem small."

Cyn headed down, determined not to hide away upstairs as if she'd done something wrong.

"Hi, Cyn. Thank you for letting me come over."

"The house isn't mine. It belongs to the church."

"That's one of the things I wanted to talk to you two about."

They went to the family room and for the first time in her life, Cyn did not offer refreshments to a visitor. She understood Wilburn, but she still took issue with Stephen for putting them in this situation—at least his part of it. Maybe one day she'd get over it, but right now, she couldn't force herself to treat him like a friend.

Stephen sat across from them, hands on his knees. "Have you heard from anyone at the church?"

"Not a word." Wilburn looked in question at Cyn.

"Not me."

Stephen avoided looking at Cyn any more than necessary. Instead, he kept his eyes focused on Wilburn. "I heard the deacons met last night—and way up into the wee hours of this morning. Seems they want both of you out of the parsonage, plus, they officially unelected me as chairman and voted Harris Harrison in."

"Wow." Wilburn shook his head. "I guess I'm next."

"I figure now that we've made the local and soon the national news, it's only a matter of time, yes. Seems our church has become the laughing stock of the denomination. Folks aren't happy about that."

"So do they have the next move, or do we? If so, what do you suggest we do?" Wilburn stood and paced the floor.

"They mentioned some retired preacher they wanted to serve as interim pastor. Of course, they won't let you fill the pulpit or even the doorway, I imagine."

"So what do we do?"

"Right now, I think we sit tight. I suspect you'll hear something soon." Stephen scratched his head as though deep in thought. "However, you might as well start packing." This time, he looked at Cyn. "Do you have any plans? Somewhere to go?"

Cyn looked Stephen in the eye. "Yes, I have somewhere to go—to see your wife. Meanwhile, Wilburn has something to tell you about her." She looked at Wilburn. "No more secrets. None."

CHAPTER TWENTY-SIX

The clouds dissipated as Cyn walked up the driveway of the sprawling ranch-style house surrounded by an immaculate, now rain-saturated lawn. Water dripped off of a bronze statue of two boys playing, arms outstretched towards each other. That hit a chord with Cyn. Of all the times she'd walked past the statue over the last five years, and she'd never picked up on that clue.

However, she'd never felt the same as she did today, either—fired up and ready to have her say. She took a deep breath. The pungent smell of rosemary near the front door welcomed her.

She pushed the doorbell and waited.

Footsteps, then the door swung open.

"Cynthia? I...I didn't expect—"

"I'm sure you didn't." Cyn waited, letting Ginger

process her suspicions about the visit.

Ginger acted nervous, but she swung the door open and stepped aside.

Cyn waltzed in.

"Want to sit in the kitchen? Maybe have a cup of coffee."

"Why not?" Cyn thought about apologizing for dropping in unannounced, then realized Ginger had done her own share of dropping in without notice.

The kitchen gave off a friendly aroma of freshly baked chocolate chip cookies. A plate of them lay on the sideboard.

Cyn always admired Ginger's décor. The rich yellows and bright blues added cheery warmth to the room. A ceramic, bright-colored rooster stood on the island in the middle of the kitchen, posed to crow the arrival of morning.

She pulled a bar stool from under the island and sat while Ginger dropped a spoon, rattled the sugar bowl, spilled coffee grounds on the cabinet, then, after she wiped them, had to clean the floor while mumbling something about clumsiness.

The discomfort of the woman Cyn once considered her friend brought a certain amount of pleasure.

"I have another pan of cookies ready to come out of the oven. After they cool, we'll have one with our coffee, okay?" Ginger laughed, but the laughter sounded anything but funny.

Cyn waited until Ginger had no more excuses to bustle around the room looking busy. Cyn hadn't decided exactly how she'd start the conversation, but she knew how she intended to end it.

However, Ginger didn't wait. "I guess you came to talk about our husbands."

"Not really."

"Oh?" Her smile faded.

"I'm not sure I ever thanked you for the chicken casserole you left at my house a few days ago."

"Oh?" Ginger's eyes went from a twinkle to a dark place of uncertainty. "Uh… that's… no problem," she stammered. "Wilburn—he thanked me that day." She splashed coffee into two mugs, passed one to Cyn, and then grabbed a paper towel to clean up the spatter.

"Yes, that's what I hear." Cyn spooned sugar into her coffee and added milk.

The room grew quiet for a few seconds before Ginger said, "Oops, my cookies smell ready," and turned to collect the pan from the oven.

The overwhelming delight of the hot, sweet delicacy filled the room.

Cyn stiffened herself against the sweet temptation—the bribe.

Ginger rested the cookie sheet on a metal rack to cool, hands shaking anew.

When she turned back to Cyn, her gaze darted, as if she expected something to zap her at any minute.

Still, Cyn waited.

With all avenues extinguished once again, Ginger pulled out a barstool and sat, her arms resting on the black granite countertop. "I guess you came to—"

"Talk about your behavior? You bet your sweet patootie I did."

Silence. Ginger jumped up and switched off the oven, then sat again. The silence in the room grew deafening. Still, Cyn said nothing, just watched Ginger.

"I am so sorry, Cyn."

"Sorry for what? I'm so sick of that word. If I hear it one more time, I'll throw up all over your precious cookies. Give me something else."

"What?"

"Come on. You know what." Cyn slammed her fist on the counter. "Say it, damn it. At least have the guts to admit what you did—that you betrayed me."

"If I'd known about him and Stephen..." She let her words drop as if things would have been different if she'd known about their husbands.

"Do you really mean that?"

Ginger intertwined her fingers. "I guess not. I didn't mean that the way it came out. Let me start over." She leaned forward and propped her arms on the counter. "When Stephen and I married, we agreed to have an open relationship—"

"What do you mean, open?"

"We didn't want an exclusive marriage, so we agreed each could see other people as long as we kept it private—so no one knew about it."

"I don't believe that."

"It's true. You can ask Stephen. The thing is, I didn't know he preferred men."

"Meanwhile, you spent your time getting in bed with God knows who. I heard what you did to the last pastor."

Ginger didn't respond.

"What is it with you and preachers, Ginger?"

"I have feelings, too. I have needs."

"Didn't you think about the needs of other women— those men's wives?"

"We had an understanding."

"You mean you and Stephen had an understanding— that you could screw any pastor that came to the church?"

"No, nothing like that."

"All I can say is, you are a sad excuse for a friend." Cyn got up and paced the floor. "Dee warned me the first time she saw you. Said I couldn't trust you. You know what I did? I defended you. Told her that you..." Cyn fought back tears, refused to allow them to surface.

"I don't know what else to say, but I'm sorry."

"Sorry doesn't make my pain go away—and right now I've got about all the sorry I can stomach."

"What are you and Pastor going to do now?"

"He won't be the pastor much longer. I hear the natives are restless."

"That's what Stephen says."

"One thing for certain, I'm not sad to no longer be a pastor's wife. In case you don't know, that is the toughest job in the whole wide world. Besides, from what I see between your husband and mine, you soon won't be Stephen's wife."

"What do you mean? You think he and Wilburn will stay together?"

"Count on it, sweetheart. There isn't anything to stop them now."

Both women stared at their mugs, silent; nothing left to say.

"I'm going now." Cyn grabbed her handbag and pushed the stool beneath the counter. She shoved her shoulders back, turned, and strode out the door feeling taller than she'd ever felt in her life.

Behind her, she heard sobs of a guilty woman found

out and now sorry—sorry she got caught. What was it about people who only regretted their behavior after it was too late? Why did it take that? Had people so encased their conscious actions in denial that they couldn't identify it except when it hit them in the face, reflected back from exposure?

"Let that teach you a lesson, Miss Cyn," she mumbled as she got in her car. "You know the rules you chose many years ago, things like intent, integrity, impeccability. Things Mama and Daddy taught you by example, if not in those exact words." She drove away, feeling, not self-righteous, but chastised for her own failures. And wishing she had one of those chocolate chip cookies.

She too, carried responsibility in the whole thing. For she never challenged Wilburn with her suspicions even though something didn't seem right. Instead, she bought the myth. Drank the Kool-Aid. Believed everything people told her just because they said it was true. She ignored and squashed down her own sense of knowing.

But new days made all the difference. She'd face this with Wilburn. Search for the exit that would liberate them both. Then, she'd leave. Where she'd go, she hadn't a clue. But it didn't matter. Wherever she went, she'd find herself. She longed so much to spread her wings again.

By the time she turned into the driveway, she felt ready to take on the world despite a hint of guilt over how she'd spoken to Ginger.

Then, she walked inside where all hell had broken loose.

CHAPTER TWENTY-SEVEN

Before Cyn opened the front door, she heard loud, angry words coming from inside. She went in and stood listening to several heavy voices talking all at once. It seemed several deacons had arrived. She moved to the doorway and scanned the room, but didn't see Harris and Bud. She wondered if they'd elected not to come, or hadn't been invited.

All eyes focused on Wilburn and Stephen. Accusations from first one deacon and then another flew across the room. When the men ran out of accusations, they started quoting Bible verses and shouting insults.

When the group realized her presence, they stared at her as if, before that minute, they never knew she existed.

"Gentlemen."

"Mrs. Carter," each visitor said, but not in unison.

Deacon Lambert spoke up first. "We're sorry to invade your home, ma'am. We can continue this another time."

"That's okay. You're always welcome in our home."

She glanced at Wilburn who mouthed, "What on earth are you doing?"

Unable to signal back, she continued, "I've always heard there are two sides to every story. Where's the other side? I didn't hear anyone giving it."

"The other side, ma'am?"

"Well, if you don't mind my saying so, it sounds like everyone present sits on the side that wants to run the preacher out of town on a rail. I'm sure there are others who disagree."

Several men blushed.

"If I heard right," she pushed, "you sound like these two men deserve to be hung, drawn, and quartered. What about all the years of hard work they've put into the church? Doesn't that count for something?"

"We're trying to do God's will, ma'am," one of them said.

"Hogwash." Cyn glared at the man. "I'm sure you think so, but you're most unproductive, and a little one-sided if you ask me. Perhaps if you regroup and approach this in the right spirit you might get better results."

Her friendly attitude began to work. Several men ducked their heads and gave her a sheepish smile.

"She may be right," Deacon Lambert said. "Gentlemen, why don't we adjourn and take this up after we cool off."

"Wait, I didn't mean you had to rush off." Cyn's words surprised her, along with most of the men present—including Wilburn and Stephen. They squirmed in their seats as if wondering what in the world she wanted.

Acting the hostess didn't make the list. But defusing the situation did. "I made a big batch of peanut butter cookies the other day. How about I put on a pot of coffee, and let's sit at the table and catch our breaths."

Deacon Lambert's face deflated, like he'd lost the steam he'd accumulated during the inquisition. He looked from her to the other men. "What about it guys? I reckon we shouldn't leave mad. Plus, I've tasted Mrs. Carter's cookies."

By the time the evening ended, the cookie jar and the coffee pot sat empty, but the men left with full bellies. Had she changed their minds? No way, but at least she'd called a brief ceasefire.

After she ushered the last man out and closed the door, she went back into the living room where Wilburn and Stephen sat side by side, white-faced, exhausted.

"You pulled off a miracle," Wilburn said to Cyn.

Stephen laughed. "If not a miracle, at least a stay of execution."

Cyn took a chair near the fireplace. "That group sounded like the tar-and-feather committee. What did they want—other than to run you out of town?"

Stephen glanced at Wilburn then cleared his throat. "They demanded Wilburn's resignation on the spot."

She looked at Wilburn. "And you said?"

"I said hell no."

"You didn't?" Cyn guffawed. "Really? I'm proud of you."

"They want this to go away like nothing ever

happened," Wilburn said. "Well, it did happen, and I refuse to slip out of town in the dark of night like they seem to want. We must talk about it."

"Talk about? Talking sounds pretty mild if you ask me." Stephen pulled a handkerchief from his back pocket and wiped his forehead. "Can you believe they're actually threatening to put both of us on trial—to sue us for fraud. They plan to demand reimbursement for the salary they paid Wilburn over the last five years."

"Five years? Is that all? Here I thought they wanted to run him out of town on a rail like they did in the Wild West."

Stephen continued. "Plus, my work as deacon chairman didn't cost them a dime. I'm thinking about a counter suit for all the hours and costs for gasoline." He laughed. "Not really, but I'm sure tempted."

"By the way, where were Harris and Bud? I figured they'd be the first ones in the door."

Wilburn chuckled. "We didn't ask."

A look of sincerity smoothed the lines in Stephen's handsome face. "I don't care what happens to me, but I will never regret my relationship with Wilburn. However, I do regret the pain my actions caused you, Cyn."

Wilburn looked at Cyn. "And I've been an asshole, haven't I?"

"Yes, you have." She smiled, surprised at how easily he said it, and how easily she agreed.

While they talked, dusk came, and the room grew darker.

Cyn switched on a couple of lamps while Stephen asked how her visit with Ginger went.

"As expected."

"Did you mention..."

"That I knew both she and her husband had seduced my husband?"

"Ouch." Stephen squirmed. "I guess we had that coming."

"Is that really necessary?" Wilburn looked embarrassed—whether at the thought of being seduced or by Cyn's blunt comment, she didn't know.

"It's okay." Stephen defended her. "She has a right to say it. It's true."

"But she doesn't have to be ugly about it."

Stephen stared at the floor, fiddled with his pants leg. "What do you think we've been to her?"

Chagrin colored Wilburn's face. He looked deep in thought then nodded his agreement. "Good point. Besides, instead of fighting between ourselves, we need to talk about how we're going to handle what's before us. I suspect—"

The phone rang, interrupting the awkward conversation.

Wilburn answered it and even in the dim light, his face blanched. "I'm on my way."

When he hung up, he turned to face them. "That was Bud Harvey. Their son, Marcus, is in ICU and doctors don't give them much hope. He wants me to come."

"What happened?" Cyn and Stephen asked in unison.

"Hung himself." Wilburn kneeled next to Cyn's chair and grabbed her hand. "He left a note. Seems he's gay. Never told his parents."

"Oh, no. All this must have taken a toll on him." Cyn's thoughts went immediately to Justice, and how much Marcus meant to both him and Sophie. The three had been inseparable until Justice went off to State, Sophie left for a university in California, and Marcus enrolled in the local community college to improve his GPA. Next year he planned to join Justice.

"We've got to let Justice know," she said, sick to her stomach at the thought of how the news would hurt him, especially on top of everything else. "He'll want to come home for sure. And it sounds like if there's a chance for Marcus to pull through, he's going to need Justice."

"Let's hold off until I get to the hospital and see what the situation is, and then we'll call Justice." Wilburn grabbed his coat, straightened his tie. "I'll be back."

"I'm going with you." Cyn jumped up. "Lorene will need me."

Bud and Lorene were one of those couples that turned their self-righteous noses up to the whole issue of gay marriage—gay anything. But this changed things. Against had nothing to do with loving your son. Or would it to them?

Stephen left when they did, but said he'd stay away from the hospital for now, since Bud and Lorene could handle only so much at one time—but to call if they needed him.

Cyn drove, giving Wilburn a chance to steady himself for what he faced.

"How are you going to handle this?" Cyn stopped at the red light, then pressed her turn signal.

"I have no earthly idea. This pushes all my buttons. Bud said one thing Marcus included in his note ripped him apart. Marcus overheard his parents attack me because I am gay. He knew that when they found out about him being gay, they'd disown him. He'd rather die than have that happen."

A cold shudder washed over Cyn. "Oh no. What a burden of guilt to carry—knowing your words and actions forced your son over the edge."

Silence.

"Well, he's not dead yet. We can only hope and pray."

"I couldn't live with myself if I thought I did something that caused Justice to end his life." She paused. "Do you think Justice knows Marcus is gay?"

Wilburn laughed—as if to agree stated the obvious.

"Yeah, I guess he does. He knew about you." She didn't say anything, but she wondered about Sophie. Could she be a lesbian, and if so, had she and Justice used their friendship as a cover-up? Cyn pulled into the parking lot and the two hurried up to the ICU floor where they found Marcus's parents in hysterics.

Lorene's eyes were almost swollen shut, her cheeks bright red. When she saw Cyn she grabbed at her like Cyn was the sole floatation device between heaven and hell. "He's gone, Cynthia. He didn't make it. He's dead. He's dead. He..."

Cyn wanted to say something—anything—but all those pious phrases she'd used before didn't fit. She held Lorene in her arms, mumbling, "Oh, sweetheart, sweetheart. I am so sorry."

As a pastor's wife, she had ministered to a lot of people during times of grief, repeating the words Wilburn taught her. Word's like, He's in a better place. God wanted him to be with the angels. God never gives us more than we can handle.

Bullshit. No one could handle this, no one, and if

God thought differently, then...Cyn wasn't handling it—not at all. Marcus had been like a son—in and out of her home almost as much as Justice. His contagious laughter never failed to lighten her day. He always helped her prepare food for the youth group when they met at the parsonage; then he'd hang around to clean up after everyone left. Her own pain came as close to Lorene's as possible. She carried as much of Lorene's grief as one person can carry for another.

She had to call Justice now, before someone else did. It would be tough enough. He needed to hear it from his mother.

She looked over Lorene's shoulder and saw Wilburn, broken too, clasp Bud in a tight embrace—both men locked in the pain of unbearable, senseless loss.

In an instant, Lorene went limp in Cyn's arms. Cyn squeezed tighter, hanging onto the dead weight the best she could while easing Lorene to the floor. "Wilburn, get a nurse, help me."

The two men rushed over and grabbed Lorene from Cyn's weakening arms. A nurse walking down the hall saw them and ran over. "Let's get her into a bed. They're getting a doctor for her."

After what seemed like forever, the attendants settled Lorene in a room and sedated her. By then, other church members heard the news and came. Some gave Wilburn a wide berth, ignoring his presence. Others embraced him and thanked him for coming.

Meanwhile, Bud Harvey looked like death itself. He sat in the corner of Lorene's room staring at his lap, talking to no one.

Cyn moved closer to Wilburn and whispered,

"We've got to call Justice."

He nodded. "I know. Would you go call him? I'm afraid to leave Bud."

"I'll go outside and call. That way, I can be honest. You know him, he'll insist on the truth." Cyn took the elevator to the first floor then stepped out into the cool, damp air. Pulling her beige jacket tighter, she turned her back to the wind and dialed, hoping Justice answered. She would not leave a message—no one should learn they lost their best buddy by voice mail—let alone suicide as a result of prejudice and judgment.

"Mom? Is that you? Pops okay? He didn't try again did he?"

"No, sweetheart, your dad is fine—well, as fine as he can be with the mess he's in, but no, I'm calling about..." Her words stuck in the back of her throat. She choked.

"Mom? What is it?"

"Son, did you know Marcus was gay?"

"Marcus? Sure, I know it. All the kids in school..."

Silence, she knew he worked on the past tense of her sentence.

"Why did you say was?"

"His parents...they found him in...his..." She choked on the hideous words.

"Mom, spit it out," he yelled. "What happened?"

"He hanged himself, sweetheart. He's dead."

"Oh no, not Marcus. He couldn't have. I talked with him two days ago, he..."

"He overheard Bud and Lorene talking about your dad. About gay people—how they were doomed to hell..."

"Aww, Mom, he knew they'd think the same thing about him, didn't he?"

"Listen to me, Justice. I have to ask this. I need to know—"

"You want to know if I'm gay."

"Yes. I want you to know I love you; I don't care if you are, or not. I love you without conditions. I don't care—"

"Thank you, Mom. I knew you did. But, like I've already told you, no, I'm not gay. Sometimes I wish I were," his voice reached fever pitch, "so I could stand up and scream at people's stupidity."

"I understand, but I had to ask you again to make sure, so I could assure you that has nothing—"

"Thanks. That means a lot to me."

"Something else..." Cyn hesitated, not knowing how to ask about her next suspicion.

Justice read her mind. "You want to know about Sophie."

Cyn choked, but managed a weak, "Yes."

"No, Mom, Sophie isn't a lesbian."

"It's okay, if she..."

"Take my word for it, Mom, she isn't. But I wish Bud and Lorene could have had parents like..." The line fell silent for a couple of seconds, then, "Mom, you know I've got to come home again. I'm sorry for the expense, but—"

"Don't worry about that, of course, you must. I hope the university will understand."

"They will. Besides, we're off all next week for Thanksgiving."

"Thanksgiving? Wow, I hadn't even thought about it. Not a lot to be thankful for this year, but—"

"I'll call the bus station then text you my arrival

time."

They rang off, and Cyn grabbed the elevator and headed upstairs.

However, on the way up, she worried whether or not Justice had been honest with her. Had he used his relationship with Sophie as a cover-up? If so, for Sophie or him?

"You've never known your son to lie to you, Cyn," she mumbled.

Then again, she hadn't known Wilburn to lie either—until now.

She stepped off the elevator and hurried to Lorene's room.

Lorene still slept under the effects of sedation. Bud had gone to sign papers of some sort. Church members lingered in the waiting room down the hall from Lorene's room, each lost and grief-stricken. They sat in silence, as if dumbfounded and up to their eyeballs in doubt and confusion. Wilburn stood in the corner, his back to Cyn. She walked over, ignoring the nosy stares from the others, and put her arm around him. "How you holding up?" She rubbed his back.

"Not so good. I feel like I failed so many people. If I'd been there for Marcus…"

"How could you? You didn't know."

"I suspected as much."

"What about Justice? Have you ever suspected he might be? Or Sophie?"

"Good grief," Wilburn said, "now you see gays coming out of the woodwork."

"I just want to know. If he is, I don't want him to do something like Marcus."

"The answer is no." Wilburn emphasized the last word. "So stop worrying about that. We've got enough to deal with."

Numb by now, Cyn stared out the window at the leaves scattering across the parking lot, the wind kicking them into the air, then moving on, the leaves drifting, looking for a place to land. When the wind beneath her let go, where would she land? Where would any of these people land? But even more, how would Lorene and Bud live with themselves and the price they paid for their prejudice?

A noise sounded behind them, then a man said, "What the hell are you doing here, Preacher. You're the cause of all this." The man jerked Wilburn around to face him. Mr. Harrison stood red-faced, his hands balled into fists.

"Let's get out of here." Wilburn jerked his arm free, grabbed Cyn's hand, and tried walking away, but Harrison blocked his path.

"One thing I need to tell you, preacher. Don't bother planning a sermon because if it's the last thing I do, you won't ever preach in our pulpit again. You are hereby suspended until further notice."

Wilburn stepped closer. "Get out of my way, you bigot, before I knock you to the floor. You have no power to suspend me or anyone else. All you think about is your own arrogant opinion. Know how I recognize it? I did the same thing, and all in the name of God. Besides, I'm not here at your invitation. I'm here for Marcus' parents. I will leave when they ask me, or when there isn't anything more I can do for them. Now, get out of my way."

When Harrison didn't move, Wilburn grabbed Cyn's

hand and knocked into Harrison's shoulder.

Harrison stumbled but regained his footing, evidently too startled to retaliate.

Wilburn kept going, still holding onto Cyn. She turned and glanced back at Harrison, who stood with his legs spread, mouth open, and eyes wide. He yelled at Cyn, "Why are you going with him, Mrs. Carter, you don't have to do that."

A woman, Cyn couldn't tell whom, called out to her, "Tell Pastor to go to hell. He's already cavorting with that forked-tail devil anyway."

A ripple of anger coursed through Cyn, quickly replaced by pity for every stinking one of them. A few short weeks ago, she might well have felt the same way. When she'd been ignorant.

Not now. Not after she saw the pain in Wilburn's eyes. She couldn't help but compare how Wilburn felt about Stephen, versus what he never felt about her—or any woman. The same connection that seemed missing from many couples at church—like Harris and Hazel. Add that to the pain she'd seen in Bud and Lorene's eyes, and what she knew her son must be feeling right now. She may not understand all of it, but she certainly wasn't ignorant anymore.

So many questions remained. Plus, she couldn't deny the hurt and downright anger that roiled in her gut when she let her guard down. Betrayal of any kind wounded a person at their core—and her core still felt ripped up and spit out.

They had the church and the convention to face. More correctly, Wilburn had to face them. She'd stand by him because it felt right to do so. Do the right thing, even if it costs you a couple of bucks, her mother always said.

Wilburn wronged her and the congregation, but now she understood why. Truth be known, every person in that church would have kept the same secret. And, who knew? Perhaps others had kept it, and no one knew. Not yet, at least.

But why hadn't one person in the group spoken up for Wilburn? Or at least reached a consoling hand out to them?

CHAPTER TWENTY-EIGHT

Cyn and Wilburn walked outside into the night air as a text alert sounded on her phone. "It's from Justice," she said. "He'll arrive at ten tomorrow morning."

Tomorrow—another day. What would it bring? Today brought more than she could imagine. And to think, a few short days ago she'd felt bored.

They both remained silent on the way home, each caught in his or her thoughts.

Once she got past this chaos, where would she go? How would she make a living? She'd have to get a job. She still needed to call Paul Cooper. Something might work out there. One thing for certain, she'd write her memoir. There must not be too many books by women with experiences such as hers.

The idea that preachers' wives couldn't divorce now

seemed insane. Divorce became the least of her worries.

Dee came to mind. A foreign correspondent knew a lot of people. Maybe she had contacts for Cyn. Her degree in journalism should help. Wilburn never allowed her to use it, but now...

"I know I don't deserve what you're doing for me." Wilburn interrupted her thoughts. "Actually, I never deserved it—but I certainly don't deserve how you are standing beside me in all this. I'm not sure how I'm going to make a living, but I promise, I'll help you get established."

She didn't answer, just nodded. Then, a new thought came to mind. "You think Bud and Lorene will ask you to conduct Marcus's funeral?"

"Ha. I doubt it. Even if they wanted to, at this point, that's probably too risky for them. Who knows, that preacher who thinks all gays should be denied a Christian burial might show up with his supporters and placards."

"Wow, that thought hadn't crossed my mind."

"Would not put it past him."

"Justice will go to the funeral, you know that. Hell or high water won't stop him."

Wilburn chuckled. "That boy's got more guts than his dad."

"His mom, too."

Wilburn checked the traffic in his rearview mirror. "How about you? You going?"

She hadn't really thought about it before, but when she did, she knew the answer. "Yes, I'm going. They can kick me out if they want to, but Marcus became my second son. I can't *not* go. I'd never forgive myself."

"Humph." Wilburn laughed. "Looks like Justice did

get his bullheadedness from his mom."

Wilburn grew silent again, looked deep in thought for a few minutes. "Maybe I'll go too, and see what happens. Surely people will respect the dead."

"Don't count on that."

"At least, maybe the grieving parents."

"Maybe."

Something nudged her to keep the line of communication open. "I will say this. I wish you had been honest with me many years ago. I might not have understood, but it certainly would have helped me make sense of our marriage, and why I felt so alone."

He reached over and squeezed her hand. "I wish I had, too. I thought I could control it, and did, until Stephen—" He squeezed tighter. "I hope me mentioning his name doesn't bother you."

"It should, but when I see the two of you together, it helps me understand the missing piece in our marriage, and why. And actually, I always liked Stephen. Maybe if I hadn't already made the decision to leave you, I'd be more upset. But by now, I've gotten past any feelings for you—other than anger, that is."

"You have every right to be mad." He braked at a red light and waited.

Cyn glanced out the window as cars whizzed by, wondering at the lives of the people driving them, and if they had a clue hers had shattered.

"Despite the pain, though, at least now, I understand. It's like I finally have all the pieces to this monstrous puzzle I've carried on my back all these years. As I said, I'm still pissed that you betrayed me—our wedding vows. Even in the midst of all my misery, I never did that. I'm not taking this as easy as it might seem. But in a way, it helps me do what I've needed to do for some time."

"You mean, leave me."

The light turned green, and Wilburn accelerated through the light.

"It's not easy divorcing a Baptist preacher, you know. Church members might divorce, but they don't look kindly on preachers who do."

He laughed. "We won't be the first ones. There are a few."

"Then some preachers' wives just shoot their husbands while they're sleeping."

"Thanks for not doing that," Wilburn said, with a laugh. "It took us awhile before we...you know..." Wilburn's words trailed off.

"You mean before you and Stephen..."

He nodded, but didn't say anything more.

"You mind me asking about the catalyst? Not with too many details, you understand. I can only handle so much information."

"I'm not sure. It seemed like a slow build up. A touching of hands, a look." Even in the dark, she noticed a look of discomfort cross his face. He grew quiet again.

Cyn let the topic die and soon her thoughts returned to poor Bud and Lorene. Too bad they would never get to know their authentic son. Never understand his battles, his desires, and his heartbreak.

Yes, nothing could keep her from attending Marcus' funeral. Not for his parents, but for Marcus. And by God, she'd stand proudly.

While at the hospital, she'd overheard parishioners whispering that the deacons might not let Bud and Lorene hold their son's funeral in the church. Still others said his parents talked about a private graveside service.

The pain of that ripped at her heart.

At noon the next day, Justice stood outside the bus terminal, one hand on a small bag, the other holding a garment bag over his shoulder. Even from a distance, pain radiated from him. She put the car in park and waited while he tucked his belongings in the back and climbed in the front passenger seat.

"Thanks, Mom. Long time no see." He leaned over and gave her a peck. "How's Pops?"

"Not too good on one hand, then on the other, better than he has been."

"He still with Mr. Goodman?"

"Uh-huh,"

"And how are you dealing with all this...this...I would say shit, if it weren't for Marcus. That's pure hell." He pounded the dashboard with his fist when the tears started. "Damn it, Mom, why didn't he call me? Maybe I could have helped him—got him some help—something."

Justice fell apart.

Cyn pulled out of the bus terminal and found an empty parking space. Unable to do otherwise, she grabbed her hulk of a son and held him tight, her pain even greater because of his.

"Damn it, Mom. Damn it, damn it, damn it. We've been friends ever since Pops accepted the job at the church and moved us here. Marcus is the first kid who came up to me our first Sunday at the church."

"I know, sweetheart. I know."

"What the hell did his parents say that sent him over

the edge?"

"I heard Marcus' note said he feared the church might hate him because he was gay, too. I don't know exactly what he wrote, but he'd seen how much they hated your dad. He couldn't bear to face the same anger and hatred from the people he loved so much."

"Aw, shit." A fresh rack of pain tumbled out. "Mom, why do these people spend all that time and energy judging other people instead of looking at themselves? Everyone thinks they are so—excuse me—frigging perfect."

"I don't know, sweetheart. Fear I suppose."

He dried his eyes and straightened. "Come on, let's go home. I'd like to go by and see Mr. and Mrs. Harvey, but I'm afraid of what I might say."

She checked her rearview mirror, put on her turn signal, and pulled into traffic.

"Have you had lunch? Want to stop and get something?"

"Nah, I can get a sandwich or something at home." He sat quietly for a few minutes, as if his mind raced faster than he could express in words. "Have you heard anything about the services? What they plan to do?"

"No, but I assume they won't ask your dad to preside."

"I guess not. And you know how much Marcus liked Pops."

She glanced at her son. "Did he know?"

"About Pops being gay, too?"

A smile crossed his face. "To tell you the truth, Marcus told me."

"Really? When?" Without realizing she had, Cyn cut

her speed until the man behind them blew his horn for her to get moving. She accelerated.

"Three or four years ago. He even told me that Mr. Goodman had the hots for Pops."

"Geesh."

"Sorry, Mom, but that's the word Marcus used."

"What did you say? Did you hit him?"

"Actually, I did—right in the kisser." He laughed, remembering the day.

"You didn't? I've never known you to hit a soul."

"Yeah, and my best buddy, too."

Again, silence.

"I asked him how he knew, and that's when he told me about himself. Then I asked him how he knew that. He said he'd known since elementary school. Said he felt different about boys than he did girls—stronger."

"Little Marcus?"

"Little Marcus." Justice yanked a tissue from a box on the floor and wiped his nose.

By the time they pulled into the parsonage driveway, their emotions had settled into a deeper level of grief. As soon as she turned off the engine, Wilburn opened the front door as if he had stood at the window watching for them. Father and son ran to each other, both weeping uncontrollably.

"I'm so sorry, son," Wilburn said, at last.

"I know, Pops, but it's not your fault."

"It is, in a way. This whole thing should never have happened—at least not this way. My actions led to this. I'll carry this weight the rest of my life."

Their grief tore at Cyn's heart, but she needed to honor their pain. "I'll make us a pot of tea," she said and headed inside.

By the time the kettle whistled, Wilburn and Justice came into the kitchen arm in arm. "Son, I apologize to you and your mother—and to Marcus, if he can hear me."

"I don't blame you, Pops, and I know Marcus wouldn't blame you either. He, more than any other, knew what it felt like to hide in a closet. If you came out, you lost everything. If you felt free to be yourself a long time ago, none of this would have happened."

Cyn poured the boiling water in the heated teapot and rested the kettle on the stove. "Yes, but then we wouldn't have you."

Justice laughed. "Hadn't thought of that."

"Why don't the two of you go sit in the family room, and I'll bring tea."

Father and son walked off while Cyn poured the tea and laid biscotti on a plate.

So much had happened since she'd made them.

After passing cups of tea to Marcus and Wilburn, she collected hers and settled nearby. They sat in silence, dunking biscotti, and nibbling the softened ends.

Justice broke the silence. "Mom, I have to say this again. I need to tell you how much I admire how you are handling all this."

Speechless, uncomfortable, unfamiliar with such praise, Cyn said nothing. She gave her son a smile, wondering what she and Wilburn did right to raise such a neat young man.

Wilburn cleared his throat, glanced at Cyn, then at Justice. "She should have kicked me out a long time ago, son."

"I know that." Justice grinned.

She and Justice laughed at the startled look on Wilburn's face.

"Okay, well, you likely know I've also acted like an ass."

Before Justice could agree with him again, Wilburn chuckled. "You can agree with me on that, too, son, but you don't have to say it out loud."

Their laughter lightened the tension in the room.

"The more I think about the whole thing, how I've treated her just because she's not a man is inexcusable."

"If I'd known you wanted me to be a man." Cyn smiled "I'd have worn jeans more often."

"Funny." Wilburn grew quiet for a minute, hesitated over his words. "Your mom tells me you always knew I was gay—or have for several years. Is that true?"

Justice didn't answer. Just nodded.

"How?"

"Marcus told me. He knew."

Wilburn's mouth dropped open. "I wonder how many other people knew? And here I thought no one did—except for Stephen, that is."

"Marcus couldn't have been the only one," Justice said. "You might find a number of people in church who will support you. Everyone isn't closed-minded about that today. Of course, they wouldn't like you cheating on Mom." He rested his teacup in the saucer and refilled it from the teapot. "By the way, Pops, how is Stephen handling all this? Or should I ask in front of Mom? For some reason, I'm rather tired of walking around family secrets. If I can't talk about it in front of Mom, then we don't need to talk about it at all. She's—"

"It is okay, Justice. I feel the same way. No more

secrets."

"Do you and Stephen know what you're going to do after this?" He looked at his mom. "I assume you will divorce Pops."

"We haven't gotten that far, yet," Wilburn said.

"Let me assure you," Cyn piped up. "There will be a divorce."

The men laughed.

"With all this going on, Stephen and I haven't had much time to talk. But I suppose Ginger will want one too, although the two of them had an open marriage, she didn't see him as gay."

Cyn didn't mention Ginger's attempt to seduce Wilburn. Not to keep it secret, it just didn't seem relative to the topic. Besides, it made no sense to drag Ginger's name into the situation.

"Your dad has some pretty angry parishioners." She switched the subject. "We don't know where this is going."

"I do know I'll soon not have a paycheck. I've heard rumors there's talk about a lawsuit."

"A what?"

"Fraud, I've heard. Said I sold myself for something I'm not."

"That's the most ridiculous thing I've ever heard." Justice set his cup down with a bang, then caught it before it toppled to the floor. "Surely they won't go that far. That's stupid."

"We'll see. Of course, the convention has something to say about it as well. I'll likely be blackballed."

"But Mom told me you were invited to speak at the state convention this year."

"Was invited, was as the operative word in that sentence. Invited before they knew all this. They withdrew the invitation."

"Shit. Self-righteous bastards." Justice pounded the sofa.

Wilburn's ringing cell phone interrupted the conversation. He checked the caller ID. "Mind if I take this? It's Stephen."

Both nodded.

Wilburn stood to answer but didn't leave the room. No more secrets, he'd said. Whatever Stephen had to say, evidently Wilburn determined not to exclude her.

After he hung up, he looked at them, took a deep breath, and said, "Well, it looks like Bud and Lorene have decided not to hold a public service for Marcus. Instead, they've elected to have a private graveside service this afternoon. They plan to invite no one but the family."

"What?" Justice jumped to his feet. "That's it?"

"Seems so, son."

"They are not going to keep me from paying my respects, I'll tell you that." Justice paced the room. "I didn't come home to be shut out this way." He looked at his dad. "Did Stephen say when the graveside service is taking place?"

"Today at four."

"Where?"

"Westlawn Memorial Gardens"

"That's the one over near the church. I know how to get there."

"Son, are you sure?"

"Positive."

"I'd go with you," Wilburn said, "but I'm afraid that

would only make matters worse."

"I'm going." Cyn hurried to her feet. "That's only a couple of hours from now."

CHAPTER TWENTY-NINE

When it came time to leave for the cemetery, Wilburn beat them to the car.

"Hey, Pops, I thought you decided not to go."

"I won't get out. But I can't let this kid be buried in shame, or hidden away from those who loved him for himself. I can at least wait in the car."

Clouds moved in, and it started drizzling by the time they arrived at the cemetery. Marcus's family had already gathered under a green tent. The group looked small, maybe ten people. Cyn didn't recognize the man officiating. Perhaps the family called a pastor of another local denomination. One who either didn't know Marcus was gay or didn't judge him because of it, she thought uncharitably.

Wilburn waited by the car while Cyn took Justice by

the arm and the two started across the grass, heads up, as if they belonged there. One lone floral spray covered the simple casket—the simple, closed casket.

Bud saw them first and even from a distance, Cyn noticed a change in his jaw line. Lorene noticed them next, and placed a hand on her husband's arm and said something to him, evidently warning him he'd better not cause a ruckus.

Cyn and Justice eased behind the family as the pastor read from Psalm 23. Then, he invited everyone to join him in prayer. He'd only said a couple of words when he stopped mid-sentence. At first Cyn thought he stared at them, but then realized he looked beyond where they stood.

As people do, others began to turn and look as well.

Uncomfortable, confused, then curious about the growing sound of shuffling feet, she started to look, but as she did, Wilburn stepped between her and Justice. He grabbed their hands. "Look behind you," he whispered, indicating over his shoulder.

The three of them turned to see a couple hundred solemn-faced parishioners holding hands and walking down the long gravel road towards the casket.

At first, no one at the gravesite moved, but then a piercing wail ripped from Lorene's gut. She tore loose from Bud and hurried to greet the crowd now running towards her. Once they met, those closest to Lorene grabbed her tight, while the others encircled them. Deep, gut-wrenching sobs filled the air.

The rest of the family at the gravesite appeared undecided. Should they go to Lorene or stay with Bud?

"Looks as though half the church members felt like

us, Mom." Justice whispered across his dad.

Wilburn's face had softened. "I saw them coming and figured if they could crash the funeral, then I could, too."

"Did you see Stephen? Is he with them?"

"Bringing up the rear." Wilburn strained his neck to see.

"Wow, wow, wow, is all I can say," Cyn whispered.

"Not me, I got something more to say." Justice made no attempt to soften his voice. He let go of their hands and strode to Bud and the officiating pastor who stood side by side.

Justice stared straight at Bud Harvey, who still hadn't moved or spoken loud enough for everyone to hear.

Justice did. "If you don't mind, I want to say something."

Bud appeared encased in concrete.

"With your permission, Mr. Harvey."

Even the birds stopped singing as if awaiting Bud's reply.

"Let the kid talk," someone yelled from the back while the throng of people surrounded the rest of the family.

If ever love became tangible, it did then. Cyn felt like someone came and wrapped a warm blanket around them. She hoped the family felt it as well. She looked from church member to church member, surprised to see who had come. Not the ones she'd expected. Not the so-called leaders—and not the men always ready to crucify Wilburn—but certainly the faithful. Not a single eye looked dry, but of course, she told herself, maybe it seemed that way because she looked through her own tears.

The birds waited with Justice. A squirrel that had been hop skipping across the lawn stopped and gave pause. Cyn could swear he, too, looked straight at Bud Harvey.

By now, Lorene rejoined her husband. However, she looked different. She no longer appeared to carry the weight of grief by herself, like she'd accepted the offering from the crowd to help her carry it. She pulled out a tissue and wiped her face. After tucking it in her pocket, she pulled on her dress, straightened her askew black hat, and then stood resolute.

Determined.

Ready.

Bud looked at her, but she didn't flinch. Nor did she give in. Instead, she nodded ever so slightly at Justice, but only once. If Cyn hadn't been looking straight at Lorene, she would not have noticed. Even then, she wasn't sure.

Justice saw it too and took it as permission.

He looked from the casket to the gravesite, then back at the casket as if trying to figure out what in the world to say that might bring peace to his own soul, and to this heartbroken family. He raised his eyes and looked at Marcus' parents, his own, then at others present.

Cyn's heart felt like it might burst wide open—if not with love—with pride—and pain.

Justice cleared his throat for the second time and then spoke. If he struggled to express himself earlier, he didn't now.

"Folks, you are my family, as surely as my parents who stand behind you offering nothing but love and compassion to every single one of you."

Heads turned. Eyes looked at Wilburn and Cyn, who still held hands, but now moved closer to the other attendees.

"I love each of you. I apologize, Mr. and Mrs. Harvey, for crashing what you hoped to be a private family gathering, but I'm family too. Marcus and I were brothers as surely as if we shared DNA. You see I knew Marcus was..."

Go ahead, Justice, put it out there. Say the word no one else is brave enough to say.

"...was gay. Knew it for years. To tell the truth, Marcus and I talked about it frequently. I respected that he was homosexual, as Marcus respected that I'm not. We accepted each other the way God made us. I didn't choose to be straight. I just am. Marcus didn't choose to be gay. Fact is he had nothing to do with it. Neither did his parents. Neither did you. But no one, and I mean no one, ever loved folks as unconditionally as Marcus did."

Justice went on to recount childhood antics that the two boys got into, like the time they accidently ran the car into a ditch, and how a carload of sailors stopped, picked up the car, and swung it back onto the road. How they slipped home in the dark of night, turned on the water hose and washed the mud off the fenders, hoping not to wake Bud and Lorene.

"Hey, Justice. My bedroom window faces the Harvey driveway," yelled the family's next-door neighbor. "I saw you guys out there washing the mud and grass off that car. You didn't know it, but Bud and I waved at each other from our bedroom windows."

At first a twitter went through the crowd, then the

group roared with laughter.

The tension broken, Justice smiled. "As you well know, over the last few days, I've learned a whole lot about family secrets, and the damage they do. And of the healing power of love, acceptance, and forgiveness."

The squirrel scampered up a pecan tree, then stopped, and looked at the crowd.

"I want to say Marcus was one of the neatest guys I've even known. His spirit will always be with me, and I know it will be with you, Mr. and Mrs. Harvey."

With that, he stepped aside and rejoined Cyn and Wilburn.

The funeral attendant removed two roses from the arrangement on top of the casket, walked over to Marcus' parents and with solemn dignity, gave one to each. Afterward, he invited each who wanted, to pluck a red rose from the arrangement and take it with them, to remember a young man who loved greatly.

No one moved. The air felt charged with electricity, whether from the brewing storm or the unexpressed feelings of others in the group.

Justice tucked his chin and moved to the front once again. He stepped to the casket, plucked a rose and returned to stand by Cyn.

She took a step forward, but Wilburn caught her arm, gave her a look that begged her not to go. She stepped back in line.

The top of a man's head showed above the throng as he made his way to the grave.

It looked like the same blond-haired man she'd danced with at the charity event. He marched to the casket and collected a rose. When he turned, his eyes found

Cyn's and stayed on them until he stood right in front of her.

He glanced at the rose. "Marcus would want you to have this," he said, and handed the long-stemmed red rose to her, gave a slight bow, and then disappeared into the crowd—a crowd that watched his every move.

Nothing like attracting attention she didn't want.

Wilburn nudged her in the side and whispered, "Isn't that the same man you said pulled you to the dance floor at the charity event?"

"Shh," she said, nodding.

Grief released, one person after another came forward, took a rose, and returned to their place.

The arrangement grew smaller and smaller until only one rosebud remained.

Silence.

Except for the squawk of a mockingbird overhead.

No one moved. No one wanted to leave the young man. Lorene and Bud sat silent, tears streaming down their cheeks. Their only child, soon to be lowered into the earth.

All eyes, it seemed, focused on the one single rose...waiting...

Instead of growing restless, people stood, patient, reverent. Cyn glanced at the funeral director, who stood with his head bowed, hands clasped behind his back, frozen in time.

After what seemed an eternity, Cyn felt a movement beside her, then realized Wilburn had taken a step forward, and with slow, deliberate movements, strode to the casket.

With his back to everyone, he appeared to be doing

something.

What? Cyn wondered. Why does he just stand there?

The quiet crowd grew even quieter. The mockingbird stopped its song and waited. After what seemed like forever, Wilburn turned to face them, the rosebud in his lapel. He looked over the group and settled on Bud and Lorene.

Anxiety built in Cyn's chest.

He cleared his throat, and started to speak, but choked on tears.

Justice grabbed Cyn's hand and without either of them saying a word, the two moved forward until they stood on either side of Wilburn.

He looked first at one, then the other, took their hands and squeezed.

Cyn expected people to turn and walk off at any minute.

They didn't. Not a soul moved.

"With your permission, Bud and Lorene..." He looked at Marcus's parents and when Bud nodded, Wilburn continued.

"Marcus was our second son."

Cyn looked past Wilburn to Justice, on the other side. He smiled at her.

"Marcus carried his pain all alone—except for a few like Justice here." Wilburn nodded, indicating his son. "He felt undeserving of our love because our society— while best intentioned—mistakenly believed him unworthy. Worse than that—without realizing it, we taught him he was unworthy. I, of all people, should have known better." He gazed at the casket. "Marcus, buddy, your pain is no longer; it is now ours to carry for you."

Tears flowed from Wilburn without any apparent attempt to control them. When they slowed, he wiped his eyes and nose with his handkerchief and began again.

"Likely, many of you can't begin to understand Marcus, but I know he loved you anyway. Bud and Lorene, he loved you deeply. God loves Marcus as much, maybe more, because of the pain he suffered at our hands."

Wilburn glanced at the casket, and then scanned his surroundings.

"Perhaps in sharing our pain with each other in an honest open way, Marcus' death will count for something greater than the whole. I invite you to open your heart and embrace people's differences without fear or judgment."

With that, while still holding their hands, Wilburn turned and walked the three of them to their car. Cyn got behind the wheel and off they went down the long winding driveway lined with cars.

CHAPTER THIRTY

Once inside the parsonage, Justice swept them in his arms. "Just want to say how proud you two make me. Pops, you blew me away. I know my path differs from yours. But you stand head and heart above any other man I know."

Wilburn shook his head, "No, I don't, son, but thank you. I've been unfair to you and your mother, especially your mother. I've locked this damn secret so deep in my soul it seems like only one thing eased the pain. Make everyone else's life as miserable as mine. Guess I thought if I acted normal, marrying, having a child, everything would be okay. I couldn't have been more wrong—"

The doorbell interrupted him. It also stopped Cyn's heart. For the first time since she and Wilburn married, she felt like she knew the man she lived with for twenty years. The man she would soon divorce…and move from a house that never felt like home.

Wilburn looked out the window. "It's Bud and Lorene."

Cyn's heart resumed its beat. "We must invite them in." She looked in question at the other two.

Wilburn nodded.

"I'll do it." Justice turned and stepped into the foyer.

Evidently, neither Justice nor the Harveys said a word before Justice ushered them into the living room.

At first, they all stood looking at each other as if no one knew what to say, until Cyn moved to Lorene. "Won't you sit? Please?"

Lorene moved to the sofa, her steps slow, halting as if her knees refused to hold her upright much longer. Bud grabbed her arm and the two sat, thighs touching, hands clasped, each a lifeline for the other.

"Pastor," Bud spoke, his words abrupt, painful. "We need you to help us understand our son. We can't bring him back, but we sure do want to honor his life. We don't want him remembered as a, a faggot—the same word me and some of the other men called you—even painted it on your house. That's an awful word to call anyone."

The room fell quiet.

Bud focused on the floor as he confessed, but now, he raised his pain-filled eyes to Wilburn. "I hated you a few days ago." Bud choked on the words.

Wilburn nodded. "I know you did. And to tell the truth, you had a right to feel betrayed. That is exactly what I did."

Bud nodded in return. "That doesn't excuse us saying those awful things about you—I'm ashamed to admit I had a part in it. We've been friends, and our sons have been almost brothers. I had no right to attack you that way—at least without giving you a chance to help us understand. You shocked us, yes, for sure, but that's no excuse. We call ourselves Christians—Christians, mind you..."

Bud shook his head as if incredulous at his behavior. "We knew God's mind, by God," he slammed his fist into his other palm, "God sided with us and no one could tell us any different. We didn't know Marcus stood in the other room listening to us talk about you. We had no clue what our ugly words did to our son. Today, we learned how wrong we've been. We can never forgive ourselves for that. It is our fault, and no one else's that our son is dead."

Cyn couldn't stand to see the look on Lorene's face. She moved over and sat next to her, wishing to ease the woman's pain, knowing she could not.

"You see, we've always thought God hated—well—people like you."

Lorene slapped her husband's hand.

"I know how it is." Wilburn smiled. "But you see, you didn't hate me any more than I hated myself."

"Really? You mean Marcus likely hated himself?"

"Possibly. However, young people today seem a little more accepting of who they are, thanks to the love they receive from others their age." Wilburn looked at Justice.

"He couldn't help who he was." Lorene's voice squeaked, but she maintained her composure. "If it had been possible for him to change that about himself, I'll bet he would have. He didn't want to die. He had everything to live for. He loved life."

"There's a whole lot about this me and Lorene don't understand." Bud touched his wife's hand. "But we want to. No, change that. We must understand it. Thank you for what you did today."

"You don't owe us anything, Bud. We wanted to be there," Wilburn said. "I feared my presence might offend you. I started not to go. I'm glad I did."

"Us, too." Lorene smiled. "After you left, others came up to say how they grieved our pain, how they supported us, and how they loved Marcus, and—get this—and how they loved and wanted to support you."

Cyn looked from Wilburn to Justice.

Bud scooted to the edge of his seat. "Now's not the time, preacher, but there's a bunch of members who want to understand. We've got to before we lose another son or daughter. Will you help us?"

Wilburn swallowed hard. "Anytime you're ready, Bud. Let me know."

"One more thing." Bud pulled an envelope out of his coat pocket. "We found this bill in the envelope Marcus left behind. He asked us to pay it for him, out of the money he'd saved for college. Thought you might want to see it." He handed it to Wilburn.

Cyn looked over Wilburn's shoulder as he unfolded the paper—a statement of services due from the security company guarding the parsonage.

Bud took the bill out of Wilburn's shaking hands, replaced it in the envelope, and tucked it in his pocket. Without another word, he and Lorene walked out with their shoulders held high.

After Wilburn closed the door, he, Justice and Cyn

stood in the middle of the entryway looking at each other with surprise and shock.

"I never would have guessed Marcus hired the security guard to protect us." Cyn shook her head. "Incredible. What's next?"

"I'm wondering too, Mom. I wish I didn't have to go back to school. Keep me posted. By the way, do you know that man who brought you the rose?"

Cyn shrugged. "I don't have a clue. I met him at the charity ball your dad and I attended."

"Yeah, I leave the table for a few minutes, and when I come back, your mom is on the dance floor in the arms of another man."

"Mom?"

Cyn shrugged. "He asked."

"I didn't know you danced? Pops, you always called dancing a sin."

"You're right, son, I did. The reason was because that's what I was taught."

"Really? By whom?"

"The youth director of my home church had this list of fifteen reasons why a Christian shouldn't dance. That list looks mighty ridiculous today."

"Like what?"

"Here, let me." Cyn assumed an air of superiority. "No healthy young man or young girl can go through the motions of the modern dance for any length of time without thinking impure thoughts."

Justice broke into hysterics. "You've got to be kidding."

"I swear. Got the faded green piece of paper in my files."

And are the rest of them equally ridiculous?

"Come to think of it," Wilburn said, "they are."

The heavy tension of the day, now broken by their laughter, made the room lighter. In the midst of it all, however, Cyn knew they each grieved the loss of Marcus.

CHAPTER THIRTY-ONE

Thanksgiving came and went without incident. Justice returned to school after making them swear to keep him abreast of the goings on. First thing Monday, Wilburn left for his office at the church. The situation didn't look good to start with—being accused of job abandonment would not improve the situation, and no one had taken away his key yet.

Meanwhile, Cyn called Dee and gave her an update. As a part of the telling, she mentioned the ball and the same good-looking blond-haired gentleman who gave her a rose at the funeral. Dee demanded to know his name, disappointed to learn Cyn didn't remember. "Find out," Dee demanded.

"Okay, busybody, I'm hanging up now. You're giving me a migraine, and I'm out of meds. I need to get the prescription refilled." She gave a heavy sigh. "With all the chaos going on, I've run out of almost everything."

After the call to Dee, Cyn's headache improved but the prescription still needed refilling. She grabbed her wallet and left.

Disappointed when she arrived at the drugstore and didn't see an empty spot, she waited until a vehicle on the end backed out, and then pulled in alongside a beige sports convertible.

As if fate joined forces with Dee, Cyn and the sports car driver exited their vehicles at the same time. They looked at each other and stopped.

The good-looking blond from the charity ball and the funeral flashed her a heart-stopping smile.

"Well, hello," he said, maintaining the grin. "My day just grew officially brighter."

With little choice but to proceed, but furious at her stupid, wobbly knees, she closed her door and walked around her car.

He met her at the front. "Say, are you still married? Did I see your husband at the funeral?"

Thankful she still wore her wedding band, but unsure why, she held out her left hand.

"Aw, shucks. Guess my luck's not holding."

The two walked through the automatic doors, and she collected a shopping cart.

"I didn't expect to see you at the funeral." Cyn grabbed a sale paper from a wire bin and placed it in the top part of her cart to peruse while she shopped. "So, are you related to Bud and Lorene Harvey?"

"Lorene and my dad are cousins. Sad about Marcus. Neat guy. I always suspected the kid was gay, but I had no idea Bud and Lorene didn't. What a waste."

"Yes, it is. Marcus grew up with my son. He felt like family, always coming in and out of our house." She paused, remembering. "Oh, and thank you for the rose. I don't think I said so at the time. To tell you the truth, it shocked me when you did. I hadn't seen you there."

"I could see you wanted one, so..."

They pushed their carts further into the store. Uncomfortable with the encounter, Cyn wanted to escape but didn't know how to without looking rude.

"Was that your husband and son?"

She nodded.

"I've heard the rumors going around. You doing okay?"

No way did she care to get into that conversation with this stranger. She shrugged but said nothing.

"Sorry, I'm prying."

"You are. I don't mean to sound rude, but that's personal."

"My apologies." He tipped his hand to his forehead and smiled. "Okay, but we'll meet again, I promise you."

Not if I have anything to do with it. No need complicating my life any more than it is already.

However, as she walked away, she put her hand on her chest to calm the pounding. She'd never had a man look at her the way he did. *Just friendly, that's all*, she told herself.

She turned in her prescription for a refill then walked the aisles while she waited, but the reality of her life forced aside the thoughts about the blond man. Despite their problems, she still vowed she'd maintain her end of the bargain until they moved out of the parsonage.

Moving from cleaning products to healthcare, she turned the corner and spied Handsome ahead, his back to her. She slowed her pace and waited for him to turn the corner, then stalled a few more minutes and reversed her pattern, retracing her steps to get out of sync with his.

A few minutes later, she collected her prescription, checked out, and returned to her car, both disappointed and relieved to see the convertible wasn't there.

She slid behind the wheel before she spotted a piece of lined yellow paper tucked under her windshield wiper. Her heart pounded in her throat while she stared at it. He left it. She knew he had.

Stepping out, she snatched the note, afraid to unfold it, afraid of what it might or might not say.

The page contained only one word written with a bold black marker. Cheveré.

That one word touched her most vulnerable spot—aroused her in a way no man ever had, and she didn't even know the meaning of the word. But something about it made her pelvic floor tighten, then release, and tighten again, begging for more.

She chortled. What would Dee say when—if—she told her about this—and how it matched her dream—and the impact of the note, all the way down. She flipped down the visor mirror and looked. Sure enough, her cheeks looked bright red. Her eyes sparkled.

The timing felt so off. She dealt with enough uncertainties in her life right now, and none of them were going away anytime soon. Besides, for all she knew, he could be a serial killer or a rapist.

However, she tucked the note and the memory away with a promise to revisit it after she went to bed that night.

Remembering what she and Wilburn faced, the saying, hell hath no fury like a woman scorned came to mind. Perhaps folks got that all wrong. From her viewpoint, the fury and vindictiveness of a church might supersede the former, and all in the name of God.

Little surprised her these days, but when Cyn pulled into her driveway and spotted Hazel Harrison sitting on the front porch swing, that list grew longer.

Hazel wore a white shawl around her shoulders and clutched a purse to her chest as if she feared someone might sneak up and grab it.

Cyn collected her prescription and the other bags, and opened the car door. From the corner of her eye, she saw Hazel sling her purse over her shoulder, straighten the shawl, and head down the driveway towards Cyn.

"Here, let me give you a hand with that." Hazel took one of the bags while Cyn forced herself to stay conscious. Although Hazel offered strong support while Wilburn was in the hospital, Cyn hadn't talked with her since. Did she still support them now, or had she crossed the line and joined the tar-and-feathers league?

"Thanks for your help," Cyn said, curious as to the purpose of the visit, but determined not to ask. "Let's get in the house, and I'll fix us something hot to drink. It's cold outside. I'll bet you got chilled sitting on the porch."

The two walked inside before Hazel answered.

"Shivery, yes. Didn't know how much longer I'd wait," Hazel unpacked one of the bags.

Cyn made cups of hot chocolate, and the two adjourned to the family room. "Here, sit in this chair. It's closest to the fireplace. I'll turn on the gas logs."

Hazel sat where directed. Meanwhile, Cyn tucked an afghan across the woman's lap, turned on the gas logs, then curled on the sofa across the room.

"So did you wait long? I'm afraid you'll catch your death—"

"I'm fine. Thawing out a little, but the fire feels nice."

Curiosity got the best of Cyn. "Is there something you need? Can I help you?" In five years, Hazel only set foot in the parsonage once a quarter when she and her committee came to inspect the house for damage. That and her obligatory attendance at the annual Christmas Open House—the precedent set by previous pastors' wives. Precedence Cyn dared not break. Last year, she took a short cut and had the food and drinks catered— much to the annoyance of the deacons' wives. Seemed they took pride in the slavery of homemade. Thank goodness no one expected an open house this year, homemade or store bought.

"I wanted to let you..." Hazel twisted her hands in her lap then fidgeted with a loose button on her dress. "I've never done anything like this before." Her words sounded like a prelude to a confession.

"Never done what, Mrs. Harrison?"

"Oh, remember, call me Hazel. Mrs. Harrison sounds too formal, and right now, I don't feel very formal. I'm going behind my husband's back. If he knew, he'd...he'd..."

Silence—more hand wringing and fidgeting.

"What? Hit you?"

Hazel looked up, surprised. "No, no, he doesn't hit me anymore, not since we got older, but—"

"You mean he used to?"

Hazel didn't confirm or deny. She simply stared at her hands in her lap.

"That's okay," Cyn said, "I didn't mean to put you on the spot. Go on."

Hazel waited, as if building her courage before she continued. After a few seconds, she straightened her spine and looked Cyn straight in the eye. "I wanted to let you know they have called a business meeting next Wednesday night. Instead of a prayer meeting they want to have a face to face meeting with your husband."

Okay, here it comes, Cyn thought. She had expected something like this.

"A meeting, or an inquisition?"

Hazel grimaced. "Folks are split down the middle. Half are for Brother Wilburn, and the other half are against him. The deacons felt the only way to put this whole thing to rest before it splits the church was to get everyone together and slug it out. I'm afraid that's exactly what this meeting will turn into—a free-for-all. I hate this kind of thing." Hazel looked close to tears. "Makes me want to never darken the doors of a church again."

Cyn thought about moving closer to Hazel, but feared if she did, Hazel would shut down, or worse yet, flee.

"You won't tell anyone I came here and told you will you?"

"I need to tell Wilburn. I assume you don't mean him."

"Of course not, but he won't say anything to Harris about it, will he?"

"I'll ask him not to. And I can assure you, I won't

say anything."

Hazel took a deep breath, seemed to relax a little.

"I guess you know after the deacons kicked Stephen out as chairman, Harris wormed his way into the position."

"That's what I hear." Cyn smiled inside, amused at Hazel's description of her husband's actions.

"The other deacons told Stephen not to show his face at the meeting." She paused, as if in deep thought, then roused, and looked at Cyn. "I can't pretend I understand all this about...about...Pastor and...and Stephen. But I do know what folks are saying and doing is wrong. Half of them wouldn't even go to the poor Harvey boy's funeral. That's so wrong."

Hazel put her empty cup on the coffee table, and then yanked on her shawl. "I've said all I came to say. I didn't want you and Pastor to get blindsided. I told Harris they shouldn't do that, but he didn't listen. He never..."

The remainder of the sentence went unsaid. Instead, Hazel stood as if ready to leave.

Cyn rose and put out her hand. "Thank you for coming. That took a lot of courage. I appreciate it, and I promise this will be our secret." She kissed the elderly woman on her soft, wrinkled cheek.

"Thank you, Cyn." Hazel smiled. "I like that name so much better than Cynthia. Sounds much friendlier. And you tell that sister of yours I said hello."

The two women chuckled on that comment as they strode down the hall.

After Hazel left, Cyn closed the door and leaned against it, an overwhelming sense of gratitude washing over her. She and Wilburn might soon face a tiger, but forewarned was forearmed.

She no sooner stepped away from the door than Wilburn walked through it with a puzzled look on his face. "Was that Mrs. Harrison I saw driving away?"

"It was, and despite what I thought about her, I've learned to like that woman. More than that, I admire her. Let's go make lunch, and I'll tell you why she came."

Wilburn prepared their drinks, and Cyn collected sandwich makings while she recounted the purpose of Hazel's visit and the need for confidentiality.

"I won't breathe a word." He motioned his fingers across his lips as if closing a zipper.

After a long pause, Wilburn said, "Well, I've got news for you, too. When I got to the church earlier, I couldn't get in my office. Seems they changed the lock over the holiday."

"Wasn't your secretary there?"

"Not yet. Iris got there late. Seems her son came down sick, and she had to drop him at her mother's first. Iris hated that I beat her. It's pathetic when your secretary has to tell you that not only is your job suspended until further notice, but also you can't even get in your office to collect your belongings. Seems Harris' retort at the hospital carried more weight than I thought."

"I could understand the deacons not wanting you to preach until something gets settled, but locking you out of your office is wrong—you have personal property there."

"Nevertheless, that's what they did. My secretary said the deacons are divided about all this as well as the whole church. Most of those who came to Marcus' funeral are the ones who want to understand, to give me an opportunity to explain, to...whatever. The others—

those who didn't—are the ones who...well, you get the picture."

"That's the same thing Hazel said. What about Bud Harvey?" Cyn smeared mayonnaise on their bread and piled wafer-thin slices of smoked turkey on top.

"Not sure." Wilburn collected lettuce and tomatoes from the fridge and placed then on the counter near Cyn. "Guess we'll soon know if he's rethought his feelings about gays."

"Do you think Hazel's description of the plan for this Wednesday night is accurate?" Cyn added the veggies, completing the sandwich, and grabbed a bag of chips.

"Looks so. Iris says folks want to address it now, before the Christmas holidays loom any closer."

"At least we'll know something either way."

"Either way? I've accepted the fact that I'm jobless. Right now, I'm hoping for a decent severance. Some don't even want to give me that. Others? Well? We'll know after Wednesday."

"Don't mean to hit you when you're down, but soon as this gets settled, I'll go see a lawyer and start divorce proceedings. No sense in delaying the inevitable. After we get past that meeting, we both need to get on with our lives. Plus, I know they'll want us out of the parsonage right away."

Wilburn laughed. "Yeah, they'll need time to fumigate it before the next pastor moves in." He bit into his sandwich.

"And you're right," he said, after swallowing. "There's no sense in prolonging the inevitable. I think we've got enough money in our retirement savings to help pay for your lawyer. You ask for what you think is fair, and I won't fight it. I'll make sure you have enough to live on for a while—as far as we can stretch the money."

Relieved and somewhat surprised—no, shocked—at the one-eighty turnaround in Wilburn's personality, and his attitude towards her, she said, "You know, I can't believe you're the same man I lived with for twenty years. You're actually quite nice."

Wilburn roared with laughter.

"You are—now that you don't have to pretend."

"Except for the mess at church, I feel better than I have my whole life. Here I forced myself in that closet all these years and...and...made us both miserable—and for what? So a group of people could tell me how awful I am? That I'm damned to hell? Despite what they might think, they aren't the doorkeepers of either place."

"So what do you and Stephen plan to do next?"

"Truth is, after I found out the deacons locked me out of my office, I called Stephen. I've been with him all morning. According to him, Ginger saw a lawyer."

"Wow. She didn't wait long."

"Seems she's found someone else." He laughed sarcastically, and then stopped sudden like. "I have no right to judge her. I apologize for that."

"I guess none of us do." Cyn took a sip of iced tea and put her glass on the table again. "Suppose we all do the best we can under the circumstances at any given moment. I know that because I've still got work to do forgiving Ginger's betrayal of our friendship." Cyn didn't mention the guilt she felt talking to the blond man at the drugstore—or the fantasy she planned after she went to bed later.

For the next few minutes, they sat quietly and ate.

"You know," Cyn said, "When we married, I had such big ideas for the two of us. Turns out, they were naïve dreams of the young. Now, it's hard to believe I will soon be a divorced woman, and out on my own."

"Any thoughts on where you'll go?" Wilburn stuffed the last bite in his mouth and crumpled his napkin into a ball.

"I guess a lot of it depends on what happens Wednesday night. I certainly don't intend to stay in a town where people ridicule or pity me."

"Maybe pity, but not ridicule. That would be me. But, regardless, I'll live wherever Stephen lives."

"What about your calling?"

"To tell you the truth, I'm still trying to figure out that whole thing. I'm thinking if the calling truly came from..." Wilburn shrugged, as if letting go of the control.

"And Stephen? What about his job?"

"Safe, so far. Seems no one at the museum cares about his private life. By the way, he's already found an apartment and moves in this afternoon. I'm probably going to go ahead and move in with him, unless..." He looked at her in question.

"To tell you the truth, I'm more comfortable with you doing that anyway."

"Then I'll pack a bag this afternoon. When it's time to load up and vacate the parsonage, I'll either come help you, or pay a mover to do that."

"Isn't there anything here you want?"

"Of course there is. We've got a little time to go through things. You may not believe it, Cyn, but I'm hurting over our breakup. I care about you. I hope, in time, we can be friends."

She laughed. "Well, I think I would like you better as a friend than I've liked you as a husband."

"As I said before, ouch."

"Sorry."

"No, no, I don't blame you. I've been a judgmental, controlling, arrogant bastard."

Cyn laid her hand on Wilburn's forearm. "Hey, I like you better already." They smiled, and the tension passed.

"So, I guess we'll both look for a job." Wilburn shrugged. "Problem is, there isn't a lot of transferable skills when you've been a pastor all your adult life."

"Sure there are, but that's all you ever wanted." Cyn tried to suppress any feeling of misplaced responsibility. "It's what you felt called to do. It's the main reason I stayed with you as long as I did."

"I'll be okay. I figure God made me this way, God can take care of the calling. At least I like myself for the first time in my life."

Cyn busied herself cleaning the kitchen while Wilburn went upstairs to pack his bags. Good lord, who'd have ever thought she'd be in this position at this age and at this stage. Lost as a goose about what came next, at least for the first time in her life, she'd found herself.

A few minutes later, Wilburn came downstairs carrying two suitcases. He put them at the door, and the two stood looking at each other.

"If anyone from the church calls, they can reach me by cell phone. You might not swant to tell them I've moved out. That way, you can buy a little more time."

"So, do you think they'll let you know about the trial set for Wednesday night?"

"They just did. Harris called me while I packed. Said

if I wanted any kind of a severance package, as far as his vote counted, I better show up Wednesday at seven and face the music."

"You going?" Wilburn looked at Cyn as if he cared about her answer.

"Wouldn't miss it for the world."

"Really?" He stepped over and kissed her on the forehead. "You're quite a woman, Cyn. I'm sorry I've been such a shitty husband."

"Wow, your language sure has changed," Cyn said.

Wilburn shrugged and gave her a sidewise grin. "When it smells like shit, it probably is."

"Glad to see you're not taking yourself so seriously. Anyway, I'm okay. Really."

He picked up his suitcases and walked out.

She closed the door behind him—and on that half of her life.

Back in the kitchen, she pulled down the phone book, closed her eyes and pointed to a law firm—the biggest in Mobile, the ad said. Soon, she'd call and make an appointment.

CHAPTER THIRTY-TWO

Cyn collected as many free boxes as possible, purchased a few more, and then spent the next few days going through cabinets and closets. She packed what she wanted and left the remainder for Wilburn and Justice.

Justice called every night to check on her. She told him about Harris' call notifying Wilburn of the trial. Tribunal, Justice called it. He wanted to come home and be there for his dad, but she encouraged him not to. "This battle belongs to your dad, sweetheart. He can handle it. You do what you need to do for yourself. Study. Finals come soon."

"Are you going?" he asked.

"To tell you the truth, I wouldn't miss it."

"You're something, Mom," he said, shortly before hanging up.

For the first time, she believed that about herself.

Felt dang good.

Wednesday morning broke bright and beautiful. A front came in overnight, and the air felt unusually crisp even before she slipped from underneath the warm blankets. After Wilburn moved out, she'd been sleeping in her own bed, which sure helped her mood.

She glanced at the boxes piled in the corner, thankful now that she'd stayed up late to get everything she intended to take taped and ready to move as soon as the church demanded their house back. She assumed the deacons would give Wilburn time to get his things after she moved. However, as far as she knew, the end might be as near as tonight.

Swinging her feet to the cold hardwood floor, she hurried to the bathroom, closed the door, and lit the old gas heater in the wall. Shivering, she backed up to the fire, waiting for it to take the nip out of the air before she unrobed to bathe.

While she waited, she took in her surroundings. A fantastic room, actually. The claw foot tub in the corner made the top of her favorites list from the get-go, that and the old porcelain lavatory with the original ceramic white handles and the push button light switch.

The realization surprised her—she had built fond memories in this house—home to her for the last five years—and home for how many others before her? The church purchased the building decades ago, and the wall down the stairwell held portraits of each pastor who lived in it since then.

At first, she'd pushed Wilburn to take the portraits

down, store them in the attic, but he feared the parsonage committee might object. Cyn hated looking at the portraits, so she taught herself to pretend they weren't there. After a while, in her mind, they didn't exist. But, indeed they were there—in all their glory, and likely growing roots in the wall behind them, and just as likely, Wilburn's picture would never hang on the wall with the others.

It had come as no surprise that the wall held not a single photo of those men's wives—not one. Parishioners always talked about the importance of the preacher's wife, but the words fell through paternalism's black hole. As a result of Wilburn's ouster, her turn to fall deeper into the hole and out the other side loomed, and that suited her just fine.

How many such wives stood here warming by the fire, reliving the memories? Did they, too, wonder their identity outside their role—women who sacrificed themselves on the altar of anonymous?

The chill gone, she stepped to the tub, filled it with hot water, and added bubble bath. Today, of all days, felt like the perfect day to pamper herself. She slipped her sleep shirt over her head, dropped it to the floor, and slid into warm, liquid meditation.

Where would she be after tonight? She'd checked the newspaper listings for apartments with short-term leases. One thing for sure, she didn't want a long-term lease—not on anything.

Her future spread out in front of her, taking no particular direction. As soon as things settled down, she needed to call Paul Cooper—oops, she'd scheduled a meeting with him before hell broke through the façade they'd called life. When she called, she'd explain. She needed a job, whether she could do what he wanted or not.

That thought reminded her to call Dee and bring her up to speed—she'd do that tomorrow, after the battle. Meanwhile, her role in the trial that evening remained unclear. Should she sit on the front row in her usual spot, or out of sight in the back? Where would Stephen sit? Would he even come? Would he be called on the carpet as well?

Ginger—what about her? She filed for divorce, and Stephen had moved out. So she'd likely come across as the wounded wife—like Cyn—who, although betrayed, already planned to leave. That made all this easier for her to deal with—even left her feeling relieved. Took away any guilt she might have carried if Wilburn hadn't been gay.

Then again, if she'd known Wilburn was gay, she'd never have married him in the first place. She wondered again what life must be like for a man—or woman—in a closet, hiding their identity, fearful for their life.

In a situation such as that, a closet must be so much more than the simple four walls.

At the age of five, she'd been locked in a closet by a babysitter, and suddenly, the closet became much more than a closet. It isolated her from reality. It denied her existence. Those four walls held her captive—filled her mind with demons that grew bigger the longer she remained inside. Cyn shuddered, remembering the feeling of abandonment, being forgotten, left to die. With no one aware that the babysitter's interest lay more in the neighborhood boy who put his hands inside her pants than

Cyn's welfare.

Cyn's childhood pastor always called homosexuals abominations to God. And like everything else she'd been taught, she never had the courage to question his opinion. Once again, she'd believed it because someone told her so.

She thought of Marcus. What must his closet have felt like? At least he'd been honest with Justice, who accepted him—who didn't fear contamination—or fear he might turn into a homosexual by simple osmosis.

The remainder of the day, she washed drawers and cabinets, dusted cobwebs, scrubbed walls, and cleaned out the refrigerator. When the time for the tribunal drew closer, she freshened up and was dressing to go when her cell phone rang. The caller identification showed Ginger's name. Fearful not to answer it under the circumstances, she punched it on.

"Cyn, Ginger. I know you don't want to talk to me, but I needed to know if you planned on going to church tonight."

"What difference does that make?" Cyn knew irritation showed in her voice but didn't care.

"It doesn't, I guess."

"Are you?" Cyn hoped Ginger didn't ask to sit with her like some united front.

"No, I'm not." Ginger sounded on edge, nervous. "I've had about all of those people I can stand."

"I can understand that. Truth is, I have, too. I'm going tonight to support Wilburn." Cyn looked at the clock. "After that, I don't imagine I'll darken the doors again. But I'm running late. I need to go now, but thanks for calling."

No sooner had she ended the call from Ginger than the landline rang. A newspaper reporter wanted to know what time the service started. The next call came from the Lesbian, Gay, Bi-sexual, and Transgender group. They planned to attend in support of Wilburn. The next caller didn't identify himself, but let out a string of profanities about iniquity and sinful behaviors that had nothing to do with God. Odd thing was, he said it did.

Leaving the parsonage later than intended, heavy traffic slowed her progress. By the time she found a parking spot a couple blocks from the sanctuary—which gave off the aura of anything but—the crowd overflowed out onto the lawn and down the block. She ducked her head, picked up her pace, and hurried by all the strangers. Bits and pieces of their conversations fit in two groups— those arguing for the pastor, and those against him.

Self-righteous-looking protestors paraded up and down the sidewalk carrying vile signs about who and what God hated—seems God hated everything and everyone but the people carrying the signs. It made her wonder at the audacity of reading God's mind, or telling God who to hate and who not to hate—namely, them.

Who said Hitler died? Looked to her like he lived well—at least in the hearts of those carrying the signs.

Popular belief taught that a person seeking Christ could find him at church. Today, either no one sent him an invitation, or he ran late like Cyn. Or maybe Christ wanted nothing to do with these people. She certainly didn't.

No one saw her, or at least acted like they didn't, as she eased down the covered walkway alongside the building, hoping the first pew was empty.

Cyn shoved the door open and entered the sanctuary only to realize she'd been wrong. Someone occupied Cyn's pew—a woman with a wide-brimmed hat hiding her face. Who in the world would want to sit in Cyn's place today?

Dee? On my God, it's Dee. Cyn stopped mid-stride, but her heart didn't. It pounded like a racehorse in the home stretch. She hurried forward.

Dee met her halfway, and the two embraced.

Cyn wanted to bawl in relief—wanted to, but didn't. Determined to keep the world out of her business she whispered into Dee's ear, "When did you get in town? How did you know?"

"Well, sweet sister, your husband, and your church have made the national news, you know. It's not every day that a pastor goes on trial because he's a homosexual, and even fewer when that guy's a Baptist. You and Wilburn have made all the news channels."

"Good grief. Really?" Cyn's stomach felt like a lead weight.

"Did you see the photographers outside? Yep, you're going to be famous—at least your husband is. Now you have a chance to write an exposé on what life is like living with a gay preacher and finding him in the clutches of the chairman of deacons."

Cyn's mouth dropped open. "Has it been that detailed? How awful. Nothing like having the world know your darkest secrets."

Ever the realist, Dee challenged Cyn's statement. "Might be the best thing that could happen. We never know. But one thing I do know, regardless of the outcome, things will change, one way or the other, and my boss wants to take advantage of it. When I told him you were my sister, he put me on the next plane out. After I finish my bylined feature story, we can start on your memoir. No doubt, it will hit the best seller list."

"Jesus," Cyn exclaimed.

"Well put, my darling sister. By the way, you look fabulous. Love that bright red outfit. It's new, eh?"

"I bought it the day Ginger used the parsonage as a strip club." Cyn tried to keep the words serious, but by the time she finished the sentence, she snickered at the irony.

Feeling a little spooked anyway, when someone tapped her on the shoulder and nudged her to move down, she looked up and into the smiling face of Justice and a man she'd never seen before.

"Justice. I told you not to come, sweetheart—your grades, your—"

"No problem. Got that all covered. I have an excused absence from my class today. Didn't hurt that my professor, here, who happens to be gay himself, saw it on the national news last night. He insisted I come and offered to drive me. Mom, meet Dr. Adam Alexander. Professor, this is my mother, Cyn Carter, the woman I've been telling you about."

Speechless, Cyn smiled and nodded thanks as she and the professor shook hands.

Living in a crazy world came to mind. On one hand, she felt excited, supported. On the other, she wanted nothing more than for this evening to end.

"Where's Pops?" Justice whispered.

"In the back, I guess."

"And Stephen? Will he be here, too?"

"I guess," Cyn mouthed, and gave an I-have-no-idea-shrug.

Justice leaned over and kissed Dee on the cheek, smiled, then took his mom's hand, and didn't let go.

I dread this part, Cyn thought. Nothing good will come of it. Everyone present will leave at the conclusion of the meeting with the same convictions they came in with. Most people never considered the fact that there may be more to the topic of homosexuality than they've been taught, led to believe. She knew, because she never reconsidered it either until it hit her right between the eyes.

Seemed people seldom changed without a blow from the proverbial baseball bat. Even then, many still refused. This experience taught her that change—the fear of change—drove more flawed human decisions and judgments than anything in this world. That was until life inevitably came along and smacked one upside the head.

Dr. Alexander, the proverbial tall dark and handsome, leaned toward Cyn and whispered, "I know you're scared, but don't pay any attention to the demons inside your head. You're not alone, and neither is Wilburn. We are all here for him and for you. From what I could tell walking through the crowd, there looks like as many people for him as there are against him. Just keep breathing."

At straight up seven o'clock, Harris Harrison rose from his seat in the back and paraded down the aisle, a swagger in his step, smugness propping up his shoulders. Cyn looked back to where he'd sat and saw Hazel there, head down.

Harris stepped to the pulpit, stopped, and stared at Cyn, a sneer on his face.

CHAPTER THIRTY-THREE

Harris cleared his throat a couple of times. "Ladies and gentlemen, you know why we are here," he paused, and then continued. "In this meeting, we hold people accountable for their actions—like our forefathers did when parishioners broke the covenant. We have justification for churching members, although we've been negligent in doing so the last couple of centuries. But sin is sin. People must be held accountable—even when that person is our pastor—especially when he is. As acting chairman of the deacons, I will serve as moderator."

He cleared his throat again Cyn smoothed his tie over his belly. "And I need to inform you that we are recording and filming this meeting. I ask that you keep your behavior under control. As you see from the cameramen, who asked permission to film the meeting, the world watches. Your—our actions will stand as final testimony to the world against sin, once and for all."

He paused, stepped back, and popped a mint into his mouth as he looked toward the door that led to Wilburn's office. The one Wilburn exited every Sunday before he stepped into the pulpit. An action Cyn knew Wilburn held sacred.

The door opened. Wilburn walked through first, followed by Stephen. Both men looked immaculate. Dark suits, starched white shirts, rainbow colored ties, and spit and polish black leather shoes.

Cyn saw the professor nudge Justice and whisper, "Perfect."

Harris stepped to the side while the two men walked to the pulpit, Wilburn leading the way.

Wilburn rested his hands on the podium and looked at the audience with a sideways smile. "I'd like to say, it's nice to see this sanctuary filled to overflowing for the first time in my ministry here."

Laughter rippled through the building. Cameras rolled. Journalists wrote on notebooks.

"I know many of you are confused as to why we are here, but came anyway, either to support me or run me out of town on a rail. I'm here to say, either way, I'm okay. So I invite you to allow this meeting to progress. I might add, my wife, Cyn…" he nodded at her on the front row, then smiled when he looked at Justice and Dee smiling up at him, "…and I are packing now, and plan to vacate your parsonage within a couple of weeks. We assume you will give us that much time."

"Amen," a male voice yelled from the crowd.

Wilburn winced ever so slightly. Cyn felt a prickle of

irritation.

"If you will allow me," Wilburn continued, "I have something to say. Then, afterwards, I believe Mr. Harrison plans to entertain any questions or comments."

He glanced at Harris, eyebrows raised in question. Harris nodded, his back still straight, along with his expression.

Wilburn stood in silence while he scanned the room from left to right, then brought his attention right down the middle. "From my earliest memory, my family and the people of my home church taught that inherent evil resided within me."

He scanned the room again. "Oh, they didn't put my name on that evil, but I did. You see I knew at a young age I was different. I didn't have a word for it until much later. But when I learned that word and people called it evil, a word considered dirty, filthy, and ungodly, that's when I realized they spoke directly to me—about me."

He paused, then came back to focus on Cyn.

"You know the word, but likely you try not to use it because it tastes bitter on your tongue. Even saying it makes you shudder. Homosexual."

Cyn never thought it possible for such a huge crowd to be so silent. No one moved. No one spoke. She wondered how many held their breaths. She did, regardless of the professor's advice.

"So, under the circumstances, what does a kid do but deny it. I pushed it deep, denied what seemed so natural for me. I pretended it didn't exist—this evil inside me, controlling me, making me unfit for God's kingdom."

He fisted his hand and held it to his gut.

"But..."

Cyn realized he fought back tears. His shoulders quivered ever so slightly. He blinked several times in succession.

"But...I couldn't. I couldn't. Can you imagine how I felt—how would you feel if someone told you that something quite fundamental inside you did not belong there, and you had no control over it—it could not be cut out, prayed out, confessed out..." He stopped, caught his breath before continuing, "...and that something was evil? Not only evil, but an abomination before God, worse than anything else in the whole wide world—worse than lying, stealing, being racist, a hypocrite, and to some, even murder."

Cyn noticed Harris squirm.

"My pastor called me in one day and said he'd heard bad stories about me, that I didn't have to be this way, that I could go straight—or at least live like the celibate priests."

A snicker rippled through the crowd.

He paused, stared out at the congregation.

"I tried...and tried...and...but I couldn't. I hated myself. I tried everything to make it go away, because, in the midst of it all, I felt this overwhelming call from God to serve mankind as a minister, a pastor—to dedicate my life to it.

"Some days I shook my fist at God and said, 'If you wanted me to be a pastor, why did you make me this way?'

"Then other days, I told myself, Wilburn, the only thing you can do is act like you're not gay. Marry a good Christian girl. Father a child, and everything will work out okay."

He looked at Cyn and Justice.

"I did that. I married a wonderful young woman who has done her dead level best to perform her duties like a good preacher's wife. And Justice, well, you all know him."

Another warm chuckle came from the audience.

"But you know what?"

The sanctuary grew quiet, as if everyone else stopped breathing too.

"I did not know I couldn't love God or anyone else and despise myself." Wilburn paused, looked out over the crowd. "This one thing I now know for sure. God created me this way—and I can love myself, and love God for making me so, or stay locked in a closet forever, denying that I am Beloved."

Wilburn turned to include Stephen. "And I want to publicly thank this wonderful man standing behind me. He accepts me as that creation—damaged though I be."

This time, some of the sounds from the audience sounded more like those of shock—denial.

"Don't get me wrong. I know Stephen and I were wrong—very wrong. We sinned, first of all, against ourselves, but also our wives and children, and you— God's people on mission."

His voice broke. Stephen laid his hand on Wilburn's shoulder.

This time, not a sound came from within the sanctuary.

Stephen moved in closer to Wilburn.

"We—Stephen and I—express our sorrow in bringing embarrassment on this great congregation. I publicly apologize to my wife and son first, and then to you. Not because I'm gay, but because of my infidelity and dishonesty."

He stepped from behind the podium, off the platform, and headed straight towards Cyn, his eyes locked on hers.

She wanted to avoid his eyes, to look at the floor, anywhere.

But she didn't.

When he reached her, he held out his hand. With little choice but to take it, she did. He lifted her to her feet, clasped both her hands in his and said, "My dear wife, I wronged you from the start. I lied to you. Then, I wronged you by my unfaithfulness. I so regret that and ask when you can, please, forgive me."

She looked him in the eye, and without knowing she had done so until that very second said, "I have already forgiven you, Wilburn." Like magic, saying the words out loud made it so.

Wilburn then focused on Dee, who fidgeted in her seat. "My dear sister-in-law. I owe you an apology as well," he said. "I've been unkind, acted superior to you. I knew better, did it anyway, and that makes the sin worse." He cracked a smile. "But you knew that all along."

Then he turned to Justice, who rose and stood in front of his dad. "To you, my son, I apologize for my unfaithfulness to your mother, and being untruthful to you."

Justice said not a word, just grabbed his dad in a tight embrace. They stayed that way for what seemed like an hour, but couldn't have been more than a few seconds. Afterward, Wilburn returned to the platform and stood over to one side. He indicated the pulpit to Harris.

"Brother Harrison, I offer you the podium and the meeting."

The mood shifted—the energy in the room grew tighter, like the spring on an over-wound clock. Cameramen scanned the crowd with their cameras. Children wiggled in their seats.

Here comes the attack, Cyn thought and squeezed the hands of her pew mates.

Harris moved to the podium, folded his hands atop the pulpit Bible, and looked out over the crowd. Waiting. When no one spoke, he did.

CHAPTER THIRTY-FOUR

"Pastor, what were you thinking? If you had to do it, why right here in God's house?"

Everyone shifted. The air, electrified by the verbal attack, made the hair on Cyn's arms stand on end.

Harris stepped back from the podium to make room for Wilburn, who took a couple of steps that way then changed his mind. Instead, he picked up a lapel microphone from a small table and stood to the side.

That decision seemed right to Cyn. Like he'd pulled himself out of the power spot—turned the other cheek.

"The love Stephen and I have for each other is...is not a sin. I know that. We should not have acted on that love because we were both married, and certainly not in church. I can't go back and undo any of that, but I can and do ask for your forgiveness for my behavior—but not for being gay. I can't apologize for who I am."

He scanned a silent audience.

When no one spoke, he took a step forward. This time when he spoke, his voice didn't break. Instead, he spoke with more conviction than ever.

"I wish I'd come out of the closet many years ago. I wish I'd felt safe to do so. I didn't."

Still, no one spoke.

"You know why I wish that? The more I accept myself, the more I accept God's world. I remind myself every day that God made me. My love for Stephen is holy and God-given—yes, the timing is off, that's a fact, and we've done wrong, but—"

"You're a faggot, you ass. You admit it yourself. And you call yourself a preacher."

The words—spat out and filled with venom—came from the back. The cameras spun toward it.

"Please, whoever spoke, have the courage to stand and identify yourself," Harris said, scanning the crowd.

"I'll give the Harrison guy credit for that," Dee whispered.

The man stood. He looked vaguely familiar—not a regular attendee, and as far as Cyn knew, not a member.

"I don't care what you say, you can throw out all that garbage you want to, but call it what you want—you fuck men. That's disgusting," he shouted.

A tussle ensued, and several men escorted the man out of the building, still yelling obscenities over his shoulder while everyone turned and watched the melee.

"Folks, folks. May I have your attention?" Harris banged a gavel on the podium. "That man does not belong here. He isn't a member of this church, so he has no business speaking. Plus, if you have something to say, please conduct yourself with decency and respect. Remember, this is God's house, and besides, we have children in the crowd."

Another man rose and pointed at Wilburn. "I want to know what the church plans to do about this man. We gonna fire him? And if so, what about that lawsuit folks have been talking about. Far as I can see, he's ruined this church's reputation. If we don't do something and do it fast, we're..."

Cyn didn't recognize the speaker, didn't think she'd ever seen him before either. His name might be on the church role, but he didn't attend on a regular basis. Since Harris didn't call him down, she assumed the man's right to address the group.

"The Bible teaches Christians aren't supposed to settle their differences in court," another man's voice called out.

Cyn refused to turn and see who spoke.

Other comments came from the crowd, ones like, "I don't care what scripture says, I say sue. He's fooled us. He's a phony, acting like someone he's not."

"May I speak?"

Justice turned and looked, then elbowed Cyn. "It's Ella," he whispered, "from the youth group."

The sight of another young person in pain pierced Cyn's heart anew. The youth group lost Marcus and now must go through this. Would it ever end? She squeezed Justice's hand, still locked in hers.

Ella came from an alcoholic family. The support of the church and an outstanding group of young people helped her survive—gave her hope for a better future.

"Of course, young lady, you have the floor." Harris changed his tone. He sounded gentle, inviting.

"None of this makes sense," she said, her voice barely above a whisper. She pushed long strands of dark hair off her face. "What difference does it make that our pastor is gay?"

Several in the audience yelled they couldn't hear her.

"Miss Ella," Harris said, motioning her forward. "If you would, please, come down to the front and speak in the microphone."

Please stand by her side, Harris. Please don't leave her up there alone, vulnerable.

With fear on her face, but strength in her step, Ella headed down the aisle and took the microphone.

Cyn and Justice looked at each other and smiled.

"She's trembling," Dee whispered.

"Yes," Justice whispered back, "but she's okay. She's strong."

Ella paused, then straightened her shoulders and clicked on the microphone.

She turned to look at Wilburn and then the audience. Everyone grew quiet as if in anticipation, eager to hear what this brave young woman wanted to say. Cyn wondered, too.

"Reverend Carter has been here for every one of you—us—at one time or the other. I know when my mom died from alcohol poisoning, Reverend Carter stood beside me and held my hand all the way through. He even got my dad to attend AA, and he is sober six weeks now."

A mumble of agreement fluttered through the crowd.

"You talk about setting the example for our young people. What does all this tell us? Yes, he cheated on his wife—and Mrs. Carter," she looked at Cyn, "we love you dearly. We're sorry you've been hurt, and if we could, we'd change it, but I've learned life is pain. If someone tells you different, they're trying to sell you something."

A twitter of laughter came from several in the crowd.

"Don't believe them," Ella said. "Without pain, we'd have no need for faith. Besides, none of us are perfect. We try, but we fail. Why even you, Mr. Harris—"

"This is different, young lady." Harris's demeanor changed from peacemaker to warmonger. "All that sounds nicey-nice, but—"

"Let her speak, Harris," one man called out. "Stop interrupting her."

"I don't want her to make light of this situation, folks." Harris stepped back, patted his belly, his eyes wide.

Dee leaned into Cyn. "He's afraid of something. See how defensive he looks?"

Ella's chest lifted then she exhaled a long breath. For an instant, it looked like she considered what to say next. Then, the decision made, she faced the audience square on and said, "Mr. Harrison, you and Mrs. Washington have carried on an affair for years."

"That's a lie. Young lady, take your seat. Someone get that microphone out of her hands."

No one moved.

"It's true. I live next door to her, and I've seen you slipping in her house late at night or in the middle of the afternoon lots of times."

"I did nothing of the kind."

Someone from the audience called out, "Did too. I live across the street from her. I've seen it myself, just never said anything."

"Keep the cameras rolling," a reporter behind Cyn whispered.

Ella looked around the room, a sad expression on her face. "I know secrets about many of you that you'd rather me not tell."

Cyn wondered about Hazel sitting in the back, hearing that about her husband. She didn't have long to wonder. A stir in back of the sanctuary forced her to turn around. Hazel hurried out of her pew, evidently tromping on the feet of those unfortunate enough to sit between her and the end of the row. A hymnal crashed to the floor; someone yelped, others closer to the end of the pew hurried into the aisle to make way for Hazel's escape.

However, once out of the pew, Hazel didn't flee like Cyn expected. Instead, without a word, Hazel marched down the aisle toward the front, her gray hair as tightly wound as her face.

Was Hazel going after Ella? Or Harris?

Hazel reached the front, turned left, and marched to Cyn, kissed her on top of her head and plopped down on the other side of Dee.

Harris looked like he played the childhood game of Freeze. The movement of air coming through the A/C vents sounded like a freight train roaring through town.

Meanwhile, thoughts, feelings, reactions, and fear raged through Cyn. What next? She looked at Wilburn and Stephen, who both stood with their hands clasped in front of them, their faces set like stone. With quick, almost imperceptible glances at each other, the two apparently reached a consensus—they hadn't called the tribunal, Harris had. They refused to accept the position of prosecutor, defender, or judge. Wilburn might be tied to the stake, but he didn't intend to strike the first match.

After a long, dead silence, Bud Harvey approached the podium. "Maybe I better take charge of this meeting."

The rumblings in the crowd settled as Harris slumped off stage and headed out the side door.

Bud stepped to the microphone. "Folks you know we lost our son—he took his own life because he couldn't stand hearing us talk about, about...you know.

"Call it what it is, Bud," Wilburn said.

Bud looked at Wilburn, nodded, and then continued. "My wife, bless her heart, she never cared, she just loved our son. I did. It was me. Me, I tell you. I'm the one that made my son kill himself. We, me and you—every one of us who hate homosexuals—we killed my son. We're guilty. We did it." He banged his fist on the podium.

"I can't help my son, now. It's too late, but there's something awful wrong when we judge people 'cause they're different than us." He looked Wilburn in the eye, but spoke to the audience. "Yes, Pastor did wrong, but he wouldn't have if he'd been free all his life, to be who God made him to be. Like Marcus longed to be, without the shame of living in a closet. I can't tell you I understand all that. I can't yet, that is. But I reckon Pastor can't understand why we feel the way we do." He looked back at Wilburn. "That right, Pastor?"

Wilburn smiled. "That's right, Bud."

"One thing I know for certain, my God is a God of love—and if men love men, who are we to say that's wrong? How can I say, God, you made a mistake when you made them? You either didn't make us who we are, or you screwed up, excuse my language, big time when you made these men and women. We can't have it both ways, folks."

"But how about what the Bible says?" someone hollered out.

"Well, you know we can make the Book say anything we want it to. We know that because we've done it ourselves, and we've seen other people do it. Maybe we're not as right about all that as we thought. You know, my granddaddy swore the Bible taught he had a right to keep slaves, too, and did. And look what we've learned about that."

"I'd like to hear from the preacher's wife," a man from the audience yelled. "What about it, Mrs. Carter?"

CHAPTER THIRTY-FIVE

Petrified, Cyn looked from Justice to Dee. They both whispered, "You can do it." They nudged their encouragement.

Wilburn held out his hand, inviting Cyn to the platform, helped her up the steps, and then turned to the audience. "Cynthia prefers her childhood nickname, Cyn, spelled C – y – n. Please call her that from now on."

Bud moved aside and invited Cyn to the center microphone.

Her knees felt like soft butter as she approached the podium. Inside her shead, a loud voice wailed with fear and uncertainty. In all her years of marriage, she'd avoided this position like no other. Yes, she could teach a class. Yes, she could speak with women's circles. But she'd been well taught—always the background singer, never the star.

If only she'd chosen to wear something other than the bright-colored dress—anything but red. She looked at Justice and Dee, and bless her wounded heart, Hazel. They each gave thumbs up.

From there, she shifted her gaze to the audience, thankful the hostile attitude had calmed. First one and then two people hurried from their pews and strode out. Cyn wondered if they had secrets of their own they hoped would not be revealed, and feared they might.

She searched the crowd and picked out friendly, encouraging faces and focused on them. "I came here to support Wilburn, not to speak."

"We want to hear your side, Sister Carter," came a voice from the crowd.

Cyn paused while her brain raced, not sure where to start.

However, when she opened her mouth, the words flowed without forethought.

"I do agree, one can't truly love God and hate oneself. I know, because I have hated myself for many years. I didn't think for myself. I let others define God for me. I believed what I did because someone told me to believe it, not because I'd done the internal work to get there."

She took a deep breath before she continued, knowing her next words would likely shock the congregation as much as Wilburn's self-disclosure had.

"And in that process, I lost my soul."

A stunned, inconceivable-looking expression washed over the faces of the congregation. As if they'd never heard of such, or perhaps didn't know of the possibility, or had ignored something similar within themselves.

She knew what the heart of a racehorse must feel like, coming down the home stretch.

"To find it," she continued, feeling stronger, more sure of herself, "I decided to leave Wilburn only a couple of days before...before I learned he loved another. You might not know this, but that Wednesday night after I found Wilburn and Stephen in the pastor's study, I fled town. I didn't want to have anything to do with any of this—pardon me—this mess." She held out her opened palms, including them all. A couple women near the front snickered.

"I figured all of you—including Wilburn and Stephen—could go to hell in your sanctimonious handbaskets." She felt herself blush, raised her hand to her cheeks.

Laughter rippled through the room.

"I left in a blinding rainstorm and drove all night, with no idea where I headed. By daylight, I found myself on the beaches of the west coast of Florida. I walked the beach for hours, blasting Wilburn, Stephen, my stupidity, and at times, even God. But when that didn't change anything, I wanted to die—I prayed a wave would wash me out to sea—anything, to take me out of this situation, to ease my pain."

She grew silent, breathing in, breathing out, with no idea where to go next. One thing she did know—more words waited her saying them.

"Then...then, I stopped talking and started listening. I listened and listened, but heard nothing other than the waves washing ashore and thoughts growling inside my head. I kept looking for an answer to hit me like a bolt from heaven, but it didn't. The answer came in this still small voice inside me. It said, 'Cyn, you are the answer. You must go back. You must go back.'"

All eyes focused on her as if waiting to hear what came next.

"Now, to tell you the truth, that was not the answer I wanted."

More laughter.

"As a matter of fact, that is the very last thing. But I knew running away wasn't the answer either—that I couldn't keep running. I had to come back and—"

"Stand by your man," Robert Marshall yelled from the back, his words sneering, ugly sounding.

Cyn cringed, and knew it showed, which pissed her off. Several booed the man, and a couple other voices mocked him. One man even sang the first stanza of the song until his wife yanked him back down to the pew.

Don't let them see you sweat, one of Dee's favorite sayings bounced around in Cyn's head and found its way out. She leaned toward the microphone. "Mr. Marshall that may be the only correct thing you've said today."

The crowd howled. When it settled, Cyn continued. "Don't get me wrong. I'm no Tammy Wynette, but yes— I came back to stand by—not my man, but your man— your pastor.

"Otherwise, I'd be taking the same way out as the ostrich. Like many of you are doing, or wanting to do. This whole thing bothers me as much as you—maybe more. I had this whole issue of homosexuality wrapped up in a nice neat Christian bow.

"But out on that beach, I learned that the answer I searched for would only come by me seeing this through instead of running and hiding. From me taking an honest look at the whole situation. To hear with new ears. To stop thinking I have all the answers, but rather to look for and celebrate the questions."

She looked at Wilburn. "For you see, I'm not perfect in all this either. I admit, I felt shocked, and at first, quite angry with you and Stephen. Later, however, I started making sense of our marriage, and why it never worked for either of us—because we both hated ourselves. Me, for acting like such a such a...doormat...a marshmallow, someone called me." She stopped long enough to wipe her eyes on her sleeve, to take a sip of water, and then went on. "I had no idea what I stood for and perhaps more important, what I wouldn't stand for. That's why I came back—to discover my voice, and in doing so, to recover my soul. I wanted to make my own decisions about my life, rather than run and hide from circumstances out of my control. That's why I came back."

She saw a movement out of the corner of her eye and glanced at Dee, who now stood and with slow, deliberate movements, started clapping. One by one, others joined in, building faster and stronger.

Cyn noticed Hazel also stood and clapped. Healing had begun, for some, at least.

Tears flowed down Cyn's cheeks, and when the applause quieted, she smiled and said, "That's all I have to say, except, I do know love is the theme of my existence. Over the last few days, I witnessed a deep, profound love between my husband and Stephen. A love I've never experienced. A love so strong, neither of them can deny nor ignore it. Our world needs more love. When a person finds it, surely that love can't be sinful. Yes, they went about it all wrong, but under the circumstances, I'm beginning to understand why they did."

Again, she paused, caught her breath. "And in case you're wondering, yes, Wilburn and I will file for divorce. I don't know what my plans are, but I will be fine. Actually, I'm relieved to know why Wilburn and I got to the place we did in our relationship. That helps me know what I must do. I'm packing my things and intend to move out of the parsonage soon. That's about all—"

Just then, Justice rose and walked toward her. She waited as he stepped up on the platform and put his arm around her shoulders.

"When we moved in," Cyn said, looking up at her son, "Justice here had just finished junior high, so we have neat memories of the years we've lived in that magnificent old house. I do suggest, however, that you allow the next pastor to choose where he—or she—lives. Allow them to create their own home, wherever that may be." She stepped away and then came back to the microphone. "One more thing. By all means, move those old portraits to the Fellowship Hall. Don't make the wife of your next pastor have to look at them day after day. They mean nothing to us. They mean something to you. Hang them here, in the halls, so you can see them." She gave a nervous laugh and walked off stage.

She and Justice retook their seats by Dee and Hazel.

Bud Harvey regained the podium. "I do know our world needs more people loving each other, that's for sure. Mrs. Carter, I don't mean to make light of your pain. I know Preacher done you wrong." He looked at Cyn, who nodded, encouraging him on.

"I have a question to put out to the congregation to

consider. What would we have done if the preacher here had an affair with a woman, then came, and repented?"

A man near the back stood and called out, "Yeah, that last preacher did the same thing, and then ran. Didn't give us a chance to—"

"So what do we do?" One of the other deacons stood and asked. "Let's say we forgive him—what then? He can't still serve as our pastor. What would the community say? Wouldn't anyone come here anymore."

"Are you so sure?" another man called out. "Seems to me there's a lot of hurting people out there looking for a place of forgiveness and love."

The questions kept coming—too many to track who said what.

"Yeah, but soon our church would be full of people like him. Do we want that?"

"In light of all we've said, your point is?"

"I'm not sure our church is ready for that."

"I'm not sure it is either," Wilburn interrupted. "To tell you the truth, I'm not sure this church will ever be— maybe sometime in the future, but not now. A few of you are ready to take that step, but if I were to stay, this church would split in half. I don't want that—not now. Inclusive congregations set the example, but you're not there yet. That's why I've come to tender my resignation. Here, Bud, I have it in writing."

A hush fell over the crowd while Bud opened the letter and read it. "Effective immediately?"

"Yes, but I do ask for a couple of months to get our things out of the parsonage."

"Is there a motion to accept Pastor Wilburn's resignation?"

"I make the motion," Robert Marshall called out from the back. "I don't think this church is ready for a homosexual pastor. I know I'm not."

Someone seconded.

"All in favor say aye."

A smattering of ayes sounded through the room.

"Opposed?"

"Opposed," Hazel and Justice said, along with others from the crowd.

"Well, it sounds like the ayes have it." Bud Harvey looked at Wilburn, tears in his eyes. "Preacher, this church may not be ready—like Robert said—but I got a feeling we will be one day soon. I plan to propose to the deacons that we establish a committee to do an in-depth study on this topic and bring the results back to the church."

"That's all I could hope for, Bud." Wilburn shook Bud's hand.

"Plus, as chairman of the finance committee we'll meet with you and work out a severance package." Bud glared at the crowd. "And I dare anyone to object to whatever the committee recommends."

Quiet.

Bud surveyed the crowd, waiting. When no one said anything, he held his palms to the ceiling. "Then I guess that's about it. The show is over, folks. Looks like a lot of us still got work to do on ourselves." He turned to Wilburn. "Preacher, we wish you the best."

Cyn stood and put her arms around Hazel, who by now looked wilted as a plucked flower left too long in the sun.

"I don't know what to do now, Cyn. Do I go home?

If I do, what will he say or do when I get there?"

At a loss for words, Cyn held her tight while considering alternatives for her new friend.

"I'll tell you what. Why don't you join Dee and me? Let's go get coffee and pie—or maybe even a beer." She snorted at the idea, making Hazel laugh.

"That sounds nice."

Cyn pulled Dee aside. "We're going to spend some time with Hazel tonight. Would you take her and wait at my car? It won't take me but a minute."

Dee gave her the biggest smile and grabbed Hazel around the waist. "I'm delighted. Hazel and I are old friends, you know." The two touched foreheads, snickering.

Cyn waited for Wilburn and Stephen to join her, then the three, along with Justice and Professor Alexander, slipped out the side door.

"Guess it went as well as expected," Wilburn said. "Wish it could have gone otherwise. But that's okay. I've learned one thing. Everyone has their own spiritual path and their own timing on that path."

Outside, Justice grabbed his dad and hugged. "Proud of you, Pops," he said, squeezing him tight, then said, "And I'd like to introduce you to one of my professors. This is Dr. Alexander."

The professor grabbed Wilburn's hand. "You might consider teaching," he said. "You express yourself well, and I think the students would respect that."

"We'll see." Wilburn scratched his head. "Right now, I'm enjoying the feeling of freedom—freedom to be myself instead of hiding in a closet."

Stephen laughed. "Buddy, we didn't come out of the

closet, we got caught in the closet."

"True." Wilburn laughed. "Guess that's not quite the same thing." He took Cyn's hand and looked her in the eye. "However, I do regret my dishonesty with you, and the pain this has caused. Thank you for forgiving me. I hope we can stay friends."

Cyn shrugged. "Of course. Besides, I'm tough. At least now my life makes sense. What's next for you, do you think?"

"Not a clue. But that's the way it is. I'm not going to let fear control me anymore. Besides, the convention will likely blackball me and take away my ordination."

"Not if I have anything to say about it." Dr. Nathaniel Powell stepped up, surprising them. Cameramen followed him, cameras still rolling. "I wish I had the authority to reissue that invitation as our convention speaker, but I don't. Perhaps in time folks will get there, but like some in this congregation, they aren't there yet." He handed Wilburn a sheet of paper. "Take a look at this. It might interest you."

Wilburn scanned it. "Look here, Stephen, it's a job description." He read from the page: "Searching for a senior pastor who knows what it is like to be wounded. I have never seen an ad like that before. It sounds perfect. I'll check this out."

Dr. Powell looked at Dr. Alexander. "You know what, Professor, I've done some research, and I found out—to my surprise—that Jesus never said a single word on the topic of homosexuality—that tells me something. He did teach us to love our neighbors as ourselves. Didn't say a word about loving only straight people and hating homosexuals. Actually, neither one of those words ever came up. The new commandment supersedes all else. So, if Jesus didn't say it..."

Wilburn looked from Dr. Alexander to Dr. Powell. "You two know each other?"

"We met out front before the meeting started," both men said at the same time.

Before long, Dr. Powell excused himself and left.

A number of members searched out Wilburn and Cyn.

Others didn't bother. They left the church without a backward glance. Still others couldn't get away fast enough.

Stephen stood on one side of Wilburn while Cyn claimed the other. After the crowd thinned, Justice said, "Mom, I hope you don't mind, but my professor and I would like to spend the evening with Pops and Stephen. That won't hurt your feelings will it? What about I catch up with you in the morning before we head back to school?"

"That's perfect. Dee, Hazel, and I are going to paint the town red." She gave him a hug, thanked the professor, and headed to find Dee and Hazel waiting at the car.

When she found them, Dee said, "Okay, ladies, I'm starving. Let's go out for dinner."

"I'm starving, too." Cyn grabbed their hands. "That kind of work really takes it out of a person. I'll go, but this time, I'm buying."

"You mean it?"

"Yep."

"Cool. I like this." Dee looked from Cyn to Hazel. "Where we going?"

Hazel spoke for the first time. "Somewhere near the

water, and I know just the place. Trust me?"

"With our lives." Cyn and Dee said in agreement.

The three women got in the car, but as they started to drive off, Harris knocked on the rear passenger window where, inside, Hazel sat buckling her seat belt. At first, the sight of him startled Cyn, but one look told her they had nothing to worry about.

"Can I talk to you, Hazel?"

Cyn had sight of Hazel in her rear view mirror and saw her shaking her head.

"Please, give me a minute," he yelled.

"We've got time, Hazel, if you'd like to," Dee said, turning towards the back.

Hazel rolled the window halfway down. "Whatever you've got to say you can say it right here and now."

Harris shuffled his feet, stuttered, "I wanted to tell you I'm sorry. I never meant to hurt you."

"What makes you think I'm hurting? I'm going out to dinner with the girls. You go do whatever you want to do, and we'll talk tomorrow. In the meantime, you might want to call your lawyer." Regardless of her words, Hazel's tone oozed the pain of betrayal.

"Aww, Hazel, don't act that way. You know I love you, always have. That other woman didn't mean nothing, just a—"

Hazel rolled up the window. "Let's go, Cyn, I'm hungry."

Soon, the three women arrived at a seafood restaurant near the gulf. A chilling sea breeze planted salty brine on Cyn's lips as they hurried inside.

After the host led them to a table overlooking the water, Cyn unfolded her napkin and spread it across her lap. "So, what's your new assignment, Dee?"

Dee smiled, but ducked her head and mumbled, "Imbedded in the middle east."

"You what? Isn't that dangerous?"

"Life is dangerous, sweet sister."

Cyn chuckled. "You can say that again. Who would have thought those people who look so holy on Sundays could be so vicious?"

"Or screw your husband behind your back." Hazel tucked her chin into her chest like a turtle. "I'm sorry, Cyn, I wasn't talking about you, rather..." Tears dripped off Hazel's chin and into her lap.

"I know that, sweetheart." Cyn didn't know what else to say, so she didn't. In silent agreement, she and Dee gave Hazel time to recover.

After a couple of minutes, Cyn said, "So anyway, enough about men. How much time do you have before you leave the country?"

Dee looked at the clock on her cell phone. "Three hours and forty-eight minutes."

"That soon?" Panic slammed into Cyn's voice.

The waiter approached their table to take drink orders. When Hazel didn't respond, Dee ordered frozen margaritas all around.

"I feel like I'm barging in on what time you two have left before Dee leaves the country." Hazel spoke so softly Cyn wondered if she'd made a sound.

"It's okay, sweetheart." Dee reached over and patted Hazel's shoulder. "We'll stay in touch even when I'm halfway around the world. There's always Skype."

"Thank you for supporting me at the meeting, Hazel." Cyn scooted her chair closer to the table in order to better hear.

"That's the least I could do, especially after what you did for me."

"For you?"

"I'm leaving Harris. He bullies me. Always has. Now I learn that's not the half of it. My daughter has begged us to move near her in Hot Springs, Arkansas. I've decided I'm going to do that, regardless of what Harris says. Fact is, I don't want him to come. He can go visit his sweetheart all he wants."

"I understand how you feel," Cyn said. "But don't make any hasty decisions about Harris. Why not go to Arkansas and spend a little time there without him? Allow yourself to heal before you make any life changes. Give yourself time to process your feelings. Talk to a therapist maybe."

"That would be best, yes," Hazel said. "Could you excuse me a minute? I think I'll go call my daughter right now and tell her I'm coming—by myself."

After dinner, they dropped Hazel at home. Harris sat on the front porch looking contrite and holding a bouquet of red roses.

"Humph, he thinks a few flowers will fix this, he's got another think coming." Hazel got out and prissed up the driveway.

"Way to go, Hazel," Dee said, a smile in her voice. "I wonder what she's going to say when she gets close. Right now, I wouldn't want to be Harris."

"Sounds like a lot of good came out of this tribunal tonight." Cyn pulled away from the curb. "I dreaded it like the plague, but you know—I feel a lot better now."

"You made me proud, big sister." Dee rubbed Cyn's

shoulder. "Wilburn didn't do half bad himself."

"I thought he acted magnificently. Even thought maybe he and I still had a chance—"

"What? You're kidding. I don't believe this."

Cyn cracked a smile. "Of course I'm kidding. Give me a break."

Dee gave her a playful slap on the shoulder. "You had me going there for a minute."

Cyn dropped Dee at the airport—again—but this time gave her an extra tight squeeze. "You take care, sweetheart. And stay safe. I'll watch for you on the news channel. Tell that good-looking photographer to keep his hands off of you."

CHAPTER THIRTY-SIX

After Justice and the professor left the next morning, Cyn made three appointments.

First, she dialed Paul Cooper's office, gave her name, and asked to speak with him. In short order, he came on the line.

"Cyn Carter, I thought I'd scared you off for sure," he said as he picked up the phone. "I'm so glad you called. I read the news, so I understood why you missed our appointment. Sounds like you've had a tough time."

"I have, but that's okay. I'm eager to meet with you."

"Name the day and time."

"How about nine o'clock tomorrow morning?"

"That could work, but I have a better idea. How about we meet a little later and make it lunch? I always talk better with a full belly."

She accepted, and they agreed on a time and place.

After punching off the call, she sat for the longest time and considered what he'd said about her going through a painful time. Simple words for such a complicated experience.

No easy answers, just a long, hard road ahead. Then again, the incubator she'd lived in for twenty years hadn't been easy, either. Nor had it protected her from pain. But it dang sure fed her fear.

Could she keep living in the midst of the pain she still held? Denying it hadn't worked. She did that for years and failed miserably. In fact, it paralyzed her. Stepping into her fear and pain did work. If nothing else, it led her off dead center.

She pulled out the second, and toughest number, and dialed.

No turning back.

"Ginger? This is Cyn."

Silence.

"Hello? Cyn said again, unsure whether or not she'd lost the connection.

"I'm here," Ginger said. "I'm in shock. I didn't figure I'd ever hear from you again."

"I'm sure you didn't. Truth is, I didn't either. But I've called to see if we could meet. I'd like us to talk."

More silence. But after the longest couple of seconds, Ginger said she'd come.

"Good." Relieved and nervous at the same time, Cyn suggested the coffee shop near the mall within the hour and headed that way as soon as she punched off the call.

The small coffee shop sat tucked into the corner of a larger building. At the moment, only a few customers occupied the room. One couple sat at the small round table near the front window, elbows on the table and nose kissing. Love.

Cyn bought two lattes and found a place at the rear, right next to the storeroom.

Her stomach cramped something awful. Her chest felt like an elephant camped right in the middle of it. Everything she'd been through with Wilburn and Stephen hadn't made her feel that nervous.

When Ginger walked in, Cyn signaled, and Ginger headed that way. She looked as cautious as Cyn felt.

"I bought you a latte. I hope that's okay."

"Perfect," Ginger said, sitting across from Cyn.

"I imagine my call surprised you." Cyn passed a packet of sugar across the table.

"That's an understatement. After your last visit, I figured we became enemies."

"I'm sure—"

"Before you say anything." Ginger stirred the latte, fast. "I thought you might want to know—when you called an hour ago, Hazel Harrison sat at my kitchen table talking with me."

"Oh?" Cyn remembered a similar visit.

"So, if I come across a little overwhelmed, it's because I am. When I saw her at the door, my defenses went up big time. I thought she'd come to blast me, to accuse me of everything imaginable."

"Did she?"

"That's the thing. She didn't. She came to apologize. To me." Ginger's voice screeched out the last words.

"Said after everything that happened with Stephen and Wilburn, and what she learned about Harris, she realized she'd sat on her high horse pointing fingers at everyone else while she lived in a self-constructed bubble. Her apology went all the way back to the last pastor, and the rumors she'd started that forced him to leave the church."

"Whew," Cyn said, "I didn't see that coming."

"Neither did I. My head still reels."

Neither spoke for a few seconds. Every word Cyn practiced saying to Ginger disappeared from her mind. What did she replace them with?

She wanted peace—some way to shut out all the noise, all the problems.

Then again, perhaps a sense of peace didn't mean an absence of those things, but rather a calm, forgiving heart.

Cyn clasped Ginger's hands in hers and looked her in the eye. "We've both traveled quite a journey. We've learned a lot about ourselves. Why don't we both forgive and start over."

"You mean forget what happened?" Ginger tried to smile.

"I'm not sure forgetting is the best way to go." Cyn struggled to express what she felt. "Perhaps it's better if we remember. That way, when we're tempted, we won't likely repeat the same mistakes."

"Maybe so," Ginger said, and then looked up, confused. "I don't understand. Wilburn, Stephen, and I wronged you. Tell me one mistake you made."

Cyn wrapped her hand around her cup. The latte had grown cold.

"I didn't stay in my shoes," Cyn said. "Instead, I spent years walking in Wilburn's—forcing myself to act like he wanted me to act."

She squeezed Ginger's hands, remembering her fear when she first suspected Justice might be gay and using Sophie to cover it up. She didn't have all the answers when it came to homosexuals or anything else.

"I'm still working on my mistakes, Ginger, but I do know, regardless of what you or Wilburn or Stephen or anyone else does… that does not nullify my commitment to treat you with respect and dignity."

"What commitment—to whom? I don't understand."

"I guess it's not a commitment, really, more an action or attitude due to a choice."

"Now, I'm really confused. I have no idea what you're talking about." Ginger played with the cup, then took a sip and shuddered. "It's tepid," she said and rested the cup on the table.

In her mind's eye, Cyn saw herself explaining the same thing to Justice many years ago. How did she sum it up now without sounding like Pollyanna? Or like she had all the answers.

She ended up recounting the incident between Justice and the rude man, and the resulting conversation she and Justice had that evening.

"That night I learned more about the person I wanted to be—someone who treats people with respect and dignity—not because of who they are, but because of who I choose to be."

"Hmmm. Never thought about it that way."

Cyn took the paper cups, heated them in a nearby microwave, and returned to their table. "One thing I'd like—and that's for us to resume our friendship. Not like before—like now. Think we can start over?"

"I like that. I like that a lot." Ginger smiled.

Ready for the third call, Cyn dialed a law firm she'd found in the phone book a few days ago and requested an appointment with a lawyer.

"Which one, ma'am. We have seven." Although polite, a twinge in the woman's voice made it sound weary of asking that question.

"It's regarding a divorce." The word still felt odd on Cyn's tongue.

"Okay, but which lawyer do you want?"

"The one with an appointment available this afternoon."

"I see. One moment, please."

A couple of minutes later the secretary returned. Yes, there was one slot at four. Cyn grabbed it and made a mental note of the time. Afterward, she realized she'd not gotten the lawyer's name but decided against calling back to disturb the overworked woman.

Wilburn promised not to fight for anything. She had first choice of their possessions, and he offered her a monthly allotment as long as she needed it—banking on the fact he'd find a job himself. All a matter of getting the paperwork started.

A few minutes before four, Cyn drove downtown, parked, and rode the elevator to the top floor of the tallest building in Mobile. On the ride up, reality hit. Soon, she'd be single and on her own for the first time in her life. Her knees almost buckled, but then she remembered what she'd recently been through. She could do this.

Trust the process, she told herself as she stepped out of the elevator and into the law firm's reception area.

Along the rear wall of windows, Mobile's skyline

glistened in the late afternoon sun. To the left, an older woman sat at a large reception desk pounding on a keyboard. She looked up and smiled at Cyn.

"Good afternoon. I'm Cyn Carter, I have an appointment at four, but I forgot the lawyer's name."

The white-haired receptionist checked her calendar. "It's with Mr. Benjamin. Please have a seat, and I'll let him know you're here."

In less than five minutes, a buzzer sounded on the receptionist's desk. "Mr. Benjamin is waiting for you. Follow me, please."

The receptionist led Cyn down a short hall and ushered her into a plush office with bright sunlight streaming through an equally large bank of windows, an energy Cyn felt, but didn't understand, and a man with his back turned, looking out the windows.

"Mr. Benjamin, this is Cyn Carter," the secretary said. "She has an appointment with you concerning a divorce proceeding." The woman then stepped out and closed the door.

With his back still to her, the lawyer said, "I thought you'd never call. I've waited so long, hoping you would." Mr. Benjamin swung around, his smile spreading larger— the blond man—the colorologist from the charity ball.

"You?" Cyn felt her mouth drop. Excitement charged through her veins. "I...I thought you worked with color?"

"I do. My hobby—my passion—is research and writing on the topic of color and its impact on our lives. This lawyer job pays my bills."

"So, you're a chameleon," Cyn joked with the man she'd shunned and fantasized about.

"Changing my color to fit the surroundings? Close, but not quite."

"Oh? How so?" She'd lived with one chameleon too many. A protective shield formed around her heart. Maybe she needed to choose another lawyer and someone else to...

Mr. Benjamin inspected a spot on his desk and swiped it with his hand. "This may sound strange to you, even off the wall perhaps, but did you know we change color all the time?"

"Excuse me?"

He looked straight at her. "It has to do with the amount of light we can handle at any one point in time."

"I have no idea what you're talking about. The amount of light?" The man didn't sound anything like what she expected from a divorce lawyer—didn't come close.

He moved back to his desk and sat. "The way I see it, it's like we are born anew every day. It's like I change my skin clothes, trade in my habits, and prepare for a new voyage each and every day because of that changing light."

"You mean like a caterpillar changing into a butterfly?"

He nodded, but said nothing for a few seconds, and then pulled out a yellow notepad and a black felt-tipped pen. "Now that you've changed your skin clothes, let's talk about your new voyage."

She felt her wings spread wide, and that familiar feeling return.

"Oh, by the way," he said, "people call me Tommy Lee."